Rumblings in the Reef

Charles K. Summers

Rumblings in the Reef by Charles K. Summers

This is a work of fiction

Names, characters, places, and incidents are the product of the author's imagination or are used factiously. Any resemblance to any persons, living or dead, or events is entirely coincidental.

Library of Congress Control Number: 2025906768

Paperback: ISBN-13: 978-1-7349129-5-1
e-book: ISBN-13: 978-1-7349129-6-8

Washington – USA

Teen & Young Adult 2) Science Fiction & Fantasy 3) Science Fiction
First Edition

Dedication

For those who put forth their imaginations to
explore all the worlds that are - and that may be.

Table of Contents

Chapter 1 Rumblings

After several days of not enough food, Richter knew he wasn't starving but he never quite managed to convince his stomach. The rumblings were loud enough that he woke with a start, rising to hover over his nesting hollow, his tailfin flicking something onto the floor of his small campus room. Now fully awake, he glanced back to see what had been knocked to the floor. It was a small trophy that he had received in Fifth Year. It wasn't much of a trophy - third place in a marathon - but he received few enough awards that he still treasured it.

He repositioned the trophy onto its narrow shelf. Now in Tenth Year at the campus, his living space was at maximum capacity for a single unit. Next year, having graduated, he would be out of the campus housing and hoped to secure a larger living space.

His stomach rumbled again. He was famished! A growing male, he needed his meals. This reduction in rations was truly painful. Fully awake now, he was acutely aware of the urgent need to swim out of the campus building to relieve himself in the unconstrained water currents near the doors. Only First, and sometimes Second, Years voided in their rooms where the water was tranquil and unable to carry away waste efficiently.

The hallways were wide enough to allow three to swim in parallel either direction but, when in a hurry, it was easy to get off center. And, right now, he was in a hurry. It was early enough in the day that there weren't many others in the hallway. He went over one group and swerved to the left of another. Finally, a sharp move to the right, grazing his soft dorsal fin against the smooth pearlescent wall. He saw the exit and burst out into the open relishing the strong current that swept past the entrance.

"Hello, Richtor," greeted another male who had also just left the building, swimming past Richtor before pausing. "Quite the party last night wasn't it?" Richtor managed a smile and gave him a thumbs up. He had forgotten just how much he had had at the party last night – but his body hadn't forgotten. He just wished that the party had included more food to go along with the generous amount of bladderweed. So far, there was no rationing of bladderweed - fermented or otherwise.

Feeling relieved in more ways than one, Richtor headed back into the campus building to return to his room. More students were stirring and the hallways were becoming increasingly crowded. The ceilings were high enough to allow at least one person to go under, or over, another if needed. The tiled walls had bowls of bioluminescent algae hung at intervals and at intersections. He changed directions. Richtor decided that he didn't need to go back to his room before breakfast and the sooner he had breakfasted the better.

~   ~   ~

As he swam towards breakfast, his thoughts drifted back to when he had first learned about the rationing. It had been completely accidental. He had asked to leave class for elimination and was taking his time returning when he overheard a mental conversation from farther down the curved hallway.

Not wanting to be noticed and have to explain why he was there, he found an empty classroom and glided through the open doorway - hovering there waiting for the conversation to pass. As they got closer, he detected two distinct mental signatures involved with the conversation. Almost definitely teachers. He would prefer to not be found by them.

The conversation was on a broadcast mental channel so he could hear it. That was peculiar. It was probably an accident. Using a private channel for mental discussion was considered good manners if only a couple of people were involved. Still, he was lucky - he could hear their conversation.

"The harvests have continued to be smaller for the past three currentflips," said one male whose mental signature seemed to be familiar to Richtor. He couldn't quite place the signature but the conversation sounded like it might be interesting.

"Yes. Does the Council have any idea why?" replied another male with a different signature.

"Not that I know of," the first voice replied. Richtor recognized the mental signature as that of his fifth period math teacher. Teacher Gregov was really firm in his handling of the class. But the subject held his interest. If he delved into a problem in depth, Richtor could focus better than anyone. Redirecting his attention was always a challenge.

"All I know is that we have been told to reduce rations for the entire campus," continued Gregov.

"Everyone? Even the teachers?" The second signature seemed more concerned with his own meals than that of the students. It must be Teacher Malov. Richtor had never been taught by him, but rumors had reached him. Easy to butter up with flattery. His larger build might benefit from a reduction in rations.

"Yes, even the teachers," said Gregov. "Starting at the beginning of the next quarterflip."

Richtor could tell the teachers were continuing down the hallway by the waning signal strength of their conversation. He carefully peeked around the doorframe. He could see their tailfins moving around the far curve.

~   ~   ~

Thus, he had been one of the first students to know about the rationing. Thoughts still in the past, he came close to colliding with a Fourth-Year student. He apologized and continued. Almost to the cafeteria and breakfast!

The cafeteria was just a large room with pedestals scattered around where food could be placed. The food bins were located along one wall. Luckily, he was still early and the lines were short. The menu had a fairly large variety of wild and cultivated food. The trays containing the various preparations of Gordies and Bluntnose were about half in number from the number that had been present a currentflip ago. The vegetables were still available but their quality had decreased noticeably.

Richtor loaded his plate with his ration of fish and then filled the plate with vegetables, trying to pick the ones which were the most filling and lasted the longest.

Richtor turned and looked around the cafeteria. He spotted Lichten, his best friend, hovering near a pedestal near the doorframe leading to the classrooms. Lichten looked up and waved. Richtor, hands occupied with his tray, nodded back to Lichten and started to swim over.

"Hey, Lichten. What's up?" Richtor asked as he approached his friend.

"Not much. You're going to regret getting that blue orb seaweed. It looks good but it isn't even close to ready to eat."

"Oh." Richtor looked down at his plate which he had placed on the pedestal and noticed that he had quite a lot of blue orb. "Do you think it'll make me sick?"

"Nah," replied Lichten. "But if you are susceptible to getting gas, I'd avoid it."

"That's not me. I think I'll eat it first while I'm at my hungriest."

"Good idea." Lichten picked up his fork and resumed eating. His plate was mostly empty but of the same size as Richtor's.

"Don't you get hungry? With all this rationing going on?" asked Richtor.

"Sometimes," Lichten replied. "But I get some supplemental rations at the stables. The Council has allotted a few more rations to those doing heavier physical work and my work at the stables counts."

"Lucky you." Richtor looked down at his tray and noticed it was empty. He didn't even remember eating it. He wasn't too hungry now but he knew it wouldn't last.

~ ~ ~

Physical History was his first class of the day. He didn't need to retrieve anything from his room so he was free to directly go there. He left the cafeteria and proceeded to the classroom where Teacher Jonal was already hovering at the front, making notes on the front writing board.

Class today should be as usual. In his last currentflip of Tenth Year, he should be graduated by the time the ocean currents changed direction again. This term, he had five classes instead of the usual six, as last term was mostly finishing courses that had been pushed off.

"Hello Richtor," said Teacher Jonal as he turned to see Richtor hovering around his assigned pedestal in the room. "to what are we to thank for this early presence?" Jonal smiled as he said it. His face didn't have much movement but friendliness was expressed around his brightly shining eyes.

Richtor released a chitter, in response, indicating his amusement. The people in his shoal, as well as nearby shoals, rarely used physical sound for anything other than emphasis.

Connected to the broadband mental channel which the Teacher was using, he replied. "I woke up a bit early today – had to go outside. Then, after breakfast it just didn't seem worthwhile to return to my room before class."

"We have the second test for the class coming up endweek," answered Jonal, "do you have any specific questions that might not be gone over in the review today?"

"No, but I am a bit confused about how our arms developed from the lobe-fins in other fish. I think that might be useful to the whole class, though."

"You're right. We will be covering that in class. Anything else that might not be relevant for the entire class?"

"Not unless you can tell me why I sometimes lose focus. I like the class. I really do. But sometimes I just can't concentrate."

"I've noticed, Richtor. But you also come up with some really good questions and you usually seem to remember the material even when I see you looking elsewhere in the room. Try not to worry about it too much. You're a good student."

"Can you tell that to Teacher Gregov?" replied Richtor. "I think that some days he is ready to herd me right out of class."

Jonal smiled. "I'll try to have a word with him. But I can't actually interfere with whatever he may do."

"Right."

"Right what?" asked Lichten, who had apparently finished his breakfast and was moving into the room. Lichten was more athletic than Richtor but he also did well in his classes. He excelled in open water work which wasn't Richtor's prime area of achievement.

"Right on time," said Richtor. "Good to see you. Ready for the test?"

"No, am I supposed to be? I thought we were doing reviews of the work this week."

"Until endweek, yeah," Richtor clarified. "Hey, Teacher Jonal. That's something maybe no one else cares about. Why do we have weeks? Why endweeks? Why startweeks?"

"Tradition, more than anything else, I think," said Jonal. "I really don't know. You might want to ask Teacher Lorell in Oral History. A day is from dark through light back to dark. Some people call two successive currentflips a year because that period brings the current back in the same direction. And of course, we divide the days and currentflips into smaller sections for convenience. But I don't know of any physical reason why there are seven days from startweek to endweek followed by three weekend days. Ask Teacher Lorell."

At this point, the class had filled up. Lichten, who had been swimming near to Richter's place, moved back to his pedestal. A few more stragglers entered, and the class was ready to begin. Januelle, known as one of the smartest in the class, moved in and hovered at a pedestal close to Richtor.

"Alright, class," said Teacher Jonal. Test on endweek." The class erupted in a mix of chitters and rumbles.

"Ah, yes. I see you're looking forward to it as well. This test is primarily concerned with the physical development of the People. Who can tell me what animal, still swimming around, is probably closest in appearance to our oldest ancestor?"

A female with blue overtones on her dorsal fin shot her hand up. "A protozoa?" The class let out a series of chitters.

"That's a good point, Dorala," said Jonal while giving a stern glare at the rest of the class. "We probably did start as protozoa or something even smaller. However, although protozoa have some movement with their flagella, I doubt most of us would call that swimming. Any other suggestions?"

"Great Outer Lobe-Fish," said Januelle.

"Right, Januelle. We consider them to be the progenitor of the People because of their dominant lobe-fins."

"Now, lobe-fins allow the Great Outer Lobe-Fish – or GOLF as I like to shorten it – to move with greater precision on the sea bottom. The lobes provide both joints for easier movement as well as added strength for support. Some researchers have seen them using their lobes to leave the water."

"The lobe-fins, or pelvic fins, on the GOLF are basically moveable sticks that possess the resilience and ability to be positioned more accurately. They are the basis for our much more developed arms and hands. Our front pectoral fins used to be located closer to the front of our bodies. However, as our arms and hands developed, they moved towards the back, allowing more space for optimal arm usage."

"Now, can anyone tell the class of another major difference our bodies now have from existing GOLFs?" Januelle's hand shot up.

"Anyone other than Januelle?" inquired Teacher Jonal. Januelle lowered her hand.

A female at the back of the class put up her hand. "Yes?" called out Teacher Jonal.

"Our bodies are thinner than that of the GOLF," the student replied with a flick of her tailfin.

"Thank you, Loralei. That's true, but that's not quite as important as another difference," replied Jonal.

Januelle's hand shot up again. Jonal looked around the classroom and, not seeing anyone else's hand up, looked towards Januelle. "Yes, Januelle?"

"Our heads have changed from that of the GOLF. There is space for our larger brains in addition to a hard crest bone to protect them."

"Anything else," asked Teacher Jonal.

Januelle spun around her pedestal in a contemplative manner. "Oh, yes. Below the crest bone, our faces have developed more muscles to allow more flexible use of our mouths and the ability to express some emotion. But, that isn't that big of a difference, is it?"

"Well, if you had the same face as a GOLF, you might appreciate the significance of the change." A round of chitters arose from the classroom.

Teacher Jonal continued in his review for the test. As the class ended, a large pulse was emitted from a device near the doorframe signaling it was time to head to the next class.

As usual, Richtor was one of the first to leave and, having left his pedestal area to swim back and forth in the rear of the classroom, was in a good position to be able to do such.

Chapter 2 Plans in Progress

Richtor found it difficult to not take the rationing personally. The decrease in fish harvests puzzled him and it was difficult for him to leave any puzzle alone – much less a puzzle that affected everyone within the shoal. Food and eating weren't topics that he often dwelled on. Some people might have been surprised at that since, being in constant motion, it would be expected that he would use more food. With ongoing rationing, his hunger had become more pronounced and it had become a frequent focus of his thoughts.

The scarcity of food posed a real danger to the shoal. They might rebalance their diets to include more cultivated crops but that wasn't a solution that would satisfy anyone except the bed farmers. Of course, it would be even worse if rations were reduced further. Richtor couldn't remember a time when any of the People had died of hunger but there was an account of such, as relayed in

Teacher Lorell's Oral History class, caused by a disease that went through the food supply.

The week had passed and Richtor had successfully completed an oral presentation to Teacher Lorell, one of the most respected teachers within the campus cluster. Most of the teachers were very good and he felt guilty being a source of extra problems for them.

He truly didn't want to cause problems. He just couldn't remain hovering around in the classroom if he wasn't actively involved in a project, doing in-class homework, or making a presentation or something else that required his immediate focus. Listening to lectures definitely didn't qualify.

But there was nothing he could do about the food supply right away. What could he do today? He didn't want to just keep going from place to place all over the shoal. He decided to head over to the residential chambers at the dormitory and see if he could find anyone else who wanted something to do. Maybe, as he had told Teacher Lorell, he could find someone to join him on an expedition to the seaweed jungles.

Arriving at the dormitory chambers, he thought he would see if Januelle and Lichten were interested in joining him.

The hallways of the dormitory chambers were rather plain. Since they were temporary quarters, the Council saw no reason to invest work credits on decoration. Few of the student residents had any reason to add decoration and, if they did feel like it, there wasn't any particular place to add them.

Januelle and Lichten's chambers were both located on the next to top floor but at different ends of the spiral hallway. He decided to check on Lichten first as there was an exterior access tube that went close to his chamber. Januelle's chamber was close to the center of the spiral.

Richtor swam through the access tube, carefully staying away from the sides as the dormitory tubes sometimes got somewhat dirty from the younger children coming up to visit or to play games of hide and seek.

Lichten's door had a plain '762' on a plaque on the door. Below it, in ornate script, was Lichten's name and an intricately drawn sketch of someone perched upon a sharrell and moving through a seaweed jungle. Lichten was very good with the domestic sharrells and he continued to improve that by helping with the animals after classes. Lichten's expertise with the domestic sharrells earned him extra work credits, experience, and also currently included extra rations.

While he spent most weekends pursuing other interests they often aligned with his work with the sharrells. Doing additional work was not mandatory as all students had sufficient work credits to be able to do a bit extra and the community pantry was open to all, albeit with rationing in effect. Many got part-time jobs after school hours to extend the extra offerings. If they were fortunate, like Lichten, the work might be related to their eventual interest upon graduation.

Richtor pressed on the pulse plate beside and Lichten welcomed him with a smile. "Hey, aren't you tired of getting in trouble yet?" he queried as he slid the door open. "This is the last currentflip for classes. Hang in there. Come on in."

Lichten moved to the side and Richtor swam in. Lichten's room had many sketches all over the walls. A lot of them had sharrells or quarrells as a prominent part of the piece. There were sketches of the seaweed jungles and the fissures with their craftsheds near, or over, some of the cracks. There were even a couple sketches of the campus – interior and exterior though the exterior wasn't really that distinctive.

Each time Richtor came into Lichten's room, the sketches on the wall changed as Lichten gave away some, put some away, and created new ones. There were a few that always seemed to be present. There was usually a sketch of a herd of sharrells near the door across from his nestle. His nestle was almost always messy but it looked really comfortable too. Lichten was almost as well known for his deep sleeps as for how hard and well he worked with the shoal's herds and work animals.

"I know it's hard to believe," Richtor said with a sigh. "But I really don't try to get into trouble. I like almost all of the teachers on campus and I'd settle down more if I could."

Richtor wandered over to a set of shelves on the wall, admiring Lichten's collection of sketches and trophies. He picked up a small trophy that Lichten had won during his early years for gentling a wild sharrell. He had heard rumors of places where they still broke the spirits of the sharrells while getting them ready for service but it was widely acknowledged that gentling the animals was better all around. The animals tended to be more content, live longer, and be willing to learn more complex tasks. Lichten was a member of a group trying to eliminate the more violent breaking of animals.

"I don't seem to be able to settle down," Richtor continued, his voice tinged with frustration. "As you say, I just need to make it through this last currentflip. I'm sure I can make it that long – all of the teachers, except possibly Teacher Watfor, want me to graduate successfully."

Lichten nodded, understanding Richtor's struggles. "I don't know why Teacher Watfor seems to have a dislike for you. You've had fewer incidents in his class than most other classes and your work is always on time."

"And my grades are OK," Richtor added. "They're even better than average in the class. But, sometimes, my grades on tests seem to still be marked down," said Richtor.

"We probably won't be able to solve all the problems of Ocean today," said Lichten. "What's up for today? Did you have something in mind or did you just want to drop by? We can play a game of Glick if you want. I get shells."

Richtor chittered, shaking his head. "No, I don't quite feel like being demolished today," said Richtor with a smile. "I thought maybe we could check out some sharrells and have an excursion into the seaweed jungle."

"Sounds OK," Lichten replied. "Just you and me?"

"I thought maybe we might ask Januelle if she would like to join us."

"Fine with me," Lichten commented. "She's usually better at keeping you restrained from your stupider acts than I am."

Richtor grinned, defending himself. "Hey! I admit that sometimes they don't end up being the best ideas but we do have fun, don't we?"

"That we do, friend," Lichten added a chitter. "If we're going to be heading out on sharrells, I'm going to grab my personal tack - the stuff they issue at the public stables does the job but it can be a real pain in the tailfin to adjust."

Lichten gathered harnesses and other mysterious items from hooks on his wall near the shelves and turned around to Richtor. "Alright, let's go see if Januelle wants to come or if she'll talk you out of whatever you are planning. Oh, and I should grab a trident while I'm getting stuff. It could end up being useful if we're going into the seaweed jungle."

They headed out the doorway, sliding the door shut. The only lock that existed in the shoal was on the weapons depot door panel and that was primarily to keep the younger students from hurting themselves or others. Personal items were private and of little use, or interest, to anyone else.

They passed a few students heading the opposite direction. When this happened, the person swimming on the upper level went to their right and the person swimming on the lower level went to their left.

Luckily the spiral they were navigating was a gentle one – though, as they proceeded closer to the center, the spiral became tighter. Januelle's room was very close to the center of the spiral. It might have been faster to proceed via one of the spokes until they got closer to the center but sometimes it was just good to swim – especially when there was sufficient room to swap vertical positions.

They reached room '707'. The odd-numbered rooms were on the opposite side of the hall from the even-numbered rooms. Richtor pressed the pulse plate by Januelle's door while Lichten hovered close behind. No response. Richtor waited for a while, exchanged a glance with Lichten, and then pressed the pulse plate again. After waiting a bit more, Richtor turned to leave. At that point, they noticed Januelle coming down the corridor towards them.

"Hi guys," Januelle greeted them. "You here to see me?"

"Januelle," said Richtor. "Hey! I'm glad that you're here. Are you interested in joining us for a trip to the seaweed jungle? Lichten and I thought we might spend a day doing a bit of exploring." He paused and added, "There might be something new for you to study."

"Doubtful," said Januelle, with a twist of her mouth. "It's been studied too often, even by me."

"But you'll come?" Richtor asked.

"Sure," responded Januelle.

"That's great," Lichten chimed in. "Maybe you can keep this guy under control and we'll all come back in the same condition in which we start off."

"Hey. I'm not a miracle worker," Januelle retorted.

"Okay, okay," said Richtor. "It's pick on Richtor day. That's alright. I do kind of deserve it. But it's fun, isn't it? And we've only had one broken arm among us."

"Don't forget that lacerated tailfin," said Januelle.

"That could have happened to anyone," Richtor defended himself.

"Maybe," Januelle said with a playful smile. "Let me just go in and get my sample cases and instruments. Lichten, I see that you are carrying quite a bit. Is that for all of us, do we need to grab our own, or will we just be checking out tack at the stables?"

"This is for me," said Lichten. "If you want to bring your own tack, that's fine. I don't think you or Richtor have custom harnesses and leads so I would just use the stuff from the stables."

"Sounds reasonable," said Januelle. "Just wait here a moment. It gets a bit crowded if there are more than two in my chamber."

Januelle opened her door. As Lichten and Richtor looked in, they saw many shelves of displays of various sea life – much of it fossilized but there were a few live pets in cages too. Between her nestle and all of the shelves and displays, she probably had less than half the free space that Lichten had in his chamber. As for Richtor's chamber, it was a good thing no one tried to nestle on the floor but just swam above. If one ignored all the mess and clutter, there was plenty of room. He had a chambermate for a while but they parted in good spirits when she just couldn't stand his mess any longer. She found another chambermate and he moved into a single chamber.

Januelle grabbed a small purse bladder and looked through different shelves. She examined one item and put it back. Then she looked at a different shelf and put a couple of items into the purse. She finally nodded and swam over to the door. "I'm ready. Shall we go?"

Richtor looked at Lichten, who nodded approvingly. Richtor told Januelle. "Let's do it."

Chapter 3 Ready to Ride

Leaving the dormitory was quick and easy. Since Januelle's chamber was near the center, they could go to the central vertical tube and head up and out. That placed them high enough over the various sections of the shoal that they could orient themselves swiftly.

Lichten was the first to locate the public stables, of course, as it was very familiar to him since he went there to work a few days each week. The main difference in architecture from the other buildings in the shoal was that the corrals had latticed tops as the sharrells would panic if they were within a completely enclosed area. Glowbowls were acceptable for light but did not help with their claustrophobia.

The three friends swam in the direction of the stables. Januelle spoke to Richtor. "Do you have anything specific in mind?"

"Not really," said Richtor. "I need to keep myself moving and I thought I might see if the number of fish in the jungle has reduced."

"Reduced?" asked Januelle. "Why do you say that?"

"You know about the rationing for meals – particularly the fish. I overheard Teacher Gregov and Teacher Malov talking in the hallways quite a while ago. Teacher Gregov said that rations were going to be reduced because of a drop in the numbers of fish in the herd farm. And then it happened."

"Wow, I didn't know that" said Januelle. "I hadn't heard of a reason. They just announced the decision to reduce rations temporarily."

"I wonder why they didn't give any reasons for the reduction," Lichten said. "A reduction in the fish herd seems like a straightforward reason."

"I don't know why they didn't pass that along," mused Richtor, "maybe they thought it would raise even more questions. But, I had the thought maybe it is just affecting the herd and the jungle still has the same number. If so, maybe they can just increase the hunter quota."

"That wouldn't work," said Januelle. "The quota is there so that the hunters won't reduce the population to below recovery levels. We almost wiped out the jungle once upon a time before the Council stepped in and started regulating the hunts."

"Well, even if that idea is no good," said Richtor. "I want to see if there is any change in the jungle."

"If the herds are diminishing, maybe there are more poachers in the jungle," said Lichten. "That would cause a reduction in the number of fish in the jungle."

"You're right, Lichten," Richtor replied. "That's another reason why I wanted Januelle to come along. I'm wondering whether this affects all fish, just the herd fish, or the herd fish and some substitutes hunted by poachers. If it is affecting all fish then that is a different problem than if it's just the herd fish. She may have ways to determine what the precise situation is."

"You thought of all that, yourself?" asked Lichten. "I didn't think you paid enough attention to get much of anything out of science class."

"I like science. I just don't have the passion for it that Januelle has," Richtor protested. "Just because I have to leave the class from time to time, or I'm swimming around the aisles and back more than the others doesn't mean I'm not listening."

"OK, OK," said Lichten. "You know I'll always be there for you. I just didn't think you took classes very seriously."

"Well, you're right that I'm not a scholar like Januelle," Richtor said with sadness in his eyes. "But if I find something interesting, or practical for my purposes, I pay close attention. Sometimes too much attention."

Richtor regained his smile and said, "There have been times when I was so focused that the Teacher had to tap my hand for a cycle before I noticed. I don't know which bothers them more – too deep of focus or not paying attention at all."

"You're certainly unique, Richtor," said Januelle.

They had now reached the stables. There was a complex of enclosed work rooms used for office space, supplies, and areas where harnesses could be stored and put onto the sharrells ready for a day's ride. Connected to the stables, there were several corrals – with the latticed tops – in which the sharrells spent most of their time. There was enough room for exercise but not enough room for them to build up speed and knock out a wall. Some of the early corrals had that problem but problems existed to learn from.

Lichten took the lead when they went to the manager's area and started planning for the day. "We'd like to take out three sharrells for the day, Diplodus," said Lichten. "Is Brightglow available by any chance?"

"Aye, she is. We haven't had very many people come in to check out the sharrells today yet. Do you need tack for the sharrells too?"

"Just two sets. The normal set of harnesses. We don't expect to be hauling anything back."

"Aye, you brought your own tack, Lichten?" Diplodus asked.

"Whenever I can," Lichten replied.

"Are you still thinking about doing your apprenticeship here?" asked Diplodus.

"Yes," said Lichten.

"We'd be glad to have you here."

"Thanks. Can we head to the corral? What are the names of the other two sharrells?"

"Noseo and Widefin. Have you worked them before?" asked Diplodus.

"I've worked with Noseo but not Widefin."

"Then I'd better come along with all of you," Diplodus commented. "Widefin is relatively new in the group. She was gentled and brought into the stables about a halfflip ago."

"I'm glad she … is it a female?" asked Lichten.

"Yes, she is."

"I'm glad she was gentled," said Lichten.

"We don't add to the group with anything other than gentled sharrells. It's not worth it. They either depress the others or they're still on the edge of rebellion and fire off at the worst times," said Diplodus.

"Do we harness them in the corral?" Januelle queried. "I've only ridden out with groups from campus or the Academy and they had the sharrells ready for us."

"No. We'll shift them from the corral to the stables and harness them there. They can stand to be enclosed for a little while and the stable chambers have tack on the walls and tools to scrape off parasites and keep them in good health. Once they get into the stable chamber and the harnesses are attached, we can lead them from there to the open water," said Diplodus.

Diplodus led them outside and around the building to the corral areas with the latticed sides and tops. There was one large area where a number of sharrells were idly swimming. There were also a set of smaller chambers each of which were packed with nestles. A few sharrells appeared to be resting in the nestles. Most of the sharrells were on a diurnal cycle but the stable encouraged a few to shift to nocturnal so there would be well-rested mounts if needed during the night.

They swam through an opening in the corral which was too small for the sharrells to use as an exit. Lichten went up to a larger sharrell that had some dark bands, probably some type of orange if they were closer to the surface, which ran diagonally on its sides, starting lower towards the front and rising to the rear. Lichten took it by a blunted lobe fin and guided it towards the stables.

Diplodus led two other sharrells towards the stables as Richtor and Januelle followed him. Richtor and Januelle had been talking to each other on a private band but hadn't thought they had much to contribute to the business of getting the sharrells. Now, Januelle spoke up.

"Which sharrell do you think would be better for me? I don't have a lot of experience," said Januelle.

"You should go with Noseo," responded Diplodus. "Widefin may be a really great mount but we don't have as long of a history with her. Noseo is a pretty calm sharrell. She probably couldn't survive long in the wild as she seems to have lost most of her reflexes, and instincts, to react when something might startle her. Here, in the stables, that's a positive thing but being able to respond quickly is a necessity in the wild."

They entered the stable and positioned their sharrells near the walls near the tack. Lichten immediately started to set up his harness with Brightglow.

For young adults such as Richtor and his friends, the harness could be attached towards the arms. But older adults, who might have grown almost as large as the mounts, had to have modified harnesses that connected farther back so their tailfins did not disturb the mount's dorsal fin.

Lichten finished connecting the harness to Brightglow. He motioned to Richtor to come close. "Hey, can you help me with my harness? I can do it by myself, if I have to, but it's a lot easier with two people. I'll help you with yours later."

"Sure, Lichten," said Richtor. Lichten put his left arm through the harness and Richtor took the rest of the harness and swam over Lichten so it would wrap around his top. Lichten put his right arm through and motioned to Richtor that that was all he needed. "Thanks," said Lichten.

Diplodus was putting the mount harnesses on Noseo and Widefin. His experienced hands got them attached quickly. Januelle started putting her harness on by herself, tossing the harness across her back to allow the second arm to make it through the opening.

They all connected the straps on their underbodies, making sure the magnets were facing the correct direction and that they were firm against their bodies. Loose straps usually didn't cause much of a problem but it did tend to scrub away mucus and leave the skin more open to infection.

"I think you're all set up," said Diplodus. "You said you didn't need load harnesses?"

"Not for this trip. No need to pull anything behind them," Lichten responded.

"I might collect a few samples but I can easily carry them in my own travel kit," Januelle added.

"Well, then. You're all ready to go. Make sure you sign out with your planned destination and time of return," said Diplodus.

"We certainly will," Januelle and Lichten spoke at the same time. They chittered and Richtor swam over to join them, pulling his mount along by the lobe fin. "You guys go sign out in the journal. Mark the destination as the Jordech Jungle. I'm not sure when we'll get back. Just mark it as 14th hour and that should work well. We'll probably be back before 12th hour and in time for the dormitory dinner," Richtor said.

"I didn't pack any food for midday," said Lichten. "Did you?"

"No," said Richtor. "I didn't think about that part of the trip. I guess I'm not used to thinking about food that much."

"I have some snacks but not enough for a meal. Certainly not enough for meals for all three of us," said Januelle.

"Then I guess we need a side excursion before we head off. Since this trip is my idea, I'll pay for the lunches," Richtor said with a smile.

They led their mounts along towards the center of the shoal. There didn't seem to be any reason to attach themselves for such a short distance and no reason to tire out the sharrells.

A small snack shop was open not far from the stables. Richtor swam in and purchased four large seaweed wrapped sandwiches which contained a combination of ground fish meat, spices, and a spicy seaweed usually called picantos. He also got a bunch of sea grapes. He brought them over to the counter in front of the store worker who added them up and then handed Richtor a bill of work credits to be signed over to the shop. Richtor signed and the worker wrapped the purchases in cloth and tied it with string before handing it over.

"Here's lunch," said Richtor as he came out the door. Do either of you have a bundle strap? I can carry it by hand since we aren't hunting but connecting it to the harness would sure be easier."

"Let me look," said Januelle. "I often have one in my lab kit."

Januelle looked through her lab kit. After looking under a neatly folded cloth, she nodded her head and pulled out a long strap with a wide, ratcheted loop on one end and a set of snaps on the other end.

"Thanks," said Richtor as he put the strap around the package and through the loop. The ratchets held the strap firmly around the package. He looped the other end around an upper part of the mount harness and snapped it shut.

"All ready?" asked Richtor.

Januelle and Lichten nodded and they all mounted their sharrells, aligning the magnets which clicked together with a mild pulse. Taking hold of the handles, they directed the sharrells back past the stables and towards the Jordech Jungle.

Chapter 4 Onward to the Jungle

Diplodus wasn't visible as they rode past the stables. Widefin tried to return to the corrals but Richtor succeeded in keeping him on the correct path. Lichten often had his sharrell swimming above Januelle and Richtor. This gave him a bit more freedom of movement and also allowed him the opportunity to more easily help manage Januelle and Richtor's sharrells if they had any problems.

Once they had reached the edge of the shoal, there was more varied life on the seabed as well as areas of kelp and other seaweed in spots. The primary differences between within and without the shoal were a matter of buildings and the presence of wild seaweed. There were actually a lot of ground plants within the shoal area but very few animals. Except for a few deliberate spots, taller growths were not permitted within the shoal boundaries. Some people in the shoal thought that it might be more interesting to have taller plants around and thought that maneuvering around them might make journeys more interesting. So far, they were still in the minority.

This close to the shoal, about all they really had to do was to direct their mounts in the direction of the Jordech Jungle. The jungle was in a much shallower section of the seabed and, continuing on that path, would eventually lead to the surface. They should be able to get there in a couple of hours.

Richtor loved being in the open water. Even more, he loved to be on the move. He found it hard to imagine taking on a long-term work assignment that would have him hovering around the same space all day. But those types of jobs were in the majority. Even the people who worked with the sharrells, like Diplodus, spent most of the time hovering behind a counter.

There were those who headed out and found pods of wild sharrells, gentled them, and brought them back. That might be a type of work he could handle but the shoal only needed a limited number and people, such as Lichten, had the essential connection with the sharrells. The shoal was still growing but that growth only mandated perhaps one more sharrell each year. He wondered just what the wranglers did when they weren't finding, and gentling, sharrells. Maybe they worked at the stables. He should try to find out. Maybe Lichten would know.

"Hey, Lichten," said Richtor. "Do you think we'll encounter any wild sharrells along our path?"

"It's possible, I suppose. But I suspect that they mostly know not to hang around areas that people visit. There are always strays away from the pod. I see some of them from time to time."

"How about predators?" asked Januelle. "Do we have to watch out for any of those? Perhaps a sharpfang?"

"Probably not until we get to the jungle," said Lichten. "Look around. There are a few fish here and there but they aren't abundant and they don't group together. Sharpfangs prefer to be able to dart into a cluster of fish and not to chase after individual fish. They aren't that fast."

"Do you ever encounter Widemouths when you are moving around?" asked Richtor.

"No. I've only seen one in my life," said Lichten. "It swam through on its way to warmer waters. It did eat a few quarrells but we are too small to appeal much to it. My aquaculture class went on a well-guarded field trip to observe it from a distance. Goodness! Even from a distance they are huge."

"Even bigger than old man Gregritch?" asked Richtor.

Lichten chittered. "Yes, even bigger than elder Gregritch. You know, growing that old and big isn't something that is easy on a person. They have to eat a lot and the normal residential chambers aren't large enough for them"

At that moment, they passed a cloud of green algae. The sharrells turned their heads and tried to head for it. All three worked to maneuver their sharrells away from the cloud. Richtor's magnetic connection gave way and he was pulled through the water on the safety strap.

"Whoa!" said Lichten. His sharrell pulled up and started to turn away but Noseo and Widefin both ignored their riders and Richtor was unable to get his magnetic connector refastened.

The two sharrells reached the cloud and darted around trying to suck up all of the algae. Richtor finally was able to reconnect his harness connector and that gave him a firm perch upon which to try to persuade Widefin to head away.

Lichten came up with Brightglow in a calm, only slightly hurried proceeding. "We might as well let them all have a snack. I don't remember any other clouds on the route to the jungle. Just watch them and, when they seem to be slowing down, try to head them out of the cloud. If they eat too much, they'll be sluggish for hours."

Lichten allowed his mount to enter the cloud with the other two and the sharrells moved around while sucking in the algae. It must have been a pretty rich cloud as their eating didn't seem to affect the density or size of the cloud very much. After quite a few cycles, they appeared to start slowing. Lichten maneuvered Brightglow behind Noseo and Widefin and called out to Januelle and Richtor. "Time to head them back out."

With their appetites reduced, and Lichten urging them from the rear, Noseo and Widefin allowed themselves to be enticed from the cloud and continue their journey towards the jungle.

They had travelled perhaps half the distance. It had been a little over a half-hour ago that they had left their path to allow their mounts to eat. With the sidetrack into the algae cloud, they would arrive slightly later than expected. Not that it mattered just when they arrived.

Richtor surveyed the area from the back of his sharrell. The area had few rocks scattered around the seabed, and this limited the variety of sea life. However, the slope of the seabed was bringing them closer to the surface. By the time they reached the jungle, they would be only about seven or eight bodylengths below the surface.

Here, they were eleven or twelve bodylengths down. Of course, this was according to a standard bodylength – a typical young adult's length – since the People never completely stopped growing, Lichten's body length was not the same as

Diplodus's body length. But, the measurement of a bodylength was a standard length.

The blue tint of his back would be visible now although, of course, he could not see his own back. Januelle and Lichten also had blue tinted backs which was part of the reason the shoal was named the Bluefins. The red on his sides was not yet apparent and wouldn't be unless they got very close to the surface.

He saw a rock on the seabed with many corals arising from its surface. The cluster supported a fairly large number of small fish which darted in and out between the various growths of the different corals. He saw some crustaceans scuttling along on the sand. Just because this wasn't a jungle didn't mean that there wasn't a lot of life out here. A lot was hidden or had temporarily withdrawn as they drew near.

Richtor called over to Januelle. "Januelle. Is there anything you can do to check fish populations out here?"

"No, not really. I have to have a set of base numbers for the populations. I have some for the jungles which comprise a relatively homogenous area. But out here it would vary from section to section and there is no way to have a good baseline unless someone had just happened to have done a survey in a spot that was easily found again," replied Januelle.

"Oh well," said Richtor. "I wouldn't expect it to be that easy." He reached down to grab a scuttling criecraw, bit its head off, and then swallowed it. If it had been cooked, he would have eaten it more slowly but, fresh, it was better to go directly to the stomach.

"Hey!" Lichten said. "Do you have enough for all of us?"

"Find your own," responded Richtor with a chitter.

Richtor really wasn't that hungry yet. It was just the sight of the sharrells eating through the cloud that reminded him it had been a number of hours since breakfast. He saw Lichten also scoop up a criecraw but Januelle and Noseo just kept moving forward.

The seabed varied but stayed much the same too. Richtor could travel along in almost any direction for as long as it kept him moving. He was never bored or antsy as long as he was on the move. Right now, he felt very calm on the back of Widefin moving through the ocean with its continuously varying life.

He spotted a lone sharpfang heading after a small school of small fish. First, it circled the school enticing it to close in on itself and make a tighter, more compact, cylinder of fish. Then, once the density had gotten high enough, it headed into the school with its mouth jaw unhinged to scoop up as many fish as he could in one swoop through the school.

He could see Januelle looking around too. She and Noseo had taken the lead within their small group. Januelle was the smartest person he knew but she didn't rub it in. She was nice enough, and patient enough, to explain things even though sometimes you could tell that she couldn't quite understand why you didn't understand. She would never allow copying of homework or papers but sometimes, after you had obviously put in quite a bit of work, she would check it over and point out places where you hadn't understood the problem well enough.

Januelle's passion was in science and especially in biology. There was such a wide variety of life to be examined and she was always excited when she found something that no one else had ever reported. She was acknowledged within the campus, scientific, and academic communities for her insights about the life cycle of the criecraw. It was way over his dorsal fin but he was proud, in some manner, that she was a member of his hatching.

Lichten, on the other hand, wasn't a bad student, and a really good artist, but they weren't his primary interests. Lichten was larger than most of the other people within their hatching. He even had somewhat of a rigid, spiked, dorsal fin in front of his soft dorsal fin. That was rare within the shoal. It probably meant that his egg-giver or sperm-giver had moved to this shoal from another shoal. It happened on occasion. Mostly when that shoal had too many people within a particular work niche. Sometimes the Councils arranged trades of people to compensate for changes in workload or things needed.

"Hey, Lichten, what do the wranglers do when they're not wrangling?"

Lichten chittered. "What brought that up?"

"Just thinking about you."

"I hope they were good thoughts," Lichten responded. "They meander around a lot. They turn over rocks to see what's there. They go on automatic and hover and contemplate the world." He smiled. "Not that they come up with a lot worth sharing."

The Bluefin shoal, being perched on the boundary of the Fat Hole Fissures, was well known for processes that required high heat. Chemical and forging processes both made use of high heat. He wished that he would have had those talents. Lichten probably could have joined in with one of the forging groups because of his size and strength. They would have welcomed. But Lichten, though good at the biology areas in which he was interested, wanted to directly work with livestock. He was a wizard at gentling wild sharrells even though he had only a fraction of the experience that the official wranglers had.

The times that Lichten really shone, however, was when he worked with the quarrells. It was quite easy to be hurt when interacting with them. Similar to the sharrells that they used for labor and for riding, the quarrells were larger, stronger, and more intelligent in general. Their lobe fins were almost usable as arms. Usually if you left them alone, they would leave you alone but they could get aroused if you were doing something that they didn't like. It wasn't always easy to know, in advance, what that might be.

Some people liked quarrell meat of but the shoal did not allow them to be hunted. There was always the possibility that they might get mad and associate the attacks with the shoal. Then retribution might come down upon the shoal. It seemed like quarrell meat was always available, though, if you knew the right person.

Lichten could work directly with the quarrells and they seemed to accept his presence. That didn't stop him from carrying a trident with him whenever he was in their midst.

It wouldn't be fair to characterize Januelle and Lichten as the smart and the strong because they had many other great qualities – and a few not-so-great ones. Same as anyone. He was glad that they were his friends.

"Hey, Januelle! Isn't that the beginning of the Jordech Jungle?" Richtor asked.

He could now see the Jordech Jungle in the distance. There wasn't a firm boundary. There were always a few stragglers rooted here and there before the main part of the jungle, but it wasn't difficult to distinguish between being near the jungle and being within the jungle. Outside of the jungle, a person could see a reasonable distance any direction they turned their eyes. Within the jungle, you could only see as far as the next few kelps.

"Yes, that is the edge of the denser growth," Januelle replied. "At any rate, that starts the area where we group the numbers when we do our surveys."

Januelle would be the one doing most of the work while in the jungle. There were four or five species that were inventoried on a regular basis by the shoal. Januelle sometimes earned extra work credits by being part of the inventory crew. She knew the survey patterns and could take inventory in such a way that they could validly be compared to previous inventories. His and Lichten's duties would be to make sure that no predators came across them while they were handling the inventory.

Richtor called out to the others and suggested they pull up into a group prior to going in to the jungle. All were agreeable and soon they were in a triangle, with the snouts of their mounts facing one another in a triangular pattern.

"Januelle," said Richtor. "You have all the needed equipment to do the inventory?"

"Yes, I have paper, that has been marked up in a table, and a scribe to mark down what I can count."

"I am ready to check around the perimeter where you are working, Januelle," said Lichten. "How far away do I need to stay to be out of your way?"

"Try to stay at least two bodylengths away, please," replied Januelle. "You'll coordinate with Richtor?"

"Yes," said Lichten. "OK, Richtor?"

"Fine, let's go in."

Chapter 5 Into the Jungle

*T*he first thing that they noticed as they entered the jungle was a decrease in the amount of light. It was not a huge problem as all three of them were used to a low light level with the shoal being about 17 bodylengths below the surface. At this much higher level, having the light obstructed by all of the kelp still left it lighter than at home.

With the kelp practically leaf to leaf, it was hard to move freely. Yet, the difficulty was eased as the kelp could easily be pushed to the sides – coming back together after they had passed. Januelle followed a careful procedure of examination of the various fish populations in the area. It was likely that some fish were scared off and that the count was not fully accurate but that wasn't that important since she was following the same procedure as prior censuses.

It was any difference between the counts of previous censuses versus what she could obtain that was the important number. Even if the absolute number was off by a factor of two or three, the relative number should be able to be relied upon.

Lichten and Richtor did their watch while staying above Januelle by several bodylengths. This meant that, when they moved the kelp aside during their circles, it would not affect the kelp at Januelle's level. So far, there hadn't been any intruders that might be dangerous. One sharpfang moved through the area but did not head towards Januelle. Narrowmouths, which were smaller that the Widemouths, did occasionally roam about in the jungle but, so far, there had been no indication of one moving around.

After fifty cycles, or a half-hour, Lichten and Richtor reversed directions mostly to help relieve boredom and to be able to turn a somewhat fresher eye upon the area.

The seabed was still eight or nine bodylengths below the surface but they, towards the top of the kelp, were only a few bodylengths below the surface and the reds on Richtor's sides could now be seen although the colors were still subdued. Lichten had some red streaks among the spokes of his rigidly sharp dorsal fin. Januelle had some greens along her belly. They were much prettier at this depth but they had been visible for the past hour or so.

Richtor was getting bored. While it was true that he was keeping moving there was nothing much happening. Certainly nothing for which he needed to be alert. He spoke to Lichten on a private mental band to not disturb Januelle.

"What kinds of things are you doing these last couple of quarterflips to prepare for after graduation?" Richtor asked Lichten.

"Well, I know I want to work with animals," responded Lichten. "I've loved doing that since I was introduced to a sharrell in the first years after leaving the creche. I am working part-time at the stables and that is going all right and they seem to like me. How about you?"

"I don't seem to be able to figure out what direction I want to go," said Richtor. "I have pretty clear ideas as to what I don't want to do but that isn't the same thing as knowing what I do want to do."

"You have to have a source of worker's credits," Lichten reminded Richtor. "You can always go nomad for a few currentflips but people may start to forget you and that would make it more difficult to get an apprenticeship."

"Yes, I'm pretty sure I don't want to remain a nomad but, if I can't make a decision by graduation, I may not have a choice for a while. I only have enough savings for a few quarterflips until I would need to have some position making work credits to pay for room and board," Richtor replied.

"You know what I think would be great?" asked Richtor.

"That the Council would come to you with a great job offer?" responded Lichten.

"No. Well, yes, that would be great but it's not likely to happen," said Richtor. "I would like to be like Sebaria and roam all over Ocean, visiting shoals and taking notes on everything I saw."

"It hasn't been done since Sebaria did it," continued Richtor. "At least, no one from our shoal is known to have done something similar. They aren't even quite certain just when Sebaria's journey was. A long time ago, for certain."

"Wouldn't that just be going nomad with a purpose?" asked Lichten.

"Not quite. I could represent Bluefin shoal. That might make it easier to meet with other shoals. And, of course, I would get work credits so I could stay in the shoal. If I was sent by the Council, then any journal I put together would be treated as a contribution to the shoal. Maybe Teacher Lorell might teach it someday. That would be cool," Richtor said.

"That would be cool," said Lichten. "But you would need the approval of the Council. It's possible that Cheyelle, or some other member of the Council, has heard of you. You certainly aren't one to blend into the walls of the classroom. But

I'm not sure that awareness is quite the same as approval."

"Plus, if you were going out as an approved representative," continued Lichten. "You would need quite a few skills that I don't think you're quite ready for yet. Same skills as a nomad plus other skills for negotiating and presentations."

"Hunting, gathering, and protecting yourself would be very important. You would never quite know about your next meal. But the presentation and negotiating skills – those are skills you would need to keep yourself from getting killed by other shoals or nomads that you might encounter on your voyages. Plus, you would need them to get cooperation such that your journal entries would be useful."

"I'm not sure how to get those skills," said Richtor. "They certainly aren't taught formally at campus and there's no one to apprentice to who would be doing the same type of work."

At that point, a sharpfang darted past them heading downwards. Lichten pulled his trident out from the carrying tube that was connected to his back harness and thrust towards the sharpfang. Not fast enough – or, maybe, just not close enough.

Lichten encouraged extra speed from Brightglow by squeezing the harness as he gripped the handles on the sharrell's harness.

They both headed downward, following the sharpfang.

Richtor was still gathering his thoughts. Lichten was right - he didn't have the skills needed to follow in Sebaria's tailflips yet. Not yet.

Richtor decided that he would only get in the way if he tried to follow Lichten. It was better that he continue his patrols to make sure that nothing else headed down towards Januelle. Even with the two of them present, only Lichten had noticed, and reacted, quickly enough to be of any use. He would need to be extra diligent in his efforts while Lichten was gone.

Lichten came back up looking a bit flushed but not particularly happy.

"What happened?" queried Richtor.

"It quickly decided that it shouldn't keep going the direction it was going," said Lichten. "And that part was good."

"And?" asked Richtor.

"It flipped around and headed directly for Brightglow and me. Brightglow didn't like that and bucked me off."

"Bucked you off?" asked Richtor. "With all of your trophies?"

"Yes, with all my trophies," replied Lichten. "And I dropped my trident. Thank the great ancestor, it didn't hit Januelle as it fell but, between the trident falling and me chasing after it, Januelle is going to need to take a break for a while to allow the fish to settle back down before she can proceed with the next inventory."

"So, where is she?" asked Richtor.

"She should be following along soon," said Lichten. "In fact, I'm surprised she didn't get here before me. It took me a couple of cycles just to find my trident."

Richtor turned around and saw Januelle heading their direction, mounted on Noseo. All in all, she didn't look too upset.

"I had gotten three of the inventories finished before the trident and Lichten moved through my area," said Januelle. "So, I only have one more inventory to do."

"How do they look?" asked Richtor. "Is there a significant reduction in the numbers of fish here?"

"You're just going to have to wait for those answers, Richtor," replied Januelle. "I brought along the basic parameters to be followed to collect data for these studies. And I have been following those directives."

"But I did not bring along all of the data obtained from previous inventories," she continued. "Anything I might say right now might be completely false and slanted towards confirmation bias."

"Confirmation bias?" asked Lichten who had drawn up near the two of them.

"Yes. We came out here to determine whether the fish populations were reduced – or not," said

Januelle. "So, even if we try to be as honest and accurate as we can be, without the static data to compare we are likely to shift our interpretations towards situations where what Richtor suspected was actually correct."

"Hmmm," said Richtor. "I see what you mean. So, you can't give any interpretation at the moment?"

"I prefer not to. I'd rather wait and have some reliable information instead of rushing it."

"OK," said Lichten. "How long do we need to wait for things to settle back down?"

"I would give it at least an hour," said Januelle.

"Shall we eat lunch, then?" asked Lichten.

"Why not?" Januelle said with a smile. "Richtor may not be that interested in food but we can always rely on you to not miss many meals."

"I'm just a growing boy," said Lichten.

"As much exercise as you get, it would be hard for you to overeat," said Richtor. "As for me, I feel like I am always on the move but I have to watch my girth."

"Have you spotted any algae clouds for the sharrells to use as a foraging spot?" asked Januelle.

"No. I guess it was a good thing that we allowed them to fill up on the way. We'll keep a watch for another cloud on the way back. You haven't spotted any food concentrations within the jungle, have you Januelle?" spoke Richtor.

"No," responded Januelle. "There are some fish who nibble on the kelp and you can see marks on the plants as well as places where the kelp has healed and split off a new branch. But nothing that works well for the sharrells."

"It hasn't been a long time since they ate. About three hours or so," said Lichten. "It shouldn't be a hardship for them. However, one criecraw isn't much food for me since leaving the shoal. Can we eat?"

"Oh," said Richtor. "I forgot that I had our lunches leashed to Widefin's harness. Just a moment." Richtor worked at disconnecting the strap from the harness and then removing the strap from the package. He worked slowly and carefully as he didn't want the sandwiches falling down into the kelp too.

Richtor handed two sandwiches to Lichten and then another one to Januelle. He kept the sea grapes to himself for the time being. He thought they might be more easily shared after they had eaten their sandwiches.

"Thanks," said Lichten. "I see you remembered to get me two sandwiches. I appreciate it. One sandwich just isn't enough for me."

"All the better to be able to protect Januelle and me," said Richtor. "Hey, not too close." Richtor spoke to some scavenger fish who had come around once he started biting into his sandwich. Ocean's housekeepers. He wished that they came into his room. They would really be useful. He was afraid that his room had attracted a few groundfeeders that expected to be fed on a regular basis. They weren't disappointed very often. It worked out alright. They occupied the floor of his chamber and he occupied the rest. As long as they stayed out of his nestle.

Richtor finished the last of his sandwich. Lichten was halfway through his second sandwich. Januelle was looking at the rest of her sandwich as if she was wondering just what it was.

"You want some sea grapes, Januelle?" asked Richtor.

"Maybe. But I don't think I want the rest of this sandwich. Do either of you want it?"

"You can count on me to not refuse food," said Lichten. He pushed in the remainder of his second sandwich and held his hand out to Januelle. She placed the remainder of her sandwich into his hand. "Thanks," she said.

"No problem," replied Lichten.

Richtor broke off some sea grapes from the bunch and handed them to Januelle. She took them, tore off one, and popped it into her mouth. She smiled at Richtor.

"Well, I think it has been an hour," said Januelle. I am going to head back down. Try not to drop any tridents. OK?"

"No promises," said Lichten. "I didn't drop it on purpose last time. Are you seeing any sharpfangs or any other pests down there?"

"Not really. But I can get really focused when I am working. You know what that's like, Richtor. I might not see them even if they were around," said Januelle. "I do feel a lot better with you two circling around up here. When I was with the expedition from the shoal, they had several people designated to watch while the rest worked. Once, there was even a narrowmouth that needed to be chased away." She headed downward.

"I think that I can handle a single narrowmouth," said Lichten. "But not two and not anything larger. You haven't done much hunting, have you Richtor?"

"No. It never really appealed to me."

"Well, if you think you might follow in the tailflips of Sebaria you might consider going out on a few hunts," said Lichten.

"You can't be very active today without a trident," he continued. "And, unlike Brightglow, your sharrell won't be willing to approach, or be in the way of, a narrowmouth or even a group of sharpfangs. But you will be able to help if we get any large predators by just staying in the path of them if they were to head towards Januelle."

"I understand," said Richtor. Maybe being an explorer was really a bit much for him to dream about. Although he did know a little bit about a lot of things, he wasn't sure that he knew enough about anything to be really useful at it.

Richtor handed Lichten the rest of the sea grapes. He strapped up the now-empty bag and connected it to the harness. The scavenger fish would be happy to clean up some extra food but not inedible litter. Keep it clean! He wondered how many times he encountered that phrase in the creche. Not enough times for some people, he supposed, as every once in a while he encountered litter on the seabed. He picked it up when it was a small enough amount to carry or when he had a bag with him.

Lichten and Richtor started their patrol circle once again.

Chapter 6 Back to the Shoal

*T*here was no dangerous activity, and no tridents dropped, over the next hour. Januelle swam up to them. "All done?" asked Richtor. "Still can't give any guesses as to any changes?"

"I can. I won't," Januelle answered. I can probably give you some kind of results by the end of the day if it's that time critical for you. I'd prefer to just give them to you during campus time on weekstart. Tomorrow, I plan to go to church."

"That's right. You're a member of the Shrankan Church," said Lichten. "Have they said anything about any changes in food supply?"

"No. I haven't heard anything. But then, according to Richtor, they didn't even pass along what they knew to the campus. In spite of what people seem to think about the church, it doesn't always know about things first before non-church attenders." Januelle said. This was not the first time her church attendance had come up among them. Usually, they just didn't talk about it.

"Hey! No offense meant. They just sometimes seem to know more than the average person in the corridors," responded Lichten.

"Just cool it," said Richtor. "If there is any new information, I'm sure Januelle would let us know. Since the Council changed food allocations based upon the situation, people have asked and are going to keep asking questions. I bet that every network in the shoal is vibrating."

"Well, I haven't heard anything," said Januelle. "But I'm only an attender. I'll start listening more closely at after-church functions."

"I'll check with folks that come to the stables – or, at least, I will if the topic of food or such comes up," said Lichten.

"Great," Richtor said. "Let's head back to the shoal."

They had lots of time to get back to the shoal since they had put down that they wouldn't be back until late. Richtor thought that they might wander a bit crosscurrent and see if they could find a good algae cloud for the sharrells. He knew that they ate well that morning but he also knew that they hadn't eaten as much as they wanted. It would be OK for them to be a bit sluggish on the way back. It would head off any possible supplemental feed charges if the sharrells weren't very hungry when they returned them to the stables.

"At least it's not close to time for currentflip," Januelle said. "That would make everything more difficult."

"How would that make things more difficult?" asked Richtor.

"When we do studies and comparisons, we want to keep as many factors constant as possible," Januelle replied. "During the period of currentflip, the direction of the primary current in our area of Ocean changes - or flips. That can mess up someone who sleeps through currentflip as they might have trouble reorienting. But it would also introduce a number of possible factors affecting population that would be periodic. In short, a currentflip event might make a survey unusable. Certainly, no one within the academic community would ever do a survey close to the currentflip events."

Richtor considered Januelle's talk. He wasn't that interested in knowing what wasn't involved in the herd problem. He decided he was getting his harnesses all tangled. There weren't any grounds for speculation and even less for determination of a cause. Januelle's efforts would give more information but it probably was something that had already been done by the Council. The fact that the Council had not announced the reasons for the rationing to the general public was a strong indication that they did not have an answer yet.

"Hey. You're quiet," said Lichten. "Are we heading crosscurrent on purpose?"

"Hmmm. Oh. Yes," said Richtor as he brought his thoughts back to the present. "I thought we would head for that big algae cloud that is usually present about a third of the way back from the jungle and a couple of thousand bodylengths crosscurrent. You know the one I mean, right?"

"Oh sure. Everyone who hunts, or guides hunters, knows about that cloud. But do our sharrells really need to eat? Brightglow doesn't act particularly hungry."

"Noseo doesn't seem hungry either," said Januelle.

"Widefin doesn't either," said Richtor. "But we know that they would have eaten more, at the small cloud we encountered, this morning if we had let them. And it's been about three and a half hours since then. So, it's safe to say that they would be willing to eat again."

"So would I," grinned Lichten. "But that doesn't mean that I need to."

"You old garbage cleaner," replied Richtor, nudging his mount over to tap Lichten's on the side. "Are you sure your egg wasn't fertilized by a cleaning fish?"

"I've never known one to be as large as I am," responded Lichten to his friend's gibe. "And I have never known one to have a rigid dorsal fin either." Lichten, when teased about his rigid dorsal fin while in the creche, had decided that the best response would be for him to take pride in his difference and that had worked well. In addition, it may have inspired him to be more physically active and become stronger than average.

"So, why are we heading to the algae cloud?" asked Januelle.

"There doesn't seem to be a hurry and I would prefer to avoid any surcharge being tacked on. That might happen if the sharrells are overly hungry when we return them," said Richtor.

"Oh. That makes sense," said Januelle. "If you are worried about the cost of this trip, I can put some into the pot."

"No, no," responded Richtor. "This is all about my insatiable curiosity. You two shouldn't need to feel like it's any part of your responsibility. I'm just glad you both were willing to come."

As they approached the large algae cloud, their mounts started swimming faster. This time, they allowed the sharrells to move forward as they wanted. It would not matter if they overate. It was just too bad that the friends could not easily eat from the cloud themselves. It wasn't that they couldn't eat the algae but their mouths were made to open up for eating and did not have baleen to efficiently filter the algae from the cloud.

Luckily, Brightglow stayed at the edge of the cloud and Noseo and Widefin stayed close to her. If they had chosen to go directly into the churning cloud, their second eyelids might not have been sufficient to keep all of the mass of food from their eyes. None of them - not even Lichten - had brought along goggles this trip.

As the sharrells ate their fill, they got a bit slower in their movements. When it appeared that they were almost forcing themselves to continue to eat, Richtor nudged Widefin away from the cloud. She moved away readily. Seeing Richtor and Widefin, Lichten urged Brightglow away and Noseo, with Januelle on top, followed along.

The movements of the sharrells were definitely slower now as they headed towards the shoal once again. Lichten started nodding off a bit. He had eaten the most during their lunch and he was starting to feel the effects. It didn't matter as long as they didn't encounter anything dangerous - which would mean a narrowmouth or larger. The sharpfangs could be a danger if they caught you by surprise but, in the open water, that would be hard for them to do. The sharrells, especially the wild ones, were quite adept at discouraging sharpfangs from coming too close.

The journey continued in silence. Januelle glanced over at Richtor from time to time but, as he appeared to be lost in thought, she turned back to align herself with the sharrell.

Mostly, Richtor was just thinking about his future. He was curious about the food supply and what was causing it but his larger dreams were to be useful to the shoal and not be bored out of his mind. Some type of research might be good since he was able to obtain a good, prolonged, focus once his interest was aroused. But he wasn't an academic, like Januelle. He needed a current, relevant, problem to address. He hoped that he wasn't making a problem where there wasn't one.

It was true that the people on the Council addressed problems. Cheyelle, head of the Council, was particularly good at analyzing a problem and knowing who could best resolve it. But Richtor wasn't a politician himself - dealing with many different groups of people and attempting to make them all content with a solution or creating packages of things which allowed for proceeding without necessarily being heartily endorsed.

In addition, in spite of being associated with current problems, the Council was not particularly active - and he needed a job where he could be active. Aiming to be on the Council just didn't fit.

He wondered whether he could really follow in the tailflips of Sebaria. Sebaria needed to negotiate with other groups, other shoals. She needed to handle groups of people. How did what she did differ from what was done within the

Council? It felt different but he wasn't sure that it was.

"Hey, Richtor. Where are you?" asked Januelle who was not very happy at effectively being by herself after having done so much work through the day.

"Oh. Sorry, Januelle," replied Richtor. "I just can't keep myself from wondering what I will do after we graduate. You're pretty clear on your direction and Lichten has a few possible directions to choose from, with the likelihood of being accepted. I don't have either."

"There are others in that same situation, Richtor," said Lichten. "You don't do badly in classes but you don't have the best reputation as a student. You seem to be more interested in what hasn't been done than in the things that have been done and are available to do."

"True enough," responded Richtor. "My top skill seems to be getting in trouble. But I don't really want to bother anyone or be a pain."

"So, just why are you that way?" asked Januelle. "If you don't want to be that way then why not stop?"

"I can't stand to hover in one place and just listen. If I take off with a subject and start thinking about it - maybe even fantasize about doing it or being there - I get in trouble for not paying attention. Actually, I am paying really deep attention - just not to the teacher."

"If I don't get captured by the material, then it feels like there is pressure that keeps building up inside of me and I have to move or I'll explode. Then I either get in trouble for moving or get in trouble for leaving the classroom. Or both."

"Well, at least most of the teachers like you," said Lichten. "That helps. You'll probably graduate and you'll probably be able to get letters of recommendation if you decide what you want to do. Even though your attention isn't always good, there aren't too many teachers or students who don't know about you."

"That's me. Most likely to ... That's just it. What am I most likely to do? Why can't I just know what I want to do or just fall into a particular niche that is already scoped out, and has been for a number of years? This seems like the hard route. And I don't want to do the hard route."

"I'll always be around for you to talk with," said Lichten.

"Me too," said Januelle. "Hatchmates to the end."

"Thanks guys. That does mean a lot to me. Wow, we're starting to get close to the shoal. It's still early to return the horses or to eat dinner. Care to join me for a tour around the shoal?"

"A tour?" asked Lichten. "Does that make us tourists?" he asked with a chitter.

"Sort of, I suppose," said Richtor. "I thought that looking around at what is done within the shoal might give me some ideas as to what I might like to do."

"If you think it might be helpful, I'm in," said Lichten.

"I think that I'd rather head into the dormitory and start analyzing the data I collected today," said Januelle. "Unless you think that coming with you is more important?"

"No, that's fine. Thanks for coming along and thanks for doing so much work. I'm sorry I wasn't much companionship on the way back," said Richtor.

"Not a problem. I enjoy being with you, Richtor. It is rarely dull though, sometimes, it is more work than what I expect," said Januelle. "Should I take Noseo back to the stables or do you want to return her along with Widefin and Brightglow?"

"You can take her back, please," said Lichten. "Just tell Diplodus that we'll be back in an hour or two. Thanks again."

"OK. I'll see you later," said Januelle as she steered Noseo back towards the stables as Lichten and Richtor headed towards the fissures.

Chapter 7 By the Fissures

O n the currentflow side of the shoal, bright spots marked the boundaries of the shoal, appearing and disappearing intermittently. The seabed was thin here, and there was a constant movement of the crust. As one area broke and magma surfaced, another recent break was already cooling and adding to the seabed layers.

Once the magma broke through the crust, it transformed into lava. Because of the transient access to the intense heat of the lava, the scientists, craftspeople, and artisans who utilized the heat sometimes had to crack open the cooled lava to allow new magma to escape.

Richtor and Lichten moved their mounts closer to the jagged line of broken crust. As they moved closer, they could see the people gathered around the edge.

"Have you ever consider working in the fissure works?" Richtor asked. "With your strength and size, you could be of considerable help."

Lichten replied, "No, not really. Sure, I could be a grunt, even a useful grunt, but the ones who are truly appreciated are the scientists and artisans creating new ways to use the heat."

Broadly speaking, there were three uses of the heat from the fissures. The first area was scientific – both theoretical and research. People involved with these areas tended to vary the equipment that they used. The temperature they needed also varied as part of different experiments and there were finely crafted thermometers in use in each of these areas. Glass hoods were sometimes suspended above the heat source to allow trapping, mixing, and other experiments upon different mixtures of gases. Sturdy walls separated the glass hoods from the work area, protecting scientists during potentially explosive experiments.

Richtor and Lichten had their mounts swim near the enclave with the scientists but kept their distance. They knew that disturbances were not welcome and could be dangerous. Richtor had already ruled out a career as a scientist. The researchers had to have the attitudes of both scientist and entrepreneur and were not in the scope of Richtor's vision for his future.

"Do you know anyone working in the fissures well enough to answer questions?" Richtor asked.

Lichten pondered for a moment. "Maybe. But they'd be more willing to talk about their work and answer questions during non-working hours. The fissures are always in flux and it's much easier for them to work with changes as they occur."

"Okay," Rector replied. "I guess we can move on."

The remaining work areas were focused on producing various products. This was the second category. Some were used by artisans who made one-of-a-kind necklaces, rings, girthbelts, helmets, home decorations and artisanal products. Some, who had especially popular products, had a quasi-factory line set up, with a number of apprentices involved, producing a large number of nearly identical products. Nearly identical, but not completely identical, as they were still hand fashioned. These artisans also catered to the needs of scientists and researchers, creating specialized items such as custom-shaped glass hoods or containment pieces.

"Do you think you might want to do sculpture?" Richtor asked. "You're an excellent artist."

"Thanks," Lichten replied. "I hope to keep doing my art for all of my life but only on the side. My passion is to work with sharrells – maybe do something more with quarrells in the future."

The third category of users of the fissures were those of the factories. They manufactured s stream of products with multiple people working in either assembly lines or as craftspeople dedicated to a single product. Neither Richtor nor Lichten knew the full array of products made in these factories, but their production was often traded with other shoals that lacked a reliable heat source.

The factory sections were located in the regions of the fissures farthest away from the shoal. Although the Council would not allow any to poison the environment, there were still sufficient disagreeable byproducts of the factories such that their proximity to, or distance from, the shoal was an important matter.

Most of the factories had either individual shops within the shoal or combined together to sell different factory products at the same retail stall. The factories, along with associated shops and stalls, formed the economic backbone of the Bluefin Shoal.

However, not all products required heat. Those that didn't were located in a separate group of buildings perpendicular to the shops over the fissures. One such area was the nacre tile farm, which didn't need heat but required undisturbed open seabed.

The shoal's daily necessities, such as the stables, campus, shops, and so forth were confined between the fissures, the non-heat-needed factories, and the nacre tile farm. The expansion of the shoal occurred in the direction heading away from the fissures.

The factories that didn't need heat for their products tended to be smaller, unable to compete in the Oceanwide markets. They primarily catered to local consumption, except for harnessware. No one was certain how it had come about but the Bluefin Shoal was famous for its harnessware. Many people of the shoal learned to make harnessware for themselves and a number of the better ones found employment at the factories.

Continuing their swim over the fissure business section, Lichten and Richtor headed crosscurrent toward the nacre tile farm. "It wouldn't be bad to work on the farm. It's a very routine job, with almost no deviations from day to day, but it would certainly keep me active and moving. What do you think?"

"I think it's like my artwork," replied Lichten. "It's something you like, and might want to continue to do part-time when there's need, but you would go nuts doing the same thing over and over."

Richtor nodded, feeling like that was true but half wishing it wasn't.

There was no need to keep their distance from the nacre tile farm for safety, but they did not want to disturb anyone. Of course, the oysters wouldn't be upset by almost anything that they might do. They waved at the workers tending the rows of oysters.

Each oyster was about a forearm in diameter. These oysters were well taken care of and produced numerous nacred objects in their lifetime. The time required was directly associated with the thickness of nacre desired. Decorative nacred tiles needed almost a currentflip to develop a thick enough layer suitable for inhabited areas. Artisans sometimes worked with surfaces that had much thinner layers of nacre, requiring less time but of greater delicacy.

The farm had been breeding the oysters for nacre production and quality for many generations. They did export some of their work but most was used locally within the shoal. The farm took pride in their products but there were many other oyster farms throughout Ocean.

Occasionally, Richtor and Lichten worked temporarily for the farm when they needed to reseed the oysters - carefully opening them, removing the current object and then putting a new object, or objects, inside before allowing the oyster to close again.

At the moment, the workers were pulling along large nets of algae that had been scooped out of a cloud. It used to be that the algae cloud that was very close to the farm was sufficient but, as the farm had grown, they had needed to get food from more than one cloud so as to leave enough for fast repopulation of the clouds.

As the workers pulled the nets along behind them, a medium-sized hole in the end of the net released algae between the rows. The oysters fed off of the algae as the current swept the food over them and they filtered it out of the water.

Richtor observed that the workers remained in motion, but the tasks were the same day in and day out. The only variations occurred during harvesting and reseeding when the tasks changed, requiring additional staff. He could continue to be a temporary worker. That wouldn't give him enough credits to last through the currentflip, but it could serve as a supplement to other income.

Richtor and Lichten turned their sharrells back into the living area of the shoal. Richtor observed the campus building, dormitories, the stables, and a couple of office and shopping complexes. There was no specific organization of the shoal. The Council had attempted long-term planning but that never seemed to work out. More structures were built as they were needed, always expanding outward from the fissure.

Overall, the system worked well. If they ran out of room at the campus building then the distance to a new campus would automatically take into consideration the population growth. Same thing applied to shops and dormitories. The Council building and associated office buildings was the one functional unit that probably wouldn't be duplicated. If needed, they might move the structures to be more centrally located but the Council had discussed splitting the buildings and the drawbacks far outweighed the benefits.

The last two major structures for the shoal were not built by the people of the shoal. The hatching area and the creche were located at the older area of the fissures, where the seabed had built up and cooled off. These mounds had left some pockets where a natural hatching cave could be present. Another pocket had become the creche. Both had been expanded beyond their original sizes but retained the general configuration and characteristics of the natural caves.

"Let's head over to the creche now," Richtor suggested. "I could never stand to work at the hatching area but working with the wigglewarts might be acceptable."

"I don't know how you can take being with them for long," responded Lichten. "Their activity and short attention spans drive me nuts."

Richtor grinned. "Maybe that is why I like them - they're just like me. Maybe I need my own creche."

"Maybe you do," responded Lichten. "OK. Let's go." With hand waves from both of them to the workers in the oyster beds, they maneuvered the sharrells off towards the older area of the fissures and the caves of beginning.

Chapter 8 In the Beginning

As they moved towards the caves, Lichten asked Richtor more questions. "You have been about the same since our days at the creche. If fact, looking back on it, I can understand your comments on having an affinity to the wigglewarts. Of course, you know quite a bit more than they do, and you're not quite as clumsy, ..."

"Not quite?" Richtor grinned. "Being really generous there, aren't you?"

"Yes. I guess that I am," replied Lichten with an even bigger grin than Richtor's. "And you have quite a bit more experience but you fidget just as much and your focus is sometimes about the same as theirs and, at other times, it is hard to get you to pay attention to anything around you."

"Sounds about right," said Richtor. "The doctor thinks there is something different about me."

"Well, I think the doctor is right," replied Lichten, still grinning. "But do you know what?"

"What?"

"I kind of like you just the way you are," said Lichten.

"Thanks," said Richtor. "I kind of like you too." They reached out and hooked little fingers for a moment.

Letting go, they looked towards the front and saw that, during their talk, the sharrells had drifted to the right of where they wanted to head. They redirected them and continued their journey.

The caves containing the hatching area and the creche were quite a way from the shoal. After the eggs were laid and fertilized, until they hatched, the area was well guarded. Although there had not been an attack in Richtor's and Lichten's lifetime, there had been a couple attacks in the history of the shoal.

Once it had been attacked by a citizen of the shoal who was deeply upset that she had not had a chance to lay her eggs before the fertilization period. She had been under medical care during the week in which the egg-laying and fertilization rituals had taken place. She had felt that, as a highly ranked female, they should have postponed the proceedings until she was well enough to participate. Her ranking had been removed and, to the best of Richtor's knowledge, she was still under medical care to this day. Her story was used as a tale to warn about taking rank too seriously.

The other attack – quite a while ago but not quite back to the time of Sebaria – was by another shoal. They had wanted to take over the area near the fissures. Destruction of the eggs in the hatching area, as well as those in the creche, had been heartbreaking to the newly established shoal but the invaders had been driven off and the shoal was now large enough, and strong enough, that that was unlikely to ever happen again. Still, while the eggs were in the hatching area and before they hatched, there were several guards at all times. This tale was used on campus – in this case, the object was to reinforce that the shoal could not become complacent and that dangers, known and unknown, did exist.

As they approached the caves, they could see that the hatching area was deserted – the latest hatching having taken place almost a quarterflip prior to their visit. No resources were used when there were no eggs present. They drifted over towards the mouth of the hatching area.

"No security here," Richtor said. "That means no eggs present and we are free to look around."

"Great," Lichten said this with a roll of his eyes. "I wish there had been. The closer I am to the exits of the hatching cave, the less I like it."

The mouth of the hatching cave was small. There was enough room for a younger person riding a sharrell and there was enough room for a much older person, who had grown large, to pass through. It was probably large enough for two young people to go in without sharrells.

Richtor had not brought a portable glowbowl so there was no reason to enter into the hatching area. Although everyone in the shoal could see with limited light – even at night when there were no glowbowls present – the darkness within a cave was much more intense.

"Have you been inside of the hatching area?" asked Richtor. "I mean, of course, other than when you hatched?"

"Sure," replied Lichten. "We had that field trip during the sixth currentflip of classes. Don't you remember? We went together. Januelle, you, and I as part of the 'Three Tailfins'."

"Oh, yeah," said Richtor. "I had forgotten that trip. We were even able to come – very well watched over and guarded – while the eggs were present. Have you come back since then when the hatching area is empty?"

"Not me," said Lichten. "I still have winnowing nightmares every once in a while. There's nothing cozy about this area for me."

"For me neither," said Richtor. "But I did come back once. I wanted to look at the area when it wasn't busy and there weren't so many people around."

"Did you like that?"

"No, not at all. I think it might have been worse than visiting with the crowds," said Richtor. "But it helped me deal with my fears a bit so I am glad I went."

"No thanks for me," said Lichten. "I never want to go back there."

"Not even when it is time for you to help prepare for a future hatching?" Richtor grinned.

"Well, maybe then," Lichten said, blushing. "Right now, I have no urge to be part of it. But I understand that I will probably change my mind at some point."

Richtor remembered both of his visits to the hatching cave. The first, of course, was along with the rest of his hatching. He came back by himself a number of currentflips ago - with a portable glowbowl. He had started thinking rather seriously about his future at that time and something told him he should start from the beginning.

There was nothing really special about the hatching cave except that it had only one entrance large enough for people over the age of about four currentflips. It did have a number of small openings around the cave. Some of them had been cut through the cave wall. It was important that the cave have a current of fresh water.

The cave floor was now all sandy. Richtor understood that it was initially pretty rocky but, over many generations, the floor area had been smoothed and then covered with sand. Sand was one of the first things they started trading for once they had started production by the fissures. Sand could be found anywhere on the seabed of Ocean but the areas where it accumulated enough to be easily harvested only existed near the borders between the sea and the land.

The sand wasn't required for the hatching cave. He had heard of some shoals having to create a hatching area. Not all shoals were fortunate enough to have suitable caves nearby. Well, that wasn't quite correct. If at all possible, new shoals were established near an existing cave, or caves. Having a cave to be used as the creche was more of a status thing and that was a bonus for the Bluefin community.

Every other currentflip, for about a week, the cave was the focus of the yearly brood ceremony. The highest ranked females would enter the cave and lay their eggs upon the sandy floor. Usually, the high ranked ones laid their eggs closer to the entrance as, when the males came through to scatter their sperm, the eggs nearest the entrance were the most likely to be fertilized. Thus, the high-ranking females' eggs were most likely to be fertilized by the most high-ranking males. It was considered to be highly anti-social for a subsequent female to lay her eggs on top of someone else's – reducing the chances for fertilization.

Occasionally, with echoes towards those who produced their hatchlings in private, females would lay their eggs in specific locations within the cave – telling their preferred males just where those locations were. Coordinating fertilization used to be a taboo for the shoal but it was now primarily a comfortable and ingrained avoidance.

From the point of view of the males, they entered the cave in order of ranking. Ranking was not stable although those on the Council usually consisted of people who maintained a high ranking. Points towards ranking could be accumulated in various ways – through unpaid community service, through generating work credit surpluses for the shoal, for special achievements, or according to various academic and physical test results. The goal was to have the people who most contributed to the shoal, or were considered to be the most able, be best represented in the next hatching.

The hatching took place one currentflip after the fertilization. The hatchlings swam around the cave, very hungry, and would start going after the unfertilized eggs first and then, if still hungry, any non-hatched eggs. Most of the adults stayed outside of the cave at this time and held various food items that were particularly attractive to the hatchlings to entice them to exit.

The exception to this were those few couples who had chosen to have a private hatching. They were required to bring their hatchlings to the hatching cave as soon as they hatched. Some still grumbled that this gave the couples an advantage but the same winnowing occurred within the private hatching as within the public hatching and they had to bring them over to merge with the rest of the hatchlings before they were allowed to move to the creche. This was the compromise reached within the Council to allow private hatchings. Once the privately hatched hatchlings were deposited in the hatching cave, they were now part of the hatching.

Once the hatchlings were enticed to leave the hatching cave, they were lured over to the creche cave where they could be fed and monitored. It was not unusual to have an additional 40% of the hatching winnowed out after departure from the hatching cave. Although their brains were not very mature at the time of the hatching, most of the citizens of the shoal had some memories of their hatching and the winnowing that followed. There were no citizens who permanently worked around the hatching cave and it was not a popular place at which to volunteer during the period of fertilization to hatching.

"The cave floor is clean," Richtor remarked. "The cleaning fish do a good job when they are released in here after a hatching."

"And someone has to make sure that they have cleaned up," Lichten added. "But it won't be me. I'm only coming here for you."

"Thanks, Lichten."

Lichten gave Richtor a brief blink of both eyes indicative of acknowledgement.

Lichten's face indicated fear and loathing while Richtor's was rather analytical. "Hey, you really don't like the hatching cave or anything to do with the hatching, do you?" asked Richtor.

"It's not the hatching that bothers me. It's the winnowing afterward. I remember being chased by one hungry, persistent, hatchling. I barely made it outside the cave and near an adult. It veered off once I reached the supervising adult."

"Do you know who was chasing you?" Richtor asked.

"Yes. I have seen her around. I try to not have her in any of the same classes as I have but I've ended up having her in two of my classes over the currentflips."

"Does she remember you?" asked Richtor.

"I don't think so. But she's just as aggressive as ever. She was probably the prime motivation for my working out so much. So, I guess that I can appreciate her for that. Ughhh."

"I hatched early and got full on non-fertilized eggs before I headed out of the cave," said Richtor.

"That's the easiest way to do it," said Lichten. "Of course, not everyone can be among those who hatch first but I'll bet that you don't have any nightmares from the hatching."

"You'd win that bet," said Richtor. "I just remember meeting Januelle along the way as I was herded to the creche cave."

"I didn't know that's when you met her," said Lichten.

"Yep. She was really smart even then. Before she had even entered the creche, she had asked more questions than I even had words for. And, of course, her questions were broadcast to one and all. But she was one of the first to learn how to channel mental speech so that only an intended recipient would receive it."

"She was one of the first for most things, wasn't she?" asked Lichten.

"She was and she is," replied Richtor. "I don't think either she or you will have any problems finding a niche. I haven't talked with her much about it because I seem to only convey negativity about a career search and who wants to listen to a bummer like that, day after day?"

"Hey, you can say whatever you want. Anytime," said Lichten.

"I appreciate it. Well, I guess I've stared at the hatching cave entrance long enough. Let's head over to the creche," said Richtor.

"Great idea." Lichten prodded Brightglow into a fast swim. "Beat you there!"

Richtor called after his friend's tailfin. "Yes, I'm sure you will." He urged Widefin along to follow in Brightglow's wake.

Chapter 9 To Creche or Not to Creche

The cave containing the creche was very different from the hatching cave. It had several openings although only one of them went directly into, and out of, the cave. The other openings all went through various offices. One office included a doctor and two nurses. Since the creche was the single building that contained food, shelter, and education for the hatchlings, there wasn't a great deal of need for the openings except during hatching days or field trips. But the openings each had durable decorations framing them – and with other bright displays – tending towards different shades of blue, purple, and some green since reds, oranges, and yellows did not show up well.

People had complained at the Council that there was no need to spend work credits decorating the creche. The hatchlings remained inside most of the time and could not even see the decorations much less care about them. The reply was that it was a wonderful place to have public art present to be seen and touched. And, when the hatchlings did go out of the building for field trips or other trips, it was easy for them to spot the building if they got separated from the others.

One of the openings led into the office of Waveur, who was the general overseer of the creche. He wasn't present at the moment but Flondeau, Waveur's primary assistant and administrator in her own right, was present and welcomed them.

"Lichten, Richtor. Welcome," said Flondeau. "What brings you here?"

"Richtor's trying to get some ideas about apprenticeships and placement," said Lichten. "Graduation is coming up."

"Why, I guess that's so. We don't really have much of a graduation here when they are ready to move over to the dormitories and campus. We do wish they could synchronize the hatchings with the class years, however. We are always very crowded during the quarterflip between the hatching and the end of your campus academic year."

"Any reason why they can't get that done?" asked Richtor.

"Tradition. Better connected people don't want their schedules disturbed. Politics," said Administrator Flondeau. "It's the same story in most of the shoals, from what I can tell. Once every ten currentflips or so, we have a meeting of administrators and overseers of creches from a large area of Ocean. The topic almost always comes up. We hold celebratory lunches for those who have succeeded in getting their schedules aligned. But those don't happen very often. I have gone to two conventions. One had one conversion to celebrate and the other had two. But the one with two was the earlier one."

"So, it isn't getting easier to do," said Richtor.

"I'm afraid not. Is there anything that I can do for you today?"

"Well, I've been here a number of times," said Richtor. "And I have even volunteered some between weeks when I haven't been on campus."

"We certainly appreciate that, Richtor."

"You're welcome. But I'm not sure that I really understand just what is a normal day here at the creche or what roles are possible," continued Richtor. "You know about my difficulties in class – I think I may be one of the most infamous of my hatching. I'm trying to determine just what my path can be such that I can contribute and not go stir-crazy or become unreliable."

"That's very commendable, Richtor. Have you spoken with the counselors on campus? They have a lot of experience in this and I know that they are excited to help every hatching."

"I really frustrated one and he got rather angry – but most have been great. Their tests are oriented towards academic capabilities and physical experience and aptitudes. I do well enough in classes that I could pass written exam tests for most apprenticeships. Not that I'm in Januelle's league, of course. But I could pass. And, when I am focused, I have good reflexes and can handle tools and all. Once again, there are those much better than I am – for example, it would be hard to surpass Lichten, in physical abilities, within our hatching – but I could pass."

"Being accepted into an apprenticeship is more than just passing the entrance exam," Administrator Flondeau replied.

"Yes, I know. In order to get them to accept me the I have to convince them that I will do the job to the best of my abilities. More importantly, I have to convince myself."

"Personally, I think he worries too much," said Lichten. "He forgets to mention that almost everyone likes him. He's loyal and friendly and helpful. I don't think any profession would refuse him an apprenticeship if he passed the entrance exams."

"Thanks, Lichten. But you didn't mention reliable or responsible and that's for perfectly good reasons. I don't want to let anyone down and

I don't want to be miserable. But, Administrator Flondeau doesn't want to hear all about that."

"If I can be helpful in any way, I will be happy to do such," responded Administrator Flondeau. "But maybe I can be most useful today in helping you with the answer to some of your questions about the creche, roles, and so forth."

"We keep the hatchlings here for six currentflips plus that extra quarterflip from the misalignment of schedules. Each hatching comprises their own class so, except for that one quarterflip, we have three hatchings in the creche at any one time," said Administrator Flondeau. "I'd love to forget about that extra quarterflip as it is just a pain in the tailfin. During that quarterflip, we have four hatchings on site. Not only do we not have enough staff during that time but the new hatching needs much more supervision until they learn not to eat each other."

"Why won't the Council give you extra staff – at least temporarily during the extra quarterflip?" asked Richtor.

"Because we make it work," responded Administrator Flondeau with a mixture of pride and exasperation. "If it failed miserably and we lost most of a hatching or the damage extended to the older hatchings, or there were casualties among the staff then they might put it on the agenda. Even then, one event would probably not be enough for them to increase our budget or put any long-term measures into effect."

"But we don't want it to fail!" continued Administrator Flondeau. "And we certainly don't want to be hurt or killed. But it's not good for us or for the hatchlings. For that quarterflip, the older hatchings are on a reduced curriculum – almost, but not quite, a recess. That allows us to steal half of their staff to move to the new hatching's needs. Three hatchings times half of their staff gives us 150% of a regular staffing to allocate to the new hatching. And they need all that and more."

"So, it works," said Lichten. "But it's not to the benefit of the hatchlings."

"Exactly. And as long as we make it work, the Council won't do anything about it. That aspect of the misalignment is a large part of the discussion during the conventions. We have gotten some good suggestions there but it's not enough."

"Enough of that," said Flondeau. "My doctor has advised me not to get into discussions about that very often."

"On to staffing and roles. With three entire hatchings, we have a lot of hatchlings here at any one time. The regular campus academy includes ten hatchings but we have the equivalent of four of the older hatchings. The first year we lose the most students but we lose some the second year and it is mostly stable during the third. That brand new hatching group has the highest mortality rate but, by the time the oldest hatching has moved to the dormitories and campus, they are starting to become somewhat social and much less dangerous."

"We have no cleaning staff. The hatchlings are expected to clean up after themselves and classes take turns cleaning up common areas like the cafeteria and gaming areas. The staff makes sure the outside is kept clean and tidy but, with very little outside traffic, that is mostly just a daily quick check."

"We do have maintenance staff. With so many hatchlings, at various stages of domestication, there is a lot of deliberate, accidental, and natural breakage and deterioration. They are kept quite busy. Does that sound good to you, Richtor?"

"It's possible," Richtor replied. "It certainly ranks up there among the possible."

"Then, there is the cafeteria staff. They stay busy - and are responsible for keeping their area clean enough that periodic, unscheduled, inspections pass at all times. They have a challenge in providing meals that stay interesting. They do have the advantage that the cafeteria is the sole source of food. Snacks are available but there aren't many choices and all of the choices are healthy. They are generally a happy group and they are treated well by the hatchlings - who are often hopeful of getting something special and are rarely disappointed." Flondeau smiled. Her appreciation of the staff and her feelings for the creche came through clearly.

"Next comes the administration staff. There are only four of us for the entire creche. That's because we don't actually do that much within the creche. Our jobs are to act as liaison between the creche and the Council and look out for the interests of the creche in all dealings with the Council or the campus academy or any other outside agency. There is a certain degree of advisory structuring for the classes and teachers but they have a large degree of autonomy. Records and paperwork seem to take most of our time."

"Finally, there is the instructional staff – which includes academics, physical training, and – especially – social training. Our task is to take wild new hatchlings and prepare them to be passed along to the campus as educable future citizens of the shoal. It's not easy but it can be a lot of fun and there are a lot of memories built up over the years – most of them very good and precious."

"I think that I would be best suited to be part of the instructional staff. I like to eat but I don't think that preparing for lots of others is for me. I could do it but I'd rather appreciate the work of others. Maintenance could be OK. I think I would go crazy if I had to your job, Administrator Flondeau. No offence meant," said Richtor.

"None taken. Administration is not for everyone and the majority of the time is spent doing routines over and over. I agree with you, Richtor, that you are not well suited for administration – or administration is not well suited for you. I'm a bit surprised about maintenance but, as I think of it, I can see you in that role. Lots of different tasks, often requiring creativity, and lending themselves to having specific focus for a short period of time. Why do you favor instruction over maintenance, Richtor?" asked Flondeau.

"I think that it's a matter of those times of job you mention," said Richtor. "I think I could be successful, and productive, within the maintenance staff and there would surely be a sense of satisfaction seeing the building look good and be strong and to remember the various tasks needed to keep it that way. But I doubt there are those moments of joy."

"It's not always joy," reminded Flandeau. "I have heard Lichten, and others, talk about their winnowing. The winnowing doesn't stop the instant the new hatchlings arrive at the creche."

Lichten blanched as he heard this. Richtor looked at him and reached out to take his hand for a bit until he seemed to have settled down again.

"Yes, I know. Maybe, if I became part of the instructional staff, I could not be part of the wild hatchling welcome staff?"

"We couldn't guarantee that, Richtor, and during the crazy quarterflip, you are certain to be chosen to move over at least once every three hatchings – probably every two hatchings."

"Well, thanks for being upfront about it," said Richtor. "I don't have Lichten's nightmares but I don't have pleasant memories of that period either. I need to keep that in mind for any decisions that I make. But there are joys, correct?"

"Certainly! I don't have any advice to offer. The downs are just part of the job. It's not a pleasant part but it can't be avoided. So, have I given you the information that you wanted?"

"I think so. If I get permission from the campus authorities, could I come in and volunteer with an instructor in one of the classes during a regular class day?"

"Certainly! We'd be glad to have you," said Flondeau.

"Thanks for all your help. I'll get in touch with you on scheduling the volunteer day. Lichten, let's get our sharrells back to the stable before they are due."

"Thank you very much, Administrator Flondeau," said Lichten. "OK, Richtor, let's grab our mounts and go."

Chapter 10 Winding up the Excursion

*R*ichtor and Lichten mounted their sharrells and started the trip back to the stable. "Why no words, Richtor?" asked Lichten. "Did you get anything useful from our short tour of the shoal?"

"Oh, yes. Sorry. Lost in my thoughts again. I think the one new thing that occurred to me was the maintenance staff at the creche. Otherwise, it's still basically the same situation I've talked with the campus counselors about. In the long run, I'm the only one who can know what I will do, enjoyably and reliably, for the shoal."

"But did the trip do anything to help you settle those questions?" asked Lichten.

"Well, the purpose of today's excursion was really a matter of nosiness and curiosity. I am sure that the Council has people actively investigating the ongoing food shortage but I'd like to know, and understand, before they decide to tell the rest of us. I can't see any way the excursion might make a difference to my career search - but sometimes things have unexpected results."

"I see," said Lichten. "But what about the short tour of the shoal? Did that help?"

"A bit. It helped to solidify my current thoughts and - as I already said - it opened me up to another possible choice. I'm sure that I don't want anything to do with fissure production and I don't think they would want me either. A brief lapse of focus could cause serious problems very quickly when you're working with high heat," replied Richtor.

"I might be able to handle retail but I'm not sure they could deal with me. Between customers, I would need to be moving about. They probably wouldn't like that. Maybe in a larger store I could spend idle time cleaning up the shelves or stocking or such but I just don't see myself fitting in there."

"I couldn't work in the stables. I don't have the strength and affinity to animals that you have, Lichten. I can't be a scientist. Maybe I could be an explorer, like Sebaria, but, as you have pointed out, Sebaria needed to be able to deal with other shoals and people. I don't know how good I would be at that - and am unlikely to be placed into a situation from which I could find out. Sometimes,

I just feel like I'm not unique – I'm broken. No one else seems to have these questions and problems," finished Richtor.

"Well, I don't think you're broken. And neither does Januelle. And I don't think Administrator Floreau thinks so either. I don't even think our teachers think you are broken. And there are certainly others who don't know their path yet. But you are right that you seem to be working with challenges that few others seem to be having," said Lichten.

"I wish I weren't," said Richtor. "But I have to do the best I can. Thanks for all of your support, Lichten."

"Sure. You've been a great friend and I'm glad to help you in any way that I can."

"Interested in a long swim to the herd tomorrow?" asked Richtor.

"Tomorrow?" asked Lichten. "No, that doesn't work for me. Sorry." Upon seeing Richtor looking a bit sad, Lichten continued. "But I still have time today. If we take the sharrells, we can probably get there and back in less than an hour. Will that work for you?"

Richtor broke into a big grin. "Yes. Thanks a lot. I just want to get a first-hand feel for just how much the herd has been reduced."

They nudged Brightglow and Widefin on their right sides to encourage them to bear towards the non-heat-requiring factories. The herd fish were located about fifty cycles away when riding a sharrell – perhaps an hour and a half away just swimming. The sharrells could swim faster than they could but their primary advantages were the ability to pull loads and their general stamina. A sharrell could swim from light up to light down without tiring. It was considered proper treatment to allow them to feed mid-day as well as before starting on a trip and after ending.

Their sharrells had not been ridden hard that day. The total amount of riding probably amounted to about five hours. They were a bit difficult to redirect as they had expected to be continuing on to the stables. They always got eager to return when they had their stables in mind. But there wasn't that much difficulty and soon they were swimming over beyond the factory section and onward to the herd farm.

"Hey, isn't that the herd right before us?" asked Richtor.

They looked upon a swirling tower of dark looming ahead of them. As they got closer, they could tell that the column was composed of thousands of fish swimming in concentric circles starting a bodylength from the seabed to within three bodylengths from the surface.

"Does it look thinner to you, Lichten?" asked Richtor.

"Yes, it sure does."

A couple of herders waved at them from the distance. There were several large algae clouds in the general area. About every four weeks, or a third of a halfflip, they were shifted from one cloud to another, in sequence. This gave the clouds time to grow back as well as giving time for the area to rest undisturbed in case any eggs had been dispersed in the area and then fertilized.

"Do you think the herders will be willing to talk with us?" asked Richtor?"

"No idea. They're usually pretty friendly. Not a lot to do in general. If they don't want to talk, they won't. Do you want us to approach them?"

"Yes." Richtor nudged Widefin forward and Lichten, on Brightglow, followed. They gave the column of fish a wide berth so as not to disturb them. If enough were shifted out of their circles, then the entire column would move. If not, the shifted fish would return to the column. The herders were in charge of the column of fish and, especially if they wanted information, it would be good to make sure that they weren't the ones to disturb the herd.

As their mounts swam around the column, Richtor looked into the herd of fish. They looked healthy, to his non-expert eye, and he couldn't detect any strange behavior. Of course, the last time he spent much time around the herd was during a campus field trip. It seemed that Lichten agreed that the column was narrower than what they remembered. Perhaps it was taller? That would explain it as a tall, narrow, column could easily have just as many fish as a short, wider, column.

Richtor looked up. During daytime, it wasn't comfortable to look towards the surface but it seemed like it wasn't quite as bright as he remembered. No, he just couldn't remember whether the column was taller or not.

"Hello!" called out Richtor to the pair of herders towards this side of the herd.

"Hello to you. Is that Lichten I see?" asked the herder on the left.

"Martus! Are you still doing this? Not tired of it yet?" asked Lichten.

"Surely not. This is the calmest job in all of the shoal."

"Calm - truly. But how do you stop yourself from going to sleep on your mount?"

"Well, most of the time that would be perfectly OK. Yet another reason why this is the best of occupations." He turned to Richtor. "My name is Martus. I've known Lichten for a long time. Are you a friend of this wrangler?"

"Yes. And glad to be. My name is Richtor. Pleased to meet you." They briefly hooked little fingers.

The second herder was staying back during this process. Martus motioned her forward. "This is Simton. Simton, meet Richtor and Lichten."

Simton came forward on her mount and hooked fingers with each. "Glad to meet you. I have seen you, Lichten, but we have never been introduced."

"So, Lichten. You are a famous student around here?" asked Richtor.

"Well known, anyway." Responded Lichten. "I bring sharrells from the stables out to this area. I try not to get in the way but having them go through training routines near the herd is good for helping them to learn control and restraint."

"There have been a few instances when they have caused a bit of a nuisance," said Martus. "But not that much and, really, it just gives us something to actually do out here so we don't mind."

"So, what are you two doing out here today? Are these a couple of sharrells that need extra training? I recognize the sharrell that you are riding, Lichten. I don't think it needs any training."

"A quarterflip, or so, ago I overheard a conversation between a couple of teachers at the campus," said Richtor. "They indicated that the harvests from the herd are down significantly and that rations would be decreased. Now that has been happening. I'm curious about it some of my friends and I are poking our topfins into it."

"Well, I can't recommend poking your topfin anywhere it isn't invited," said Martus. "As for the herd, it definitely has gotten smaller as you can see for yourself. Beyond that, I don't know and we've been told to not speculate or gossip."

"Told by who?" asked Richtor.

"Shouldn't say."

"Oh. Anything peculiar around here that you have seen?"

"Your sharrells look healthy. Do you help the stable exercise and train them, Lichten?"

Richtor grimaced a bit as Lichten responded to Marcus. There would be no more information to be obtained here. Maybe someone else could get some more from them. He couldn't. Maybe it was a good thing he didn't have those skills. He wondered just what types of people skills Sebaria had when she was wondering around and visiting shoals.

Lichten and Martus talked for a while about the sharrells and training and places to find wild ones. Simton, after following the conversation for a while, returned her attention to the herd and moved away from the group.

"Good to talk with you again, Martus," said Lichten. "Let's leave and let him get back to work, Richtor." Lichten directed Brightglow away from Martus and the herd.

"No use in leaving things in a huff," said Lichten. "We may want more information in the future when, hopefully, they are free to say something. We got confirmation that the herds are reduced so we know that the conversation you overheard is real."

"I suppose so. I really didn't doubt that. Teacher Gregov seemed to know what he was talking about. I guess, with the reduced rations, everyone knows that something is going on."

"And you think you can do something about it?" asked Lichten.

Richtor may have blushed. It was difficult to be certain in the darkening water. "I'd like to. Maybe the Council has lots of people already looking into it. If so, they're being awfully quiet about it."

"Oh. So, you're really serious about investigating this?"

"Yes. You didn't think that I was?" asked Richtor.

"Well, sometimes you get curious about things that really aren't of much interest to many people. Usually, they end up being fun to look into and they give us something to do. But they aren't often of general importance."

Richtor was silent for a bit as they guided their sharrells back to the stables. "I guess that's fair, Lichten. They seem important to me but I guess that they usually don't have much importance to anyone else. Thanks for pointing that out."

"Sure. I'm not complaining – I hope you don't think that. As I said, it usually ends up being fun and I've learned a few things in the process that I might end up wanting to know sometime in the future. But this does look important. Why can't we just leave it to the Council?"

"We probably could. But I have an itch all along my dorsal ridge. Sure, that sometimes happens about things that are a lot less important than this. And, if the Council had found some type of reason for it – and a way to fix it – then they just would have fixed it and there wouldn't have initiated rationing. Just call it doing our civic duty," said Richtor.

"Civic duty. Sure," replied Lichten. "You mean that you want to know what's going on and they aren't telling you anything."

"Partially. But you have also heard me trying to figure out something to do within the shoal. I'm almost graduated from classes. If I can't travel Ocean like Sebaria, maybe I can just do some nearby investigation. A troubleshooter."

"How often does the shoal need a troubleshooter?" asked Lichten. "I'm not aware of that many crises that need investigating."

"I don't either," said Richtor. "It's probably all just an excuse for my restlessness and curiosity."

"We've arrived back to the stables," said Lichten. "We're earlier than we promised but nearer 13th hour than 12th hour. Do you think we'll be able to make it back to the dormitories before dinner ends?"

Richtor chittered. "I don't know. But if we miss it, I'll pay for dinner somewhere else."

"Fair enough," said Lichten. "Let's bring Brightglow and Widefin into the stables. Can you strip their harnesses or do you need me to help?"

"I can do it but wouldn't you prefer me to check back in with Diplodus? I'm the one paying – unless you're volunteering."

"I forgot about that. I want to talk to Diplodus about some things. How about you taking care of the harnesses and then coming out to the front pedestal to pay? Don't forget that the harnesses on Brightglow are mine – not the stables."

"OK. That's a deal," said Richtor. "I'll take the harnesses off of Widefin and myself first and put them away. If you finish with what you want with Diplodus, come back into the stables. If you haven't come back by the time I get done with my harnesses, I will strip Brightglow's and gather them to bring out to the front pedestal with me. Sound good?"

"Sure." Lichten headed towards the office and the front pedestal while Richtor rode Widefin and led Brightglow into the harness rooms.

Richtor worked with the harnesses. Taking them off was always faster than putting them on but it was still necessary to make sure they didn't get tangled and the parts separated properly to hang up.

Lichten had not arrived by the time Richtor finished with his harnesses so he removed Brightglow's harness. He draped them over his arm and guided the two sharrells back to the corral. Then he headed to the office and front pedestal.

"So, that's what I've been thinking," continued Lichten. "Does that sound good with you?"

"It should work," said Diplodus. "Ah, here is the master of the journey. Your fees are for 6 work credits."

"That's for all three of us?"

"Sure is. I gave you a bit of a discount because you were hiring three sharrells and Lichten brought his own harnesses."

"Thanks." Richtor signed the authorization for credit transfer. "Let's head to the dormitory and see if we've missed our dinner."

"Race you," said Lichten as he swam swiftly out of the office and off towards the dormitory.

Richtor smiled and followed.

Chapter 11 People Want to Know

*I*t seemed like a repeat of the previous week. Richtor was in Teacher Lorell's Oral History class and he was more and more unable to stay hovering in his area. Maybe he could move around in the back of the classroom for a bit and that would be better than heading to the elimination room – or saying that he was heading to the elimination room – and then not coming back until the end of the class. In the back of the room, he could still listen to the teacher and even ask, or answer, questions when he wanted to. It all depended on whether she was OK with that. He was sure that it wasn't what she would prefer.

Richtor decided that he would try to focus on the lecture more. Maybe he could get really focused on it and get past his desire to get moving. It worked sometimes.

The pulse alarm went off, signaling the end of the class. He didn't like to try to be first out the doorway so he just moved towards the back of the classroom - similar to doing what he had considered doing earlier.

As he hovered in the back, Januelle came by briefly on her way out. "Hey, Richtor!"

"Hey, Januelle. How are you doing?"

"I'm well, thanks. Do you have some time to meet during lunch or after classes?"

"Sure, what's up?"

"Well, I've got some data prepared from our trip. However, in addition, I have some more information about the entire subject."

"You mean the shortage?" asked Richtor.

"Yes. But I don't think it's time to talk about it too loudly yet. We don't want to be the focus of lots of questions. Wait until the Council reveals it, if they do, and then most of the students and faculty will be discussing it."

"Pretty mysterious. Not really like you, Januelle. There must be something special going on."

"It's not that tremendously special. I just don't want to end up as a focus for later discussion. And I would be if I seemed to be the center of information about it."

"OK. I'll meet you outside the main doorway after classes. I have to do some extra time for

Teacher Gregov to get him to acknowledge that I was paying attention in class."

"Not again. What were you doing this time?"

"I started wandering around in the back of the class. I wish I could just get permission to do it. I never know what the reaction will be – I only know that no one likes it. At any rate, we were doing some exercises in class and he thinks I didn't pay any attention."

"Did you?"

"Sure. I know the topic really well. That's why I couldn't focus as much as I, and he, would have preferred. I'll be able to demonstrate it quickly but that is likely to take up most of my free time at lunch," continued Richtor.

"I'll see you after classes, then," said Januelle.

~   ~   ~

After classes, Richtor hovered around the main doorway. It was rather fun as he was able to say hello to a lot of his fellow hatching as well as a few that he knew who were from other hatchings. He even encountered a few who remembered him from the times that he volunteered at the creche.

Lichten swam by. They exchanged hellos but Lichten seemed to have something that he was heading towards rather quickly and Richtor did not try to fill him in. After all, he didn't know what Januelle had in mind. Maybe she would need them to go back to the jungle. Maybe the one interruption made more of a mess of the data gathering than she realized at the time. That wasn't very likely as Januelle was as organized of a person as he knew.

There weren't many people heading out now. He saw a few Teachers leaving. Finally, Januelle was coming through the doorway.

"Hello, Richtor," said Januelle. "I needed to talk with Teacher Piscora about the final science project I am doing for her class."

"Not a problem. It was rather fun saying hello and goodbye to people. Maybe I'll start doing it more often. It makes a person aware of just how few people are actually seen throughout the day and how little time there is to be caught up on what is going on. I get to see a wider group at the cafeteria but we still tend to sit in the same areas and see the same people."

"I guess that's so," said Januelle. "I guess that I don't have as much interest in people as you do."

"So, what's up?"

"I've done the data correlation and interpretation from our excursion to Jordech Jungle," said Januelle. "There is a reduction in the number of fish of most varieties - at least, of the ones that we have inventory for - and it is a significant reduction."

"What is significant?" asked Richtor.

"Somewhere between a 35% reduction and a 45% reduction."

"Wow! No wonder rations are reduced. Lichten and I went to look at the herd fish after you branched off from us at the end of the trip last weekend. The herd appeared to be significantly smaller and it was acknowledged, by the herders, to be smaller."

"Did they mention any reason why?" asked Januelle.

"No. They were pretty close-mouthed about it. I don't know whether it is because they don't know much more or they have been told not to tell anyone anything about the situation. I'm pretty sure that the latter is true but it may also be true that they don't know much about what is going on. I'm guessing that it is."

"Why do you guess that?" asked Januelle.

"Because people are going to start knowing more about the situation and the more information, and the earlier they have it, the better for the general morale and response of the shoal."

"I guess that makes sense. You understand people better than I do. But, there's more. You were talking about people starting to find out about the situation. In church, they used the reduction of the herd as the main feature of the sermon."

"What?" exclaimed Richtor. "I know that not as many people are adherents to the Shrankan Church as there used to be but I would have expected people to be talking about it in the hallways."

"The elders told us not to talk to others about it. They are planning to prepare a campaign with this as a consequence of forsaking the church."

"Consequence?"

"Yes. They're preparing a plan for recruitment to the church, saying that the food supply has been reduced because there have not been enough people following the doctrine of the Shrankan Church."

"That's ridiculous. And you believe this?" asked Richtor.

"Of course not," replied Januelle. "But I don't know what the cause is - and neither do you. And, as you pointed out yourself, the Council doesn't seem to know a reason. That leaves a hole to be filled. I'm in the church mainly for social reasons. I enjoy the general teachings and the histories - when they are related accurately - and the integration of science into the church. But I certainly do not believe that some essence of Perikrakoa, the shoal's volcano, is watching over us or doing something to us."

"Well, that is interesting. It means that discussion will start popping up all over the shoal very soon. When do the church elders plan to start their recruitment drive?"

"Very soon," said Januelle. "They know, just as you do, that the news cannot continue to be kept from the general public for very long and, so, they have a small window within which to be able to take advantage. If they push forward the first explanation then that will be the one that others will have to overcome."

"I admit that I am very curious. That's pretty normal for me. But I'm more concerned about the welfare of the shoal. Why is this happening and what can we do, if anything, about it?"

"The inventory counts can't be exact," said Januelle. "They can only be used as a reasonably reliable account of increases and decreases. But if the numbers that I counted were correct – and I tried very hard to be careful and precise – then some of the fish populations in Jordech Jungle may be in danger of extinction."

"Extinction? Why?"

"Every species has a critical number. That is the number below which the species cannot produce at least as many new individuals as the number that die. The primary danger is associated with finding mates and getting eggs produced, hatched, and grown to the point of being able to reproduce. But, once a population does decrease below a certain size, any other species which is more successful may take over the niche in which the first species thrived. This will reduce their chances of survival even more."

"And some of the fish in Jordech Jungle are getting down to this number?" asked Richtor.

"Yes. And, since the entire fish population is affected, it means dangers for crustaceans, cleaner fish, eels, and all other life."

"Wow! So, what do we do about it?

"We?" answered Januelle. "I don't think that we students have much role in this matter. But, if you think that you have some ideas, I am willing to listen. I am heading off now to report my findings to the branch office of the Academy of Scientists. That was what I was discussing with my teacher. He agreed that it may be of interest, and use, to the Academy."

Richtor remained by the campus doorway, watching Januelle swim away. Januelle was probably right. It really wasn't the responsibility of students to worry about this, investigate it, or fix it. But just waiting for someone else to do things just wasn't the way he floated. That defined most of his life. If he was interested in a subject, it was very difficult to knock him off track. His teachers would certainly testify to that – almost as much as they would be willing to testify that it was very difficult to get him to be sufficiently interested to focus, and study.

There was no reason to debate with himself about something he had already decided. He had organized the excursion into Jordech Jungle based on his curiosity and that curiosity would not be satisfied without some answers. And those answers must apply to the whole problem – what, how, why, and how to remedy.

Januelle had a point, however. There was no reason to not share information. Maybe those officials might even share back and make it much easier to slake Richtor's curiosity.

Richtor decided that he would ask Januelle to accompany him to the Council. It was all well and good to give the information to the Academy and they might, or might not, study it. But if it affected the people of the shoal then it should be a primary interest of the Council. Maybe they would even release information that the herders were unable, or unwilling, to share.

Richtor had had some interactions with Cheyelle, the head of the Council. Most had been positive with a couple of rather embarrassing exceptions. He doubted they would be willing to deputize him so that people within the shoal government and supporting community would be willing to answer questions but it was worth the effort to ask. He might have a reputation as a discipline problem but he also had the reputation of being honest. And his curiosity was the prime reason why his teachers hadn't tossed him to the narrowmouths. With a couple of exceptions, it was difficult for his teachers to get angry with him when he kept asking questions that indicated he wasn't ignoring them but actually quite involved with the lectures.

He wasn't certain whether it would be useful to invite Lichten along to meet with the Council - or, at least, Cheyelle. Besides being Richtor's friend, Lichten was strong and probably better able to defend himself, and others, from danger than any other student on campus. But he wouldn't be able to provide any additional information and it was not easier to arrange for a larger party to meet with Cheyelle.

Luckily, Cheyelle and the Council had limited weekend hours available for meetings - including the public eighthflip meetings when business was discussed to include general input. He would talk with Januelle first. She would have greater impact about the information they had brought back from Jordech Jungle.

Chapter 12 Discussion in the Hallways

*T*wo days later, the news that the church had released was moving rapidly through the campus. Presumably, people were also talking about it outside of the campus but Richtor had no visibility into that. Students got involved in discussions in the hallways and the number of people tardy to classes sharply increased. It's not that anyone really had anything to say but that didn't stop them from wanting to say it anyway. It was peculiar that they hadn't reacted much to the rationing but the reduction in the herd size seemed to be more immediate and something they could focus on.

Surprisingly, at least to Richtor, there were a fair number of students that were seriously considering it to be an indication of poor following of the Shrankan Church principles.

Richtor was a believer in cause and effect and not going to church did not appear to have any correlation to a reduced food supply. Now, indirectly, maybe something about it had some connection to religion. But there needed to be something acting as a trigger and that wasn't a matter of prayer.

Richtor avoided the discussions as much as he was able to. At the same time, he did try to listen in a bit to see whether any new information had been discovered. So far, he knew more about what was going on than any of the numerous discussion groups in the halls. Januelle's science club was using the situation as a speculative topic. That was fine and he hoped that they came up with some ideas. He might even attend as a guest – their doors were open to anyone. Those who had a solid interest joined and those that didn't have that interest did not continue to come.

It was amazing that there could be so much discussion without anything to discuss. He was currently trying to get to Teacher Lorell's class early so that he could talk with Januelle briefly.

Richtor had left his science class towards the front of the students departing but all of those clusters of students in the hall made it much harder to make good time. He swam up to the upper corridor in the hall to avoid one group and barely avoided a collision as someone, coming from the opposite direction, apparently was daydreaming and did not move to the side.

This halfflip, he had only one class in common with Januelle. Each hatching took the same core courses but in the last four currentflips, they were allowed some electives such that only half of the courses were in common. Of course, that wasn't the main reason he had only one class with Januelle. The hatching was so large that it was necessary to have four classes of each common course. Having one class with Januelle hit an average. Last halfflip, he didn't have any classes with her.

He reached the Oral History classroom with Teacher Lorell only a few cycles before the start of class. He wasn't sure that was enough time to persuade Januelle if she wasn't initially in favor. He hoped she would be.

The classroom was arranged such that every hover area, with its pedestal rising from the floor, had access to the aisles. He had no difficulty swimming up to Januelle's hover area. She had, apparently, gotten there even earlier. He didn't know what her schedule was this halfflip. Maybe her preceding class was close.

"Hello Januelle," said Richtor.

"Hi Richtor. You're early. What's up?"

"I'd like to go to talk with Cheyelle, and maybe the Council if needed and possible, to see if we can get any information from them. I'm sure that they are being pestered beyond any reasonable amount but I thought that, with the additional data you collected, she might be willing to talk with us briefly."

"OK. That sounds reasonable. What do you want with me?"

"I understand the conclusions and the general data but I couldn't answer any questions if Cheyelle has any. If you could come along, the data would have a lot more weight with the Council and you could answer any questions they might have."

"When?" asked Januelle.

"I thought this weekend would be good. I don't think that our free periods on campus line up this halfflip."

"OK," said Januelle. "But, as much as I like your adventures and doing things with you, I prefer to plan out my own weekends, please.

"Sure," Richtor replied. "I understand that. I'm sorry to take so much time."

"It's not a problem at the moment. Just be aware. OK?" commented Januelle.

"OK. I'll see if I can get an appointment for this weekend and, if so, I'll tell you the time tomorrow or the day after."

"OK." Everyone was now in their hover areas except for Richtor. He quickly headed back to his space and made it just before the wall pulse indicated the beginning of class.

~ ~ ~

The last class of the day had finished and Richtor was making his way out of the campus building. Avoiding collision with one of the discussion groups in the halls, a student reached out to grab him on his upper arm.

"What," said Richtor as he turned around to see who had grabbed him. "Oh, hello Arissto. How are you?"

"I'm fine. We're discussing the decrease in the herd size. I thought that you, being in the graduating hatching, might have some more information."

"I didn't realize that the campus had announced the decrease. When did that happen?"

"Early this afternoon, some of the teachers started telling their classes. Not very well organized, in my opinion, as some classes were told and others were not."

"That is peculiar. I guess the teachers decided for themselves since people from the church were spreading the news as they heard it. They probably didn't want to call an assembly. Those are really hard to organize. They have to be held outside of the campus building," said Richtor.

"I suppose so," Arissto replied. "But what do you think about all of this?"

"I don't know that much more than you do. The herds have declined in size and that means a reduction in rations. That's about it."

"Yes, but why?" asked Arissto.

"Why are the herds smaller? Why does that require reduced rations? What is the why about?" asked Richtor.

"All of it."

"Look around you here in the halls," said Richtor. "All the time, and worry, that people are spending in discussion. I may not always agree with the campus administrators or the Council but they usually seem to be aware of cause and effect. I think they would tell us if they knew more just to keep all of this from happening."

"I think they are rattled," continued Richtor. "Some of the information was released before they were ready for it. That is why the mention of the decrease in the herd size is being released in a hap-hazard fashion. They probably wanted to wait as long as possible so that they could present it as a problem that was in the process of being alleviated. It looks like the Council has decided they can't be certain the ration reductions won't be permanent, so they released more information."

"So, it isn't temporary?" asked Arissto.

"I don't know and I'll bet that no one at the campus or the Council knows either. The unknown is the hardest to take."

"I guess that's true. Thanks, Richtor."

"For what?"

"For helping me to think about it," said Arissto. "Some people may think you're a flake but I think you're brilliant. You can think through things, and explain them, better than anyone else I know."

"Thanks. I think," said Richtor. He turned away from Arissto and moved toward a secondary campus building exit. Not many had the same attitude as Arissto but he would prefer to not get into any more "discussions" that didn't contribute to anything. He needed to get that appointment with Cheyelle.

~ ~ ~

"Hello," said Richtor to the man hovering around a pedestal ledge. There were many shelves surrounding him on the far wall with the new paper documents stacked up on them, each document separated by a woven seaweed mat to make sure the writing was not disturbed. Richtor heard that the scientists were continuing to search for some better ink that could be applied underwater but not smear easily after application.

"Hello. You're Richtor, aren't you?" asked the man. "I believe that I have seen you around here before and you were pointed out to me. Is your visit an assignment?"

"No. This is more a matter of personal curiosity and interest. I would like to get an appointment to meet with Coordinator Cheyelle during the weekend."

"Right now, everyone wants to see Cheyelle. No way."

"I have some information about the herd reduction that I think she would be interested in hearing about."

"Really? What might that be?" asked the man. An engraved plate fixed to the wall behind him indicated the name of Wayroll.

"I would prefer to talk with Coordinator Cheyelle."

"As I said," replied Administrator Wayroll, "everyone wants to see her and she is very busy. I have heard mostly good things about you, Richtor, but I haven't heard anything that would give me the assurance that you could bring any new information to Coordinator Cheyelle sufficient to fit you into her schedule."

"Well, Januelle would be coming with me. She is very good in the sciences and we did some investigations in Jordech Jungle over the weekend."

"I've heard about Januelle and even met her a couple of times. OK, I'll check with Coordinator Cheyelle but she is still very busy. Can you come back tomorrow?"

"If that's what's needed, sure," said Richtor. He thanked the administrator and swam off.

Just what did he want to say to Cheyelle? He really wasn't sure but it felt right. They really didn't have that much extra information and it could probably be relayed to the Council in only a few sentences as long as they knew the information was actually coming from Januelle.

The shoal continued to grow but it was still small enough for most people to know, or know of, one another. The current graduating class, and the next hatching, got a lot of attention from the adults of the shoal because they would soon be becoming part of the adult population. That meant apprenticeships and potential moves and expansions in different areas. The Council kept a loose eye upon the process but, in general, the merging of the graduating class into the general workings of the shoal were done via the natural process of mutual awareness. If a business, or group, started accepting more new people than they could support, it became apparent quite soon.

Businesses and groups were either supported by the shoal as an essential part of life of the shoal or they were supported by incoming work credits to be redistributed according to personnel and costs. In either case, they had a pretty good idea how much they had coming in such that they could take on more people, expand, or get equipment and supplies.

He and Januelle were well known. People were probably also familiar with Lichten but, since he had shown interest in his particular niche very early in life, a lot of people probably didn't have any direct interest. If Lichten was part of a group rounding up wild sharrells then people would hear about anything he did. A little extra to liven up an often just ongoing life.

Richtor headed back to the dormitory.

~　　~　　~

Thinking about heading to the Council offices that afternoon, Richtor was possibly even less focused than usual. Of course, that was noticed.

"Richtor," said Teacher Gregov. "Can you tell me how to measure the area that exists between a triangle and its enclosed circle?"

Richtor moved his head forward, and looked at the teacher, upon hearing his name. "Excuse me? What was the question, Teacher Gregov?"

"I will excuse you. How do you measure the area that exists between a triangle and its enclosed circle?"

"You determine the area of the triangle and then subtract the area of the circle, Teacher Gregov," replied Richtor.

"Correct. I am glad that you are, at least, learning the material. But, please, I would appreciate you pretending to pay attention in class."

"Sorry, sir."

Teacher Gregov continued with his lesson and Richtor kept his gaze focused on the teacher. His thoughts, however, continued to roam about quite freely. Would they get the appointment? What should they say? What should he ask for, if anything?

~   ~   ~

"Will Coordinator Cheyelle see us?" asked Richtor as he faced the Council administrator once again.

"Yes. For twenty-five cycles."

"When?"

"At the beginning of the weekend at 5th hour."

"Thank you very much."

"You're welcome, Richtor. I hope, very much, that this will be a valuable use of the Coordinator's time."

"I believe it will be," replied Richtor as he left through the doorway and into the open sea.

There was one more class day until the weekend. He would tell Januelle about the appointment tomorrow. He hoped the time would work for her but 5th hour was pretty early in the day. It should work.

Chapter 13 Working with Cheyelle and the Council

O n the next day, Richtor told Januelle about the appointment and it did work out for her. She promised to meet Richtor outside of the Council offices twenty-five cycles before 5th hour. She would bring a summary report, with a copy to give to Coordinator Cheyelle, as well as the original raw data – though the raw data did not have a backup copy and could not, or should not, be given away.

Now, it was shortly before 5th hour and Januelle had not shown up yet. Richtor was swimming back and forth to the side of the doorway. He had been swimming in front of the doorway and Wayroll had come out and gently asked him to please keep the doorway clear and not keep going back and forth as he was getting dizzy watching.

Of course, Administrator Wayroll had not really been getting dizzy but Richtor followed his suggestion and moved his minilaps to the edge of the doorway and out of sight. It would not help anything either now, or in a possible future, to get Administrator Wayroll angry at him. Similar to his teachers, most adults either sighed, or groaned, at his foibles but there were a few that felt he should have been considered a reject from the hatching and should never be allowed to participate in future fertilization rituals.

The water didn't change much as he swam back and forth but the smaller cleaning fish had decided to avoid the area and all of the ground animals had decided that this area was one of suspicious activity. Richtor's eyes weren't really focused as he continued to think through his arguments and get them organized. Perhaps it wasn't so bad for Januelle to be late – but he greatly hoped that she wouldn't be too late. Cheyelle might see them after the start of 5th hour but Wayroll would surely move them back out of her chambers no later than 25 cycles past the start of the hour.

Januelle swam up to the building. On her back, she had a large carrying net connected to a travel harness strapped around her torso. "Sorry to be late, Richtor. I underestimated the amount of data I had available. I needed to find my carrying net and my travel harness and I don't use them that often."

"That's fine, Januelle. I'm just glad that you were willing to come. I doubt very much that Coordinator Cheyelle would take me seriously on my own. Wayroll only agreed to try to get me an appointment after I told him that you would be coming along to present some data. So, once again, thank you."

"Are you ready?" asked Januelle.

"As ready as I ever will be. Would you like me to carry the net or do you prefer to leave it connected to your harness?"

"It should be fine where it is – I don't remember any places with tight clearance on the way into the Coordinator's office."

"That's right," said Richtor. "You were in there before when you were awarded the citizen-of-the-quarterflip citation for your services helping the Academy and the shoal."

"Yes," replied Januelle. "And one other time as part of the Science Club on campus. At any rate, unless things have changed a lot, there should be no problem with clearance while pulling along a cargo net."

They swam into the front office area where Administrator Wayroll had his domain. "All present? Ready" asked Wayroll.

"We believe so," said Richtor.

"Follow me." Wayroll headed through an interior doorway into a hallway. As Januelle and Richtor followed, they felt the pulses through the water signaling the start of 5th hour.

Stopping before a closed-door panel on the right side of the hall, Wayroll pressed an announcement button to the edge of the encircling doorway. The door panel slid aside.

"Come in," said a voice from the inner office. There were a greater number of glowbowls than were commonly found in an office. A pair were framing the inside of the doorway to light up any visitors as they arrived but most were to the back of the person hovering around a long flat pedestal. The lights illuminated whatever she studied, and looked at, but put the occupant into a considerable shadow.

"Januelle and Richtor, Coordinator Cheyelle," announced Wayroll. After his announcement, he left the chamber. The occupant, presumably Coordinator Cheyelle, touched a button on her pedestal and the doors slid shut.

"Good morning, Coordinator Cheyelle," said Januelle.

"Hello, Januelle. And I presume that you, young man, are Richtor?"

"Yes, Coordinator Cheyelle," said Richtor.

"You can just call me Cheyelle. We have little enough time to keep having to add that word to the conversation all the time. I understand you have some information that is relevant to our problem."

"Yes, Coordinator Cheyelle," said Richtor. The coordinator raised one eye ridge and Richtor repeated. "Yes, Cheyelle."

"And that is?"

"Januelle, Lichten, and I took a trip to Jordech Jungle this past weekend."

"That's nice. Did you have a good time?"

"Yes, but that wasn't the reason we went. I thought it would be a good idea to check to see if there was a problem with the fish population outside of the shoal and the herd."

"Did you? Last weekend? How did you know about the problem? There had been no public announcement about the matter and the Shrankan Church notes did not start being dispersed until four or five days ago."

"I overheard some teachers talking, in the hallways, about reduction of rations," said Richtor.

"So, there were teachers discussing it in the hallways while students were moving past them and around them?" asked Cheyelle.

"No. They didn't know that I heard them. I was on my way back from an elimination break during class and I had moved myself out of their way in an empty classroom."

Cheyelle raised her eye ridge once again. It appeared to be a favorite mannerism of the coordinator. "Was it a successful elimination? Have you seen the campus nurse about these problems?"

"Yes. But that really isn't important, is it? I overheard the teachers and starting wondering about it."

"I have heard that you often seem to be spending time wondering about something – and that it doesn't always appear to be directly related to the class material," said the coordinator. "And?"

"And I thought. If this has happened with the herd, it is only happening with the herd. Is it a herd problem or is it a general problem?"

"Those are good questions, Richtor," said Cheyelle. "I see why your teachers are willing to put up with you. What were your answers to your questions?"

"I didn't have any answers. I didn't have any data to work with besides the small fact that the herd size had reduced."

"Well said," said the coordinator. "And?"

Januelle spoke up at this point. "He asked Lichten and me to join him for an excursion to Jordech Jungle. He knew that I had participated in an Academy excursion to inventory the jungle and he thought that an updated inventory might give some valuable information. Richtor's excursions are often fun and this sounded like it might be personally interesting, in addition."

"So, you went to the seaweed jungle?"

"Yes, to Jordech Jungle. And I repeated the inventory process that had been performed three currentflips ago."

"And?" Cheyelle reached out with her left hand to press a button.

"I did an inventory while Richtor and Lichten watched for potential dangers and predators. As you know, the jungle isn't always safe for individuals."

A pulse announced someone outside the door. Cheyelle pressed the door button. As Wayroll moved his head into the room, she called out "Wayroll, do I have anything pressing until half-hour?"

"No, nothing that has to be done right during that period."

"Then keep it clear but please remind me when half-hour has occurred. I will be here with Richtor and Januelle until then."

"Yes, Coordinator." Wayroll left and the coordinator closed the door again.

"Now we have a bit of extra time in which to talk," she said.

"The Council has not explored the questions that you have, Januelle, Richtor. So, the information you have to provide may be very important."

"It isn't a lot of information, Coordinator Cheyelle." The coordinator raised her eye ridge again.

"Well, it isn't, Cheyelle. Januelle, tell her the results, please."

Januelle pulled a set of two documents, separated by sheets of seaweed netting, from the bundle she was carrying. She handed one copy to the coordinator.

"These are summaries of the data, Cheyelle. I have the raw data and the results from the previous two inventories along with me if you want to go into the direct comparisons."

"That shouldn't be necessary. They will be available if we get someone from the Academy to check through them?"

"Certainly, part of the data comes directly from the Academy themselves – both of the preceding inventories. Note that I only did a subset of the inventories that they did – I was only one person this time and I was only one of the group while doing the previous inventory. The summary is based upon the differences in the groups that I inventoried."

"And? What are the results?" Cheyelle glanced at the summary sheet but looked back up at Januelle.

"All of the inventoried animals – fish, crustaceans, and so forth had a significantly smaller presence than that of previous inventories."

"How significant?" asked the coordinator.

"Somewhere between a 35% and a 45% reduction," replied Januelle.

Coordinator Cheyelle was silent for almost a cycle. Then she spoke. "That is just about the same size of reduction of the herd that we have encountered. Did you observe anything else?"

"I can't be certain because it wasn't something that we recorded in the previous inventories," said Januelle. "But I believe that the jungle, itself, was less dense and perhaps not quite as dark in color as I have seen before."

"Truly?" asked the coordinator.

"As I said, I have no specific measurements to compare against. I can't affirm the matter but that was my impression," said Januelle.

"I would like permission, Cheyelle, to continue to investigate this problem," interjected Richtor.

"Permission? You don't need my permission. We only regulate that which affects the entire shoal or activities by individuals that may affect others within the shoal. You know that from basic civics class, Richtor. You have taken basic civics, haven't you?"

"Yes, Coordinator," said Richtor. "But, Lichten and I went to talk with the herders, about the herd, after we came back from the jungle. They acknowledged what we could see - that the herd had gotten smaller – but wouldn't, or couldn't, say anything else. If we had permission, or authorization, then others might feel freer to talk with us."

"I see," said Cheyelle. She thought for a moment and then handed three engraved shells to Richtor. "Here are three Council badges for you, Lichten, and Januelle. I expect to get them back when this problem is addressed. Is that understood?"

"Certainly, Coordinator Cheyelle," said Richtor. "I mean, you can count on us, Cheyelle."

"The Council will continue to look into the matter. It is not your responsibility to find an answer to this problem. Your responsibility is to pursue your studies and to graduate and become a productive citizen of the shoal. But, as you have already shown, your curiosity and your, sometimes interminable, questions may bring up results faster than we elders may gather, even with the help of the Academy. Is there anything else for you to report at this time?" asked Cheyelle.

"No, Coordinator."

"Then I thank you for coming to me and I do still have a lot to do so I will say goodbye now." At those words, a pulse came from the doorway indicating that Wayroll was, as instructed, telling the coordinator of the end of the half-hour allocated.

Wayroll moved to the side as Januelle and Richtor left the room.

Coordinator Cheyelle called after them. "And Richtor, I think that you are going to be a very useful addition to the shoal."

Chapter 14 In the Shrankan Church

*I*n return for Januelle being willing to spend the first of her weekend with Richtor in Cheyelle's office, Richtor had agreed to accompany her to the Shrankan Church before the start of the next class week. As part of their leafletting and other attempts to gain attendance and membership, they had made the request for members in good standing to bring at least one new person to service each week for four weeks. Richtor was Januelle's contribution for this week.

Richtor had no negative feelings about the Shrankan Church - he just didn't want to volunteer for yet another environment where he was expected to not move around. In fact, there were few people in the shoal with a truly negative view of the church. The Shrankan Church had philosophies that allowed a large degree of tolerance and had no conflicts between their beliefs and those axioms and hypotheses of science.

Attendance had fallen primarily because the church did not have any true penalty for not attending. Nothing bad would happen if you didn't attend. You weren't considered a bad person and it wouldn't cause others to question your behavior.

With this being the case, most people of the shoal had decided that there were other things that they could do with their time.

The problem with the herd shrinkage and rations reduction was a negative effect. Lack of attendance may not have had anything to do with this negative effect. But then again there was no evidence that lack of attendance did not have a negative effect.

There had been few crises within the history of the shoal. Most had been of short duration and, while the effects may have taken a large number of currentflips to repair, an exhortation of the citizens of the shoal to change their behaviors would have been hard to correlate to the events. This was an ongoing, prolonged, problem. No one could argue that a change in behaviors would not help even if the church could not prove that it would.

As Richtor entered the building, he saw Januelle hovering over near a pedestal that had a large number of flexible tags on it. As he swam up to the pedestal, Januelle smiled at him and said, "Glad you were able to come, Richtor."

"I said I would," replied Richtor. "What is the sermon about today?"

"The duties of faithfulness. It's pretty much an introduction to the faith type of sermon as we have a relatively large number of newcomers present today. Let me make you a name tag. I will put my name on the bottom right corner of the tag in order to make sure I get credit for your attendance."

"Are they serious about that?" asked Richtor.

"There's no serious penalty if we don't do it but you know me. If I am part of a group, I follow the rules. So, I'll at least try to get someone here for four weeks."

"Move this way," continued Januelle. As Richtor got nearer, Januelle pushed the concave side of a flexible tag against his forehead, allowing the suction to be created. "There, now you are tagged."

"I have to stay by the name tag pedestal until after the service starts. It's my week. You head on into the main assembly area. I'll find you. You have been here before, haven't you?"

"Sure, we were encouraged to come here during our early years on campus – that's when you started coming regularly. If I remember correctly, you gave the church's junior member education committee some credit about getting you interested in science," said Richtor.

"That's right. Strange you remember that. They don't incorporate experiments into the junior member classes as much as they used to but some of those were pretty cool. Go ahead. Head on in. Grab yourself a snack if you want."

There was a pedestal with a basket of seaweed-wrapped snacks by the doorway. Richtor grabbed a small one – he had had a large breakfast – and went through the open doorway.

The assembly room was effectively a large courtyard. The church had received a variance from the Council to allow seaweed to grow around the periphery of the courtyard. This discouraged casual swimming over the courtyard and presented an impossible-to-miss landmark to guide visitors to the church.

It had been a number of currentflips since Richtor had been in church so he had no way of knowing whether this was a large crowd or not. There did seem to be a large number today. A larger pedestal was present in the middle of the courtyard for the Clerk to use during presentations and sermons. Clerk Zaristo was new to the church and he had never heard her before. He wasn't really sure which of the people swimming around might be her.

The sides of the courtyard were occupied by younger people. This allowed them to move around more without getting in anyone else's way. Richtor wasn't that young but he thought he would probably try to stay close to the sides of the courtyard – for similar reasons.

Januelle wouldn't be in until after the service had started. He looked around to see if there was anyone that he knew. Even though church wasn't as popular as it once was, with the campaign for attenders there should be some from his hatching or others that he knew. He swam around the edge of the courtyard, trying to survey the crowd. As he moved around the third wall, he spotted Arissto.

"Hello," he said. "Do you come here on a regular basis?"

"Yes. There seem to always be a few from each hatching that continue along with the church. I'm one of those. There are three others from my hatching here. I also brought a guest today," said Arissto.

"Ah, yes. Januelle brought me as her guest today. So, when you were asking about the herd reduction, you had already heard information at the previous sermon?"

"That's right. I guess Januelle told you. We weren't really supposed to tell anyone but that's OK. There wasn't a great reason not to – some type of surprise effect they were hoping for during this campaign to get more attenders."

"I'm no longer attending the weekly education classes but Januelle often guest-taught the last year I attended. She knows an awful lot but she isn't boring," Arissto continued.

"Yes. She can be a lot of fun," said Richtor. "Has the church gotten any more information on the herd reduction?"

"I don't know. Maybe we'll find out today."

A larger person with a bright blue wrap over her top dorsal area was swimming toward the center of the chamber. The crowd parted to allow easy access. Richtor guessed that it must be Clerk Zaristo.

Reaching the center pedestal, Clerk Zaristo started a slow hover around such that she could face everyone at some point of time. She started speaking on a broadcast channel such that everyone could clearly receive her.

"Hello everyone. Welcome. And a special welcome to all who are visiting after a long absence. Some of you are here as guests of regular attenders. We hope that you will continue to come but, of course, that is up to you."

"We do have a number of general announcements." A general set of smiles occurred around the courtyard. Apparently, the announcements were still mostly just tolerated. Of course, if the announcement was relevant to your interests, it was useful. But there were always so many about so many different people, groups, and activities.

While the clerk talked about the coming activities and other church-related business, Richtor started moving around the courtyard edge again. It was as he remembered. The courtyard sides remained easy to navigate with only a few clusters of younger people in evidence.

He was just about back to the main doorway entrance when he spotted Januelle coming through it. He waved to her and spoke to her on a direct channel to not disturb anyone else.

"Hello. All done?"

"Yes," said Januelle. "Still with the announcements. With doing name tag duty, I don't get to hear them. Some consider that a blessing but I am involved with enough things that they are often useful to me. Did you notice anything that you think I might be interested in?"

"No," replied Richtor. "I dropped my attention the moment she started with them. Sorry."

"Not a problem, Richtor. I know you can't stay still for long and the announcements aren't likely to be of interest to you. I'll look at the announcement sheet after the service. Wait. I think she is about done and ready to start the sermon."

Richtor turned around to look into the center once again and listen to the broadcast again.

"And that concludes the announcements which were given to me prior to the service. Does anyone else have something urgent to relay for today. Yes, Fillipa?"

A thinner person with some red and blue vertical bars on her front trunk spoke into the broadcast channel. "I'm sorry to not get it onto the announcement sheet. The break-out session of the Science interest group will be meeting tomorrow at 12th hour rather than 13th hour due to the expectation of a longer discussion. Same room as normal. Newcomers are welcome."

Richtor turned towards Januelle. "What is that about?"

"The Science interest group has decided to have a subset of the group discuss the herd reduction. That allows regular discussion and programs to continue uninterrupted. Probably most of the regular group will attend and there may be a few new people. Are you interested?"

"Can I ask you about any new facts or conclusions even if I don't come?"

"Of course, but you might want to come to raise questions of your own or to point out things that others might miss. The point of coming to meetings is not primarily to collect information. You can do most of that by reading the notes after they have been collected. The main reason is to connect with other people and to be able to ask questions that others might not think of to ask," said Januelle.

"Yes. But I can't easily stay still for meetings that may be going on for an hour or more. Either I am uncomfortable and unable to pay attention or I am distracting."

"Don't worry about being distracting," replied Januelle. "Science attracts people who are more concerned with what is happening on the inside than what is happening on the outside. They'll get used to you."

"Well, maybe."

Clerk Zaristo had already begun her sermon on the broadcast channel. Januelle put a finger up next to the side of her head indicating a desire to pay attention and Richtor moved his attention to the clerk.

"We have a period of trial going on, as you all know," continued Clerk Zaristo who had already talked for a bit in introduction.

"I will not try to claim that attending church would have made any difference as to why this trial is happening. But I do remind everyone that we, here in the church, strive to bring together the reasonable, and knowable, areas of science into harmony with the unknowable answers to questions which we all have."

"These questions have no answers and yet we long for answers. We hunger for answers. We will continue to attempt to assign answers. Some think that science, by itself, will find the answers to the long questions - what do I think? Do I think? What happens after death? Why do accidents happen? What is the purpose of our living?"

"I will not try to tell you that science will never find the answers. Perhaps it will. But it is the normal path of science to produce two questions for every answer. This is good as it continues the push for growth in our knowledge and our abilities to apply that knowledge. But if that continues and each answer produces more questions then we end up with more and more questions."

"Perhaps, someday, science will reach that final answer to the final question. But, until then, there are many approaches to tentative, but unprovable, answers. That is what our church provides – a friendly, tolerant, and supportive exchange between what is known, what may be known, and what may never be known."

"How does this apply to the current situation of a reduction in the food supply? Speculation, faith, and exploration give the basic materials necessary to push science in directions of interest to the shoal, and Ocean, as a whole. We may make use of this common body to push to understand what has happened, why it has happened, and what may be done about it."

"Let us all join together, today and every day. And now for a short silence."

During the next few cycles, all communications over all channels ceased. Since nothing was available to receive, all were allowed the short lack of need to concentrate and, in such state, contemplate without restriction.

"Thank you all for coming. Please do check into our various interest and discussion groups. And consider coming again next week," concluded Clerk Zaristo.

"How about you, Richtor?" asked Januelle. "Do you think you will come back next week? I'm not going to push for it – I have to bring someone different each week to get credit from it. You are welcome – and maybe it will help you with some of your decisions and thoughts."

"Perhaps. I think I will try to come to the next Science interest group. Remember, though, that science is only one of my many interests and I certainly don't have anything close to the experience, or interest, in it that you do."

"Sure. Last I looked, there were still snacks in the basket outside the doorway. They cannot be kept until next week."

"Maybe I should take a couple to Lichten," said Richtor. "He is almost always hungry. It seems to go to all muscle, though."

"Lichten. Yes, he would be a good one to bring next week. Thanks for the thought."

Richtor wondered if Lichten would appreciate that but he would probably appreciate the snacks. Richtor grabbed a couple from the basket as he left.

Chapter 15 Talk and Herds

*T*he next couple of weeks were a period of settling. At the beginning, there was much discussion about the herd reduction. But, without any additional information to be used, discussion dwindled and largely disappeared. A general feeling of malaise and low morale was prevalent. The reductions of rations were not severe enough to harm anyone – and they did not apply to the ones in the creche or youngsters on campus. A lot of people might lose a bit of weight and that wouldn't necessarily be a bad thing. Teacher Malov might succeed in slimming down.

The students treated the rations reduction as a novel situation and it did not bother them a lot. However, participation in more active extracurricular activities did drop as the more active students who were already at excellent weights would no longer have quite as much stamina. Overall, everyone had had somewhat more than sufficient food so the reduction did not cause much difference.

Richtor didn't participate in many of the discussions – only the ones where someone grabbed hold of him and brought him in. There continued to be almost no new news except some of the information that he and Januelle had brought in to the Council and which they later released to keep the public updated.

The reality that it was not just the shoal's herd that was affected did not ease people's fears although it may have lessened the imperative, felt by some, from the Shrankan Church.

The Council, with the advice and studies of the local branch of the Academy, was attempting to trace back to the start of the problem. The idea was that, if it was known when the problem first started to occur then that might line up with some event that happened in the same general time period. Hopefully, some event which occurred slightly before the notice of the problem.

So far, this approach had not had any results. Largescale harvests from the herd took place about twice per currentflip. There were smaller skims of the herd for use as fresh dishes from time to time. After the largescale harvests, the fish were split up into different preservation methods.

The shoal had tried to have only live catches to distribute to the citizens of the shoal. This had led to a lot of waste. In addition, it was hard to distribute fairly. With the current method, food was stored in common for distribution according to work credits. Meanwhile a couple of shops presented orders to the herders for fresh fish and they handled distribution and allocation.

~   ~   ~

Richtor hovered outside of Lichten's door panel. He pressed the button to the side of the doorframe to announce his arrival.

"Hello, Richtor," said Lichten as he slid open the door panel. "Did we have something planned for today or are you just coming by to visit?"

"Nothing planned." He handed the deputy badge to Lichten.

"What's this?" asked Lichten.

"Januelle and I went to see Coordinator Cheyelle to tell her what we found out at the jungle. I think I told you we were going to visit her."

"Yes. I had forgotten but you did tell me about that. How did it go?"

"She wasn't aware that the fish populations in the jungle were reduced. They've released that information to the general public now. They were going to get the local branch of the Academy continue research on that analysis. Maybe they'll do an additional, expanded inventory. I don't know as they haven't told me."

"So, again, what's this?" Lichten held up the badge to Richtor.

"I was successful in convincing Cheyelle that we could be useful in figuring out what is happening. You remember how reluctant the herders were to tell us much?"

"Certainly. My memory hasn't gotten that bad – especially about the herd," replied Lichten.

"Well, these badges indicate that we are representing the Council in our questions. They won't matter much to most people but those that work for the Council should feel able to talk with us."

"I see," said Lichten. "That makes sense. But how often will we be contacting people who work for the Council? I sometimes go out to check on the herds - or I end up in the same place as the herds when I working out with the new sharrells. But I've never needed any authorization."

"That's what I came for. Are you willing to go back to the herders with me now that we do have these badges?"

"Why do you want me to go? I'm happy to do things with you - they usually end up being fun - but I don't feel that urgent about solving this problem. They'll fix it or they won't."

"No curiosity but you're sure dependable, Lichten," said Richtor. "You know sharrells, you know animals, you know the herders. You can probably ask better questions about the herd than I can - more relevant questions."

"OK. I'm willing to come. When do you want to do it?" Richtor raised his eyebrows and pointed towards the hallway.

"Now?" asked Lichten. "Why is it always 'now' for you? Can't you plan anything with a little lead time? I don't know what to do with you. Can it wait a while? Until this afternoon?"

"I suppose. I like to do things as I think of them. That way I am less likely to forget them," said Richtor.

"I guess that makes sense. My life is usually pretty predictable. I don't have to worry about forgetting things because I pretty much know what I will be doing day to day and week to week."

"And that would drive me crazy," responded Richtor. "I could probably handle it if I was kept busy during those times but if any idle times came around, I'd be ready to head for the jungles."

"So, later this afternoon?"

"Sure. And thanks, Lichten. You're a good friend to put up with me."

"Hey, I usually enjoy it – and it's not like I'm the life of the party."

"We work together pretty well. See you later." Richtor headed down the hallway.

~   ~   ~

Richtor arrived back at Lichten's room after he had completed his lunch. He hadn't seen Lichten there. He hoped that he had had a good chance to eat already. If not, there wasn't really much of a rush. He could head off to keep him company while Lichten had his lunch.

Richtor pushed the announcement button by the door. Lichten drew the door panel aside promptly.

"Have you eaten?" asked Richtor.

"Yes. Have you?

"Yes. Ready to go?"

"I guess so. Anything we need? I assume that we are swimming over to the herd - we don't need to pick up sharrells." Lichten continued.

"No, no rush - unless you need to get back quickly?" Lichten shook his head. Richtor continued. "I'm willing to head off for a long swim. It'll be good for me. Reduced rations don't seem to be hurting you any," he smiled.

"It's not really cheating but I get a bit more food than you do," said Lichten. I get the normal dormitory meals that everyone here gets. But I get meals provided at the stables when I show up for work over a meal period. It all depends on timing of course and I may be a bit more careful to time an overlap."

Richtor gave Lichten a wry look and smile.

"Hey, I'm doing heavy physical work."

"You're right. But let's see what we can do for everyone else. OK?" commented Richtor.

The two friends headed down the hall and out towards the main doorway. Lichten occasionally had to slow down a bit for the more leisurely pace of Richtor. He wasn't overly hungry or tired but didn't really want to become such. He had thought about bringing a trident or a net to grab some wild fish while they were out but it really wasn't fair to everyone else who might be on the hungry side.

Lichten finally said, "You lead, Richtor. There's no sense in me going up front and having to come back to get you all the time. We'll go together and you can set the pace."

They continued to travel towards the herd. They could start seeing the column of fish from quite a distance. They couldn't spot individual fish. Nor could they spot the herders - but they might be on the other side of the column.

As they got nearer to the column, it first started to appear to writhe and, still closer, broke down into a large school of fish swimming in a tight circle.

There was no sign of the herders and Lichten took the lead once again as they started a slow circle around the column, making certain that they were not close enough to bother any of the fish in the column.

As they rounded onto the other side, they spotted one of the herders that they had met before. It turned out to be Simton - the one that Lichten did not know as well.

"Hello Simton. Where's Martus?" asked Lichten.

"Hello. I saw you a couple of weeks ago, didn't I?"

"That's us," replied Lichten.

"Martus wasn't feeling so well today. I told them that I would be fine watching the herd today without backup. They weren't happy about it but most of the staff isn't in a lot better condition."

"What's going on? Is there a wave of illness sweeping the shoal?" asked Richtor.

"I shouldn't talk any more about it," responded Simton.

"Oh, yes. We're working with Cheyelle and the Council on trying to find causes and possible solutions for the herd reduction problem. You can talk with us," said Richtor. He handed the Deputy badge to Simton who looked at it thoroughly and handed it back.

"I haven't seen these very often," Simton said. "They showed them to us when we were first hired and being trained and then, as I recall, I saw one being used by someone who was investigating a fungal mold that seemed to be contagious in the herd. That was a scary situation. We cleared it up before it affected anyone. Unlike this situation which has gone on much too long to just keep it hidden."

"OK. I guess I can tell you," continued Simton. "The Council consulted the local branch of the Academy for a quarterflip about just how far we could cut back rations for the shoal. If we kept the level too high then the herd would continue to get smaller at an increasing rate. We needed to cut rations back to the point that it would match the population growth rate of the herd."

"So, current rations are at that point?" asked Lichten.

"Yes," said Simton. "Since there is no known cause, fix, or duration known they decided that they couldn't fix the rations at a higher amount. But distribution can't be equal for all. The younger children need as close to full rations as possible or it will affect their growth and development and damage the shoal for a long time. There are always a few who do more active physical work who just have to have the calories. What all that means is that the adults are on a barely-enough diet. Lower energy and lower resistance to disease."

"What about the Council?" asked Richtor.

"They have the same rations that we do. But they don't have a very active lifestyle. We hope it won't hurt them too much. Of course, many of them are older and larger and really need more food so the largest are suffering some," said Simton.

"So, this really is a crisis," mused Richtor. "What happens if the herd spontaneously gets even smaller?"

"The Council has started negotiations with a couple of other shoals that have had a greater amount of food. Mostly smaller shoals that have access to larger herds. But their extra has decreased too. It seems that we are not the only shoal suffering."

"You sure know a lot," said Richtor. "Thanks for talking with us about it."

"Anything to help and, as deputies to the Council, it is part of my duties to help."

"How do you know so much?" asked Lichten. "You seem to know at least as much, and it seems like possibly more, than the Council."

Simton chittered. "Not more. Probably they still know things that I don't know. But I'm curious. I ask questions and I have a lot of time to think swimming around out here with the herd."

"And do you have any additional thoughts?" asked Richtor.

"Only that I think that finding out the reason the herd has reduced is the main thing we need to know. If we can determine that reason, then we can plan for how to cope and have a better idea as to how long we will need to work with the situation."

"That sounds right," said Richtor. "Thank you very much."

"You're both welcome."

"Tell Martus to get better soon," said Lichten.

"I'll tell him but I don't think he needs any encouragement to do that," said Simton with a smile. She waved at them and went over to the herd which had moved off past the current algae cloud field.

Rumblings in the Reef

Richtor and Lichten swam off back towards the dormitories. It had been a productive trip.

Chapter 16 Gathering thoughts

*T*he next class week was soon upon Richtor. He seemed to have settled better into a focusing groove - although his focus was not always on what the teacher was teaching - and had not gotten into trouble for a while. He had been thinking about their conversation with Simton and he was aware that they really couldn't make any progress without knowing how it started. The excursion to Jordech Jungle was useful as it showed that the drop in population wasn't happening only to the herd. But that gave absolutely no indication as to how to proceed.

Richtor decided that the best way to continue was to set up a meeting with Januelle and Lichton. The reason for the choice of Januelle was because she was the best person available to work with the science aspects and the choice of Lichten because he knew animals well and could handle various situations and emergencies well. Perhaps some type of meeting the beginning of the weekend.

Luckily, Januelle and Lichten were both students in Teacher Lorell's class. He could briefly ask them before class - assuming he got there early enough.

Meanwhile, they had just begun the last halfflip before graduation. Januelle and Lichten may not have chosen their exact next steps but both were well prepared to carry through with their choices. For him, not having a great knowledge of where his path would be, grades were important to allow more cushion for choices. He might not be first choice for someone taking on an apprentice in a science field, but his grades would not preclude that. Same with factory work, or administrative work, or working in the creche. He was someone who could do most things at an adequate level but he wanted to excel and be appreciated.

Teacher Lorell's Oral History class would be the next period. Having something to do before that class did not make the waiting easier. Richtor hadn't gone on any excessively long elimination breaks for quite a few weeks but he might need to do such today. The current biology class was interesting. It might even be applicable, and useful, to the current problem.

Today's lecture by Teacher Dorasol was on the life cycle of fish. It applied to him, and his friends, and people of the shoal in general - but this class included some things that the people of the shoal did not have to be concerned about and left out some things that were relevant only to the shoal.

Since this class had just been started along with this last halfflip, the teacher was still covering basic topics. They had covered fertilization cycles and were now into the basics of sustenance and growth.

Teacher Dorasol continued the lecture for today. "So, we see that there are a number of reactions to a decrease in the food supply for schools of fish. The number of eggs laid decreases. A greater percentage of hatchlings are eaten by the adults. And the general energy of the school decreases. Who can tell me the advantages of these changes of behavior? Anyone? Richtor, if you have been paying attention, can you reply to the class as a whole?"

Richtor swung his body around so that his face was toward the instructor. "If there is a reduction in the food supply then the school either reduces in size or the health of all becomes worse. A reduction in the number of eggs and the eating of hatchlings both help to reduce the size of the school. The reduction of energy level helps to reduce the amount of food needed per fish as well as decrease likely bouts of antisocial activity within and between adults of the school."

"Well done, Richtor! You may pass this class yet."

The class chittered and Richtor shared in the laughter while smiling at the teacher and class. He knew his behavior often set up an expectation of low assimilation of the class material. He had not had Teacher Dorasol for a class before this. By the end of the halfflip, she would have a better understanding of his strengths and weaknesses.

So, food supply could reduce the size of a school. That was very interesting. But was it relevant to the current situation? And, if so, what was causing a reduction in the food supply? Richtor tried to focus. It would not do him any good to make the teacher's evaluation of him correct. Besides, this was material that could be useful.

Richtor realized that he and Lichten had asked Simton about the size of the herd but not about its activity. Was the herd sluggish in comparison to its normal activity level? He had no ideas as to how he could find out if the broods were smaller or if the adults were eating more of the hatchlings. Januelle would probably have some ideas.

~   ~   ~

He swam hard and reached his Oral History class a couple of cycles before the start of class. Luckily, Januelle was already there. Hopefully, Lichten would arrive soon.

"Hello, Januelle," said Richtor.

"Hi. Do you need something?"

"I was wondering if you might be able to meet for an hour or so at the start of the weekend."

"For what?" asked Januelle.

"I don't know what to do next."

"About what? About the reduction in the herd and reduced rations?"

"Yes."

"Why do you feel it is your responsibility to find out anything?" asked Januelle.

"I don't feel it is my responsibility," said Richtor. "Well, maybe I do – but that's because I have a feeling that I can help with the problem. If a person can help with a problem, and doesn't, then they aren't being responsible. And Cheyelle thinks I can help. Otherwise, she wouldn't have given us Deputy badges."

"I suppose. Can you think of a real use for the badges?"

"Yes. Lichten and I already used them when talking with the herders. They were willing to talk more about the situation. Can you meet this weekend? Class is about to start."

"I suppose so. But I do have a lot of homework this weekend. No excursions. No field trips."

"Right. Around 6th hour after breakfast?"

"OK," said Januelle.

Richtor turned around to head back to his hover area. He saw Lichten in his area but it was too close to the start of class to talk with him. Either after class or during math class with

Teacher Gregov should be possible. This was the only class that he had with Januelle. She was in more advanced classes in every other area. Language arts and history were just subjects in which she had to take classes in order to graduate. She had no inherent interest in the subjects.

The remainder of the class did not bring out any new information that seemed to be relevant. They were continuing with school and herd psychology - which was interesting but he couldn't see any way that would directly affect herd size. Nor, if it did, did he see any way that he could work with them about it. For schools and herds, most of the psychology was based on instincts and survival behaviors. While it was also true for the shoal, the citizens of the shoal had the ability to move away from the basics and make life much more complicated, interesting, and difficult.

With the pulses indicating the end of the class, Richtor succeeded in catching Lichten's eye to motion him to the back of the classroom. He waited a bit to allow the aisle to clear and then headed back to the area at the back. Lichten, being closer to the back of the class, was already present.

"What's up?" asked Lichten.

"Are you OK to meet with Januelle and me around 6th hour after breakfast?"

"I guess so. Another excursion?"

"Not yet," replied Richtor. "Januelle specifically asked to make sure there wouldn't be any extended capture of her time. I want to bring us all into understanding on what we have done and I want all three of us to discuss what we should do."

"Should?" asked Lichten. "I think you take things much too seriously, Richtor. We haven't even graduated yet. You heard Cheyelle. She has the local branch of the Academy looking into this."

"Yes, I know. Januelle pointed out similar reservations. But the fact that Cheyelle, and the Council, are relying on the local Academy makes me more nervous and not less nervous."

"Why? They know what they are doing. They have a lot of knowledge about their various subjects."

"True. But that's academic interest. I don't mean to put them down but we are talking about real events and not just theoretical ones."

"I suppose so," said Lichten. "But that still doesn't mean that you, or even we, are responsible to clean up messes."

"What do you mean, Deputy Lichten?" replied a smiling Richtor. "Aren't you ready to harness up and gather a posse to solve the shoal's problems?"

"I wish that was all it would take," said Lichten. "But, OK, I'll meet with you two. At 6th hour after breakfast?"

"Right. See you." Richtor headed for the doorframe.

"See you." Lichten turned and was rapidly following Richtor to the hallway.

~   ~   ~

Not having set up any other place to meet, Richtor found himself swimming down the hall to Januelle's room shortly before 6th hour. He hoped that Lichten would also head there – making the assumption that they would meet just as they had for their excursion to Jordech Jungle. There wasn't a lot of decoration so the numbers were primarily the means to know that one was travelling and the direction in which a person was swimming. As he swam, Richtor glanced at the door panels set into frames along the hall which did provide a little personalization and decoration.

Some door panels just had a small tag of paper attached indicating who the occupant was and possibly hobbies and other interests. Some, of course, had only the chamber number. Every once in a while, a door panel would display what amounted to an epic collage of events – presumably from the occupant's life.

Richtor found his eye attracted to one such door panel. The sculpted panels attached to the door were framed by finely woven seaweed basketry. Within the frame were panels depicting a versatile artist and craftsperson. One panel showed someone creating a vessel for containing oil. Such vessels always had openings on the top and the bottom. The one on the bottom was for filling and the one at the top was for access to the oil.

Another panel showed someone with their arms poking up under the edge of a bubble, welding metal to form a sculpture. This panel was done exceptionally well – with the bubble giving a true appearance of transparency. Sometimes, in order to reach areas high within the pocket of air contained by the bubble, the artist would have to use extender tools. Richtor had heard of some experiments with headgear that would allow people to enter the bubbles. That would be much easier for an artisan, technician, scientist, or factory worker when they needed to do work that required a gaseous environment. But, as far as he knew, they had not figured out a way to keep the water in the helmet usable for more than a few cycles.

There was a panel showing someone creating sculpted panels. Just in case someone might think the decorations were done by someone else. Another panel showed the person weaving.

Richtor shook his head. He was amazed at the versatility of this person. There was no name upon the door but it would be great to meet such a person. But he had no real reason for such a meeting and it was getting closer to 6th hour.

As Richtor turned around and started heading down the hall to Januelle's chamber, he spotted Lichten coming down the hall towards him. That was lucky.

Lichten had a relieved look on his face. "Thank goodness you're here. I realized this morning that I didn't know where we were going to meet."

"Sorry. I woke up realizing the same thing. I thought heading to Januelle's chamber, as we did for the first excursion, might be the best thing to do. I really should have been more organized."

"No problem. I can always use a bit more exercise. I went to your chamber first and then came this direction. What are you doing hovering in front of this door panel? This isn't Januelle's chamber, is it?"

"Not unless she moved and changed interests. I was glancing at door panels as I swam and I was struck by all of these panels. The person is very talented."

Lichten glanced over at the door. "Oh yes. This is Angella's chamber. You're right, she is very talented. Do you know her?"

Richtor shook his head. "No."

"She's from our hatching. She made my harnesses as part of a project in one of her classes. I paid her some work credits but she wouldn't have done it just for the credits. Some of the details in the harnesses gave her the chance to do some things that normally don't go onto a harness."

"The people working in the panels are pretty realistic images of Angella. She's really good. The Noveum Artistaria group offered her an apprenticeship last currentflip ahead of graduation."

"That's unusual," said Richtor. "The groups hardly ever offer an apprenticeship before graduation."

"That's right. But, hey, it's getting really close to 6th hour. That was the right time, correct?"

"Yes. Let's move." Richtor and Lichten swam toward their friend's chamber with Lichten taking the upper portion of the hallway.

Chapter 17 Discussions and plans

*T*hey reached Januelle's chamber and Richtor pressed the pulse button to alert Januelle they had arrived. It was a couple of cycles past the beginning of 6ᵗʰ hour. Januelle was always very prompt – often a few cycles early – but she would not expect Richtor to be on time every time.

Januelle slid open the door panel. "Hello. We should probably head outside. There really isn't enough room in my chamber for discussion for more than a few cycles. I'm glad you came by. I wasn't sure that we were meeting here – I just assumed such since we did so last time."

"Yes, I should have arranged something. But, I admit, I didn't really know where to meet. I still should have specified some place. Shall we go to the sculpture garden? That's a quiet place to wander and I seem to have my art appreciation stirred up," said Richtor.

"That should be fine. Any particular reason you're feeling artistic?"

"No, not me. I can draw a little. Enough to illustrate a class paper but nothing special. I was drawn to the sculpted panels on Angella's door. That's where Lichten found me as he came down the hallway."

"Oh, yes. Angella. She is part of the Hatching Elite group for the campus. The title is terrible but it is a group organized by campus where the students who are doing exceptionally well can meet on a quarterflip basis. It looks good on the graduation certificate but, otherwise, it doesn't involve much. You're part of the group, aren't you, Lichten?"

"Yes. For animal husbandry."

"Why haven't I ever heard of this group before?" asked Richtor.

"It's kept low key. We're afraid that some other students would feel that not being in the group means that they are less important. Some of us in the group have argued that there really isn't any need for such a group. Just have some kind of list that is kept and maybe listed on our graduation certificate that we had been on the list. But there are some members of the group that really like it. I think that they may not have much social life other than when the group meets," said Januelle.

"Oh. Well, shall we head to the sculpture garden?" asked Richtor.

"Sure. Let's go."

The three friends headed to a vertical exit shaft and left the dormitory. The sculpture garden was located between the Shrankan Church, marked by its enclosure of seaweed, and the shoal's government office buildings. There was a smaller sculpture garden near the outside edge of the shoal with expectations that it would keep growing until it was as large as the central garden.

The sculpture garden was moderate in size. Smaller than the area encompassed by the Shrankan Church, it was around 12 bodylengths by 15 bodylengths. There were some really nice sculptures present. The garden had two sub-groups. There was one sculpture in the center and another dozen or two scattered through the garden which were considered permanent although it was possible to replace them with others. This was not often done so calling them permanent was close to accurate.

The other sculptures were juried pieces. The sculptures were created by gifted artists within the community and then, if approved by a committee of artists associated with the Council, placed within either the central or the outskirt sculpture garden. They generally were kept on display for a currentflip and then another sculpture was voted in to take its place. In the meantime, people were welcome to make offers for the sculptures to be relocated to the buyers' household once the sculpture had been displayed for its currentflip.

The system worked well for everyone. The public got interesting art, the artists of the community had their works well displayed, and the general community was enriched in credits and in spirit.

The central sculpture was the tallest and the oldest. It had been commissioned by the Council and the shoal, to be the first sculpture of the garden and a visual representation of the shoal. The twisting columns gave a feeling of the seaweed jungle while, somehow, the use of different stones in the base, and appearing around the periphery of the vertical shaft, presented the appearance of the fissures which were such an important part of the life, and commerce, of the shoal.

Somehow, this seemed like a good place to discuss plans for something that was important to the shoal. Richtor realized that their efforts might not be needed and were, indeed, possibly wasted effort. But, at least, he would feel useful.

"Thanks for agreeing to meet today," said Richtor. "I should bring you up-to-date about our meeting with Coordinator Cheyelle, Lichten."

"Is there much beyond what you have told me? About the Deputy badges?" asked Lichten.

"No, not really, I guess. Januelle's data was news for her. She will pass them along to the local Academy branch. They are doing the official investigation of the herd reduction. But I'm not sure that they have really done that much. That is, Coordinator Cheyelle did not disclose anything and, if they were not aware that the issue was more widespread than just the herd, I don't see how they can approach the problem very well."

"I agree," said Januelle. "I have talked with, and sometimes worked with, the local branch and they are really great for discussing things but there is little field work and not a lot of incorporation of realtime input from the areas affected by a problem."

"You mean that they are thinkers and not doers?" asked Richtor.

Januelle chittered. "I guess that's one way to put it. I don't think they are doing much to actively investigate the problem. They are probably doing about the same as most of the shoal – waiting and hoping the problem will go away. They're often correct that time tends to solve problems."

"I'm not eager to rely on that. The reduced rations can be lived with but what happens if the herd undergoes another reduction? We might start having some deaths. And, since it is affecting most, if not all, other species in this area of Ocean, there is no way to significantly supplement the herds with wild catches."

"Right. We agree that it is a serious problem," said Lichten. "But why is it our problem? We know it's the responsibility of the Council. Why push ourselves to do work that may be duplication of official efforts?"

"I agree that we shouldn't have to," said Richtor. "But I'm not comfortable in saying, or assuming, that we don't need to. Januelle, is there any other likely investigation going on other than through the local branch of the Academy?"

"No. And Cheyelle, during our talk, did not mention anything else. It's possible she just didn't want to tell us but that isn't likely and, if so, she would not have encouraged us to continue to investigate and give us the Deputy badges," added Januelle.

"I don't know if it is useful. You know an awful lot more about science and biology than I do," said Richtor. "But, this week in biology class, they were talking about the feeding cycles of fish – and pointing out the effect of reduced food availability on population sizes. It struck me as possibly relevant."

"Hmmm. Yes, I think you may have something there," said Januelle. "You really are good at gleaning information from lots of different sources, Richtor. I should have thought of that. In fact, there are a lot of people in the shoal who should have thought of that. I wonder if any have?"

"Well, Coordinator Cheyelle didn't seem to mention it. But maybe, if they do know it, they aren't telling anyone until they know a reason for it and how to reverse it?"

"That's a possibility, Richtor, but I think she would have told us. No one likes wasted effort. She wouldn't have given us Deputy badges and then not given us important information to narrow our investigation."

"Remember that it isn't just the herd," said Lichten. "The fish and other life in the seaweed jungle are also affected. While it isn't required that the herd and the wild fish have the same problem – it seems like the simplest answer."

"So, a general reduction in the food supply is a possibility. Rather scary but, still, a possibility," said Richtor. "Does anyone else have an idea that we could investigate?"

"There's always the possibility of overharvesting," said Januelle.

"How would that apply to the Jordech Jungle?"

"Maybe it wouldn't. Even if we prefer to have one solution for both situations, it isn't reasonable to require one. Lichten, have you had any word back from any of the hunters that you work with? Are they having more difficulty hunting down their targets?"

"Most of the hunters only talk about what they've caught or what got away," responded Lichten. "If they don't catch anything then they fall into a couple different categories. Either they just have bad luck – which usually means they were ready to give up if their game didn't jump into the net or move about right in front of the spear. Or they just look glum and don't talk about it. I guess that I could start asking them about their trips."

"Don't they like to talk about their trips?" asked Richtor. "The hunters that I have known seem to talk forever about what trips they have been on and what they caught and every little detail."

"That's true – for the hunters who are successful. The ones who don't catch anything – or nothing that they want to talk about – tend to be really quiet. Except for the 'bad luck' ones which I mentioned before, of course. It can be bad business to try to prod the silent ones for more information. Some can get really angry about it."

"So, have you had more silent hunters coming back in of late?" asked Januelle.

"Yes, we have," responded Lichten. "But I hadn't really noticed or thought about it. As we have been talking, I have gone back through my workdays through the past currentflip or so and there have been quite a few silent customers coming back. And a lot fewer large trophies that they can't wait to talk about."

"I know that going on a hunt doesn't cost a lot. Mostly rental of a sharrell and a little equipment.

But if I were a hunter and I kept going out and not getting anything then I would become a lot less enthusiastic about trips. Have you seen any sign of that?" asked Richtor.

"Yes! Diplodus has been remarking about that a lot lately. We don't have that great of a profit margin anyway but he's thinking about reducing the number of sharrells in our corrals."

"I'll mark overharvesting down on a list to talk with the herders about," said Richtor. "Lichten, maybe you can gently nudge some silent hunters about their experiences. Maybe talk about something like 'it seems like it takes longer and longer to find the good game'. We shouldn't make any assumptions. What else?"

"There could be pollution from the fissures – or from elsewhere," said Januelle.

"I haven't seen any sign of that. Have you, Lichten? No? Well, it might be something that isn't easily spotted. OK. Another question to put on the list."

"Anything else, anyone?"

"Well, there is always disease," said Januelle. "But that wouldn't be a mystery. That would be obvious and public. I don't think that disease is a likely explanation."

"OK. So, we have overharvesting, food supply, and pollution to ask about. Is that right?"

"Yes," said Lichten. "I think so. Do you want me to come along to talk with the herders?"

"I don't think that will be necessary this time – I don't want to take too much of your time just working on my curiosity. I'll do that after class towards the beginning of this next week."

"And then?" asked Januelle.

"It looks like food supply is the most likely reason at this point. I'll talk with the herders. You talk with your science club and possibly with the local Academy branch, if you can. We will make sure that we can legitimately focus on food supply. Then we'll get together and plan a way to approach the problem. Sound good?" asked Richtor.

"OK," said Lichten. "Do we set up another meeting now?"

"Not yet. I'll talk with Januelle about what she hears back and if it contradicts our main idea. It may take us a week or two to get the information back. We'll hold off on additional meetings until then. Sound OK?"

"OK," said Januelle and Lichten in unison. They smiled and split up to each head to their next destination.

Chapter 18 Questions and a few answers

After he got back to his room, Richtor wrote down the list of items on a small pad that he used for notes. The pad was a recent invention. He could use the same waterproof marker on it that he used on other paper but he could erase it to use it over again. Paper was expensive and the markers tended to make marks on the bottom of any sheet put on top of them – so long-term storage required putting in seaweed separators between sheets of paper. Even bound books ended up being a page of print followed by a page of separator followed by a page of print and so forth.

He felt a bit silly writing down the list. It was so short and his memory wasn't bad. Still, just like writing down notes before a class exam, writing it down helped him to remember it. He put on the pad – overharvesting, food supply, pollution. They had all agreed that any disease to have appeared would have been quickly noticeable and news of it would have been spread even faster.

He didn't want to go to see the herders today. Wait until after class someday this week. He had tests coming up. It was the last halfflip before graduation, after all. Januelle studied as if she didn't already know the entire textbook and all annotations. A perfect score was not unusual for her. His grades were satisfactory – even a bit better than satisfactory. But, unlike Januelle, he needed to study again before tests. As long as there was uninterrupted time for his short-term memory to move over into long-term memory, he was fine. But there were too many times when he lost focus and the only way to know what he might have missed was to go over all of it.

Books were too scarce, and too expensive, to have individual books for the students. He would need to head to the library. It would have been so wonderful to have his own copy. Maybe that would happen someday. Richtor opened his door panel, swam out, and closed it behind him. Off to the library.

~   ~   ~

Richtor was in his last class of the day. He had reviewed his short notes on the pad in his room. He was certain that he would not forget them. So, he would head out to the herd right after class. He had strapped his travel harness around him before coming to the campus today. Most students didn't bring one to campus as there was nothing that needed to be taken between classes unless one was going to be doing a presentation that day. A few wore one every day. Januelle did. She brought a few extra study items and, sometimes, some rocks or plants or specimens to study during her free period. It seemed like she never really slowed down – same as Richtor but in a very different way.

Attached to his travel harness, Richtor had a small pouch that contained a pad and marker along with his Deputy badge. He wanted to make certain that whatever information the herders had could be written down correctly so that he could share it properly with Januelle and Lichten when they met again.

The class pulse alarm, signifying the end of class and the end of the class day, triggered. The teacher, who had been lecturing and had wandered over towards the doorframe while he was speaking, was first out of the classroom. That was strange – he must have had something special to do.

The rest of the class weren't that much slower to leave. As usual, unless there was a pressing reason for him to get to his next class quickly, Richtor stayed hovering around his area until the doorframe was no longer jammed with students heading out. He really hated being pressed together as they left. Some seemed to like it.

He moved out of the doorway and headed towards the shaft that took him up through the final roof. Being part of the graduating class, most classes were on the top floor of the campus building but a few multi-hatching types of courses might be located elsewhere.

Up and out. Free again for a while. He oriented himself and started swimming toward the herders.

It seemed that Martus had recovered. Both were thinner than they were when they first saw them an eighthflip ago. Herding was not usually a physically exerting job but it was fairly clear that they were not eating as much as they were using.

"Hello! How are you feeling, Martus?"

"Hello," responded Martus. "I'm able to stay in harness. I feel some better. Thanks. How are you?"

"Fine. Hello, Simton"

"Hi. What's up?"

"We were discussing the herd depletion situation and put together a list of possibilities. First, do you two have any ideas? Since you are here with the herd, you may have seen something," said Richtor.

Simton and Martus looked at each other. Martus spoke. "We've discussed it a lot between the two of us. The results have been a reduction in the herd size but the change in numbers has been predictable. When we harvest - say half of the herd - it is not restoring itself as quickly or to the same number as before we harvest."

"Have you noticed anything that might contribute to this?"

"Not really. There are just fewer young fish to grow up for harvesting."

"Are the hatchings about the same size? With fewer fish, I'm sure that the numbers have gone down overall but, considering the reduction in the size of the herd, has the number gone down proportionately?" asked Richtor.

"I'm not sure I understand what you are asking." Said Simton.

"OK. Sorry that I wasn't clear. Let's say that a normal hatching size for the herd would be 25,000 hatchings. With the herd half the size, we would expect around 12,500 hatchlings. Is that what you are seeing?"

"You don't ask for much, do you?" said Martus. "We don't often check on prior pasture locations. As you know, we rotate through three pastures. The herd has to rotate through three times to get back to the same pasture. We shift them from the hatching pasture to the next one soon after the eggs are laid and fertilized. They usually hatch before we rotate the herd to the next pasture. Thus, before the herd returns back to the hatchery, there is at least one rotation time for them to mature."

"That's interesting. So, you rotate through three pastures. Why three?"

"Well, typically, a rotation three times within a halfflip gives enough time for the algae cloud to replenish itself. So, by the time the herd gets back to an original pasture, the food supply is as expected."

"Is that still true?"

Martus looked at Simton who then spoke to Richtor. "No, I don't think it is. I think that they are each smaller than they used to be. But that's subjective. We really haven't any record of cloud sizes."

"OK. So, back to the previous question. How about the size of the hatching?"

"Like I said. We don't usually go back to examine the previous pastures. I can't answer the question."

"Is there a hatching due soon? If you went to that pasture to inspect it, could you tell if the size was reduced?"

"No, I don't think I could," responded Simton. "To be able to detect a size change, I'd have to know the typical size - and I don't know that. There is a hatching due in about a week."

"So, you do believe that the algae cloud is shrinking but you are not certain whether the hatching size has decreased?

"Yep. That's about right," agreed Martus.

"How about the winnowing? When the older population rotates back into the hatching pasture. Do the same number of hatchlings make it to adulthood? And, during the harvesting, how do you keep the younger fish out of the harvest?"

"No, I don't think that a larger percentage of the new hatching is winnowed out. Sure, the total numbers are smaller but I don't think that the hatchlings are decreased more than usual."

"You're sure about that?" asked Richtor.

"Pretty sure," said Martus. "When we rotate back into the hatching pasture, we can see the new hatching fairly well. So, I can give a good estimate as to how many survive to grow up."

"The hatching pasture is always the same?" asked Richtor. "You rotate among three algae clouds. Do the clouds ever move?"

"Yes, we keep the hatching timed for one specific algae cloud, or pasture. That area has some small natural caves that give some protection for the eggs as they mature and then hatch. The herds spawn about once a halfflip. We watch carefully to time the return at that time," said Simton.

"What is the sequence?" asked Richtor.

"We rotate through three pastures. One is the hatching pasture. When we reach the hatching pasture, the winnowing takes place. Then the eggs are laid and fertilized. Just before we move them away from that pasture, we do the harvesting. The hatching usually occurs shortly after we have changed pastures."

"So, the hatchings occur once a halfflip and you harvest once a halfflip?"

"Correct," responded Martus. "We try to harvest about two-thirds as many adult fish as we have young ones that have escaped the initial winnowing."

"And that amount has been going down? Is it continuing to get smaller every time or has it stabilized?"

"We think that it has stabilized," said Simton. "That's the only really good news we have. That was one of the main reasons that the rationing took place – to adjust the shoal to a new level of food that hopefully will be reliable. But it is still a smaller number. And we have no leeway for the shoal to grow."

"Yes," added Martus. "We used to have a small surplus that we traded to other shoals. And, of course, the processed fish will keep for a while so we store some in case of some type of harvesting disaster. Right now, even with rationing, there isn't enough to maintain trade levels and our reserve has been depleted and cannot be restored for the time being. We are living harvest to harvest."

"When do you rotate back to the hatching pasture?" asked Richtor.

"As I said, a hatching is due in about a week," said Simton. "Which indicates we just moved to the second pasture recently. It will be more than a quarterflip before we go back to the hatching pasture – though I can head over and take a quick peek at this hatching before we come back to it in the rotation. That won't really help though. As I said, we don't go back to the non-current pastures often. I can't say what is a good hatching size or a bad one. By the time we rotate back for the winnowing, the hatching has already been decreased by other fish and other factors. The harvest size is the primary, important, number."

"Thanks for your time," said Richtor. "I've learned a lot. One other short question. Have you seen any sign of pollution in the area, especially around the algae clouds?"

"Pollution?" asked Martus. "What do you mean?"

"Anything in the water that might hurt the fish or the algae clouds. It might affect you too." Said Richtor.

"No, nothing of that nature. We get a brief cloud of particulates occasionally, when the flow at the fissures becomes more active. But that's brief, goes away quickly, and doesn't seem to affect the herds much."

"How about the algae clouds? Could those clouds of particulates hurt them?"

"I don't see how. They are usually more resilient than the herds."

"You talked about the size of the harvest depending on the numbers of young fish from the hatching. That percentage has stayed the same? There isn't a larger die off from the new hatching to warrant a smaller percentage?"

"That seems to go well. And we have used this methodology for many generations. Something would have to really change in the herd, and individual fish, behavior for it to need to be altered."

"OK. Thanks," said Richtor. "I hope you continue to feel well enough to work, Martus."

Martus and Simton waved at Richtor as Richtor swam away from them and the herd.

Richtor moved his head back and forth a bit while he swam. Nothing new but it did seem that food supply is a very strong possibility – especially since that would be a factor that would affect more than just the herds. But what could be happening?

Next week he would set up another planning meeting with Januelle and Richtor. They could hear what he had learned and Januelle could pass along what she found out. Then maybe they could decide upon a plan that might give some answers.

Chapter 19 Plans and Preparations

*T*he three friends met at the central sculpture garden on the second weekend past the respective visits of Januelle and Richtor to the local Academy and the herds. The upcoming weekend just wasn't possible as each were preparing for final halfflip tests. Usually, around the last week of the term, the graduating class had it really easy – but that wasn't here yet.

Richtor had just finished telling his friends about his trip to the herds and his talk with Martus and Simton. "So, there doesn't seem to be any indication of pollution and if it is a matter of overharvesting then something very strange is happening to cause a higher fatality rate in the young fish. Otherwise, using a traditional formula, the herd should stay the same size. And it is stable in size now, albeit with a smaller number. So, we can assume that the harvesting formula works and they are not overharvesting. Right?"

"I think that's reasonable," said Januelle. "That leaves us with food supply. Your conversation with the herders makes that a top likelihood too. If the algae clouds are getting smaller then that means less food for the herds."

"What information did you get from the local branch of the Academy, Januelle?" asked Richtor.

"Well, as usual, there are lots of theories but not a lot of data to back up any of them. They have largely followed the same path as our logic and they know that a reduced food supply would be a good reason for a reduced herd."

"What kinds of theories do they have?" asked Lichten.

"They fall into two categories. The first is theft."

"Theft?" asked Richtor.

"Yes. They think the algae clouds may be ravaged by another shoal or, perhaps, a widemouth that has changed its migratory path."

"I suppose that is possible. I don't see how that would reduce fish populations in Jordech Jungle. Any evidence for either - or both?"

"No. According to the information that Cheyelle has passed along to the Academy, our relations with our neighboring shoals are still reasonably friendly. And Cheyelle received an envoy from the Pearly Shell shoal a couple of weeks ago."

"That was after our visit to her?" asked Richtor.

"Right. The envoy wanted to negotiate some additional fish supplies from our herd to help their shoal."

"Did they say why?"

"Apparently, they were quite reluctant to talk about it but Cheyelle gave them the idea that we might be willing to increase trade balances if there was a good reason. Their herds have also decreased in size. Their approach has been to try to find other shoals from which they can purchase more food," said Januelle.

"Was there any indication that they were having any success?"

"No. They wouldn't say just how long they had been looking. But Cheyelle indicated to the Academy that it was her impression that we were not the first shoal to be approached."

"So, we know that we are not the only shoal affected," said Richtor. "However, that doesn't mean it is true all over Ocean."

"Does that matter?" asked Lichten. "If it is affecting Bluefin and Pearly Shell shoals then it means that it is affecting our region. We are unlikely to need to find any problems or solutions outside of our region. Ocean is too large."

"Well, I would love to follow the tailflips of Sebaria and explore all of the shoals and seabeds of Ocean," said Richtor.

"Sure, we know," said Januelle. "But let's just concentrate on the current problems. Okay?"

"Right," said Richtor. "I just wanted to pulse in with my willingness to go as far as needed to find a solution."

"I'm sure that Cheyelle and the Council would be happy to hear that. I don't think that is warranted as of yet."

"Alright," responded Richtor. "We were discussing possible theft of algae."

"Theft can't be ruled out as of yet," said Lichten. "The herders don't monitor any of the pastures except for the one that the herd is currently using and, for a short bit, the one to which they rotate."

"I don't see how we can possibly monitor the other pastures," said Richtor. "The Council has the herders, who work in shifts, monitoring the herd all of the time."

"You're right. The Academy has reported their opinions back to Cheyelle and the Council. It is up to them to decide whether or not to add watchers for the pastures not currently being used," said Januelle.

"I sure wouldn't want that job," said Lichten. "Watching a herd of fish is bad enough. At least there is an occasional sharpfang diving through the herd or a tendency for the school to drift away from the pasture to keep attention alive. Can you imagine harnessed to a sharrell for a third of a day just watching a cloud of algae?"

"It might be easier to just swim without a sharrell. That way you would know immediately if you fell asleep," said Richtor.

"Yes. But you saw Martus. He had to rest for a few days because his body just didn't have enough reserves to keep going. If they have people constantly swimming, they will be burning food like mad. It couldn't be done without increased rations. It would be better to use sharrells. They can float in one spot rather than hover in an area. So, they don't need as much food," said Lichten.

"I can see that. I guess they would have to figure out some other way to stay awake."

"Okay. We can't investigate potential theft," said Januelle. "But I will point out that this situation appears to not be isolated to our shoal. If there is theft occurring, it must be for some group outside of the region or some very strange changes in harvesting behavior from a pod of narrowmouths or a stray widemouth or two. Plus, as we have discovered, the reduction in population does not just apply to the herd fish."

"So, we'll just forget about the potential for theft," said Richtor. "What was the other possibility? You said that the Academy had indicated there were two."

"The other possibility is that the algae are not able to grow."

"What does algae need to grow?" asked Lichten. "They may have covered that in biology class but I don't remember."

"Not a lot. That's why it's a basic food for Ocean. It needs non-polluted water, sunlight, and a few nutrients. Mostly, it needs phosphorus and nitrogen but a few others in addition."

"The herders said they hadn't noticed any sign of a pollution that would affect them or the herd. That should rule out the non-polluted water problem, right?"

"We should still keep the possibility in mind but, for now, we can ignore it" said Januelle. "That leaves sunlight and nutrients."

"I haven't noticed it being darker than usual. Wouldn't that preclude it being a problem with the sunlight?"

"No. If the decrease was gradual, we probably wouldn't notice any change. And this appears to have been happening over the last three or four currentflips. And, even though we can measure the amount of light we are currently getting, we have no baseline - no foundation numbers - to compare against. In my discussion with the Academy, we all agreed that that is an oversight for the community. We are going to establish a group of statistics that we think are important to the health and wellbeing of the shoal. Then we will take measurements and record them. We will know of changes in the future."

"But that doesn't help now. Right, Januelle?"

"Unfortunately, yes. That's right."

"What about nutrients?" asked Lichten.

"We are in the same situation as for sunlight," said Januelle. "We have no baseline to compare against. However, we do have a basic knowledge of just how much, and what kind of, nutrients are needed by algae. So, we can confirm, or rule out, that as a possibility. Even better, if we find out that that is a problem, we have the possibility of adding nutrients to the water in the pastures."

"But, if the problem extends beyond the herds, wouldn't that mean that there is a general reduction in nutrients for our region? What could possibly cause that?"

"Good thinking, Richtor. There are some chemicals that might be dispersed in the water that would react with the nutrients and pull them out of the water. It's not likely but it is possible."

"Wouldn't those chemicals be considered pollution?"

"Yes, it would be. But it could be something that doesn't directly hurt any living creatures. It could happen and no one was aware of it."

"Can you find out?"

"I should be able to do so, with some testing."

"So, we haven't ruled out a decrease in sunlight or a lack of nutrients?" asked Lichten.

"Yes. But we can test for the nutrients. As for the sunlight, about all we can do is to go to the source and see if there appear to be any problems."

"Do you mean go to the surface?" asked Richtor.

"Yes."

"What can we do there?" asked Lichten.

"We can't determine whether there is less sunlight up there any better than we can down here. No baseline. I will be taking notes with any activities we may do and I will pass them along to the Academy as part of a newly created baseline. We can see if anything looks different or looks like it is a problem."

"I don't know if I would notice anything wrong." Richtor looked very uncomfortable.

"Does it bother you having to go near the surface?" asked Januelle.

"I can do it," said Richtor firmly.

"But it bothers you?"

Richtor swam in a few tight circles for a couple of cycles. When he came back, he spoke over the group channel. "When we went for a field trip to the surface in the early years of classes, I wondered away from the group. I wanted to see above the water more closely. I stayed at the borderline, moving my head above water in bursts, for quite a few cycles."

"And?" asked Lichten and Januelle in unison.

"And I got something the nurses called sunburn. It hurt a lot and quite a few scales fell off. It was several weeks before I could return to class."

"I remember when you didn't come to class for a few weeks. That's what happened?" asked Lichten.

"Yes. I was ashamed to talk about it. As I was frequently reminded of by the teachers – both on the trip and back on campus – it was my fault for not staying with the class and minding the teacher. They were right, of course, but that didn't make it less embarrassing."

"When, or if, we break the surface we won't have to be in the sunlight very long."

"I wasn't out of the water much either but hovering just under the border is what made the sunburn worse. The doctor called it a magnifying effect."

"I can understand your reluctance," said Januelle. "Just being aware of the possibility should make us all more careful. We can drape ourselves when we are swimming near the surface."

"What does draping mean?" asked Richtor.

"We can take along some large sheets of woven seaweed and place them along our backs. They can have a slit cut for the dorsal fin. In you case, Lichten, it could have two slits. We probably wouldn't want to try to keep them balanced on top of us for very long but we could do that for moderately long."

"Okay. So, when and what?" asked Richtor.

"This is your show, Richtor. I don't think the Academy is doing a very good job but that doesn't place the burden of solving it upon our topsides. What do you want to do?"

"Let's wait until after our finals. I need to study and you two may not need to but I bet that you want to study," said Richtor. "Let's check out some sharrells for a while and treat it as a graduation field trip. They won't need us there for the final week of the campus academic year. We'll try to get back in time for graduation rehearsals but no promises. Does that sound good to you?"

"As long as we make it back for graduation," said Januelle.

"Same here," said Lichten. "How long of a trip do you expect?"

"Since we don't know what we will be finding or where we may need to go, I would reserve the sharrells for a week and we should prepare to be gone for a week. We can do some hunting to supplement our food. I'm sure that, working with Cheyelle and the Council, we can get a week's worth of food in advance. A bigger burden would be on you, Januelle. You will need to organize, and collect, everything you might need for testing."

"That actually sounds like a lot of fun," said Januelle. "This might end up being a graduation field trip I will enjoy."

"And you'll need to bring your trident and hunting and protection supplies, Lichten. We should basically prepare for the unexpected."

"I agree with Januelle," said Lichten. "This could be a lot of fun."

"That's a great attitude. I would really love to find a reason and a solution for our problem but I would also just enjoy a great trip with you two. So, after finals week?"

"It's a deal," said Lichten and Januelle. "Good studying."

Chapter 20 Ready to Move

For the next few weeks, Richtor didn't worry about what was causing the herd reduction. He didn't get into trouble for lack of attention in class. He was studying. It was great that Januelle, and Lichten, and many - but not all - of his hatching knew what they would do after graduation. He didn't. And that made his grades even more important to act as door openers for some type of apprenticeship.

He had no chance of getting into the Hatching Elite group. That required consistent excellence in academics. Academics did not just mean learning from lectures - it included courses in the arts and physical work as well as language, science, and math. Thus, Angella was part of the group as was Januelle. Considering how good Lichten was in husbandry, he was a little surprised Lichten was not part of the group.

But he did have a chance to receive his graduation certificate marked with a star indicating an average grade of more than 80 per cent. That would place him into the top quarter or third of the hatching class. He needed to average at least 90 per cent this term to make it. He would do it.

~ ~ ~

For better or for worse, finals were done. Richtor felt that he had done pretty well but there was always the problem of interpreting questions differently than the way that the instructor meant. Whatever was to happen was set at this point. He had studied hard and now his mind could move back to their excursion. Would they find an answer? He didn't know, but he looked forward to the trip.

The week between finals and graduation would seem very short. The graduation rehearsals were not required as, with only sixty people in the hatching class, it had little need to be very organized. Taking a very short break in studies the previous weekend, he, Januelle, and Lichten had divided up the tasks needed to prepare for the excursion. Lichten was handling getting the sharrells for the trip as well as harnesses, tridents and other hunting gear, and miscellaneous carriers and such.

Lichten and Januelle would each have a trident. Lichten outclassed both of them in this area and they were happy to leave the hunting and protecting to him. But it would not be wise for them to not have weapons on this trip. Too many dangers were possible and it might be necessary for them to protect Lichten at some point.

Januelle was preparing equipment for testing and pads for taking notes. She would have her own bundles and Lichten would get plenty of bundle straps, as well as one load harness and hauling straps. Januelle was the best organized of the trio and she had been gathering materials and packing them as she had time over the past few weeks.

That left the consumables for Richtor to work with. Displaying his Deputy badge, he had been able to withdraw a week's worth of basic rations for each of them and he had that wrapped into two bundles. One would be carried by Lichten and the other by himself. As Januelle would have an assortment of bundles for her needs, the males would carry most of the other bundles with a bit more for Richtor to help Lichten maintain mobility for any needs that might arise.

In addition to basic rations – which mostly entailed processed fish that would stay preserved for weeks – he had a bundle of smaller pouches of seasonings to let the meals feel more individualized. He would purchase about thirty snack portions and a bundle of marinated seaweed to pass around. He also checked out a scribed copy of "The Voyages of Sebaria". He debated a long time about whether the added weight was useful and decided that there were so many things that he didn't know that trying to determine, in advance, what would be most useful was not possible. He brought it.

Richtor had all of the bundles secured and attached to bundle straps. They wouldn't be much burden to the sharrells but they would be difficult for him to haul to the stables. He really didn't want to take two trips so he set the bundles in the hallway, exited through the doorway, closed the door panel, and picked up about half of the straps in each hand. This didn't make it a lot easier. Certainly, it didn't make it any lighter. But splitting the bundles between his hands allowed him to balance better and to move in the directions towards which he wanted to move rather than in the direction of the heaviest bundles.

He swam down the hallway towards one of the spokes to head outside. A week's worth of food was heavy and he felt like his arms might stretch a bit by the time he arrived. If he were wearing a personal harness, he could distribute the weight better but it wouldn't help that much. He would try to arrive at the stables still able to use his arms. He smiled – he was even being dramatic with himself.

He was swimming slower with each bodylength he travelled. He tried setting down the bundles once to take a rest but picking them back up was so painful that he decided it was better to just keep moving.

In the near distance, he saw the stables and corrals. He could see Januelle near the front entrance. It appeared that she had almost as many bundles as he had. He hoped they weren't equally heavy. He had not planned to have to hire an additional pack sharrell. He had expected that the sharrells could carry their riders as well as a distributed amount of weight of belongings.

As he swam closer, he could see that Januelle's bundles – albeit numerous – were not very large. Apparently, she had split the supplies up such that she could quickly access very specific materials depending on her need. As long as she could quickly identify the bundle from the outside, it should work well for her. Not a surprise. Januelle was very organized.

"Hello," said Richtor. "Have you been waiting long?"

"Hi. No, I only arrived five or ten cycles ago. Lichten is already inside, working with Diplodus on getting our sharrells assigned. Diplodus said that we could leave our bundles in the office. I thought I'd wait until you arrived so I could tell you." Januelle picked up her bundles and started to swim towards the stable office.

Richtor, who had not set his bundles down, followed Januelle. Once through the doorframe, he could see the tridents and nets in the corner.

Lichten probably had some other items already attached to his personal riding harness. Bringing your own gear could decrease the amount of time needed to prepare to leave. He lowered his bundles into the corner beside the tridents. Oh! That felt so good.

Richtor flexed his arms different directions, attempting to get them limbered up and avoid lingering soreness.

Januelle had a smile on her face as she asked Richtor. "Doing exercises? We'll probably get plenty of exercise during this trip."

"The supply bundles were heavier than I thought they would be and, with each stop, they got heavier."

"You do remember that we will be hunting along the way? Most of our heavier meals will be fresh."

"I was always taught to prepare for the worst. Plus, the rations will add a bit of variety and balance out our diets."

"I guess it doesn't matter. But it will slow down our sharrells."

"It doesn't look like your inventory is that much less," said Richtor.

Januelle looked at her bundles which she had just set down along the wall rather than in the corner with the tridents and supplies. "Perhaps I overdid a bit. Like you, I don't know what is going to happen or what we will need. The Deputy badge persuaded the Academy to loan me quite a bit of equipment that doesn't often go into the field."

At that point, Lichten moved into view, followed closely by Diplodus.

"We have three sharrells picked out. Besides Brightglow for me, we have Widefin once again. Widefin worked well for you last time, didn't she, Richtor?"

"Yes, she was a good mount," said Richtor.

"For a third sharrell, we have chosen Lumbor. Lumbor is a larger male. He should be ridden by the one who has the heaviest load. That will probably be you, Richtor. Right?"

Richtor looked at the corner and the wall and responded. "Yes, that's right. So, you'll be on Brightglow. I'll be on Lumbor. And Januelle will ride Widefin?"

"Right," said Lichten. "Is that okay with you, Januelle?"

"I liked Noseo last time. Is she not available?"

"She's available but she's fairly young and small. She's not well suited for a long excursion. You didn't ride Widefin last time but you were around her. Are you agreeable to ride her?"

"I guess so. She's probably gained some experience since we were last out."

"Definitely," said Diplodus who spoke for the first time. "Since your excursion is on shoal business, Lichten has persuaded me to let you check out the sharrells without any work credits.

However, I have to charge you for the harness rentals."

"Thanks. That is good of you. Charge my work credits since this trip is primarily my idea."

"Will do," responded Diplodus. Follow me and we'll get you matched up with your sharrells and you can get harnessed. Richtor, you are going to be with Lumbor, correct?"

"Yes, that's right."

"He is larger and maybe a bit slower than Widefin or Brightglow. We'll set him up with the load harness just in case you need it. It's not that much different from a regular harness but it has extra-long, heavy duty, strap lines that can extend past the tailfins. Keep them coiled up and tucked under the harness until you need them."

"Got it," said Richtor. The three of them headed through the interior doorframe and the tack rooms to get to the corrals.

"Lichten and I already rounded them up. You probably recognize Brightglow and Widefin. Lichten certainly does. Brightglow swims over to him whenever Lichten shows up. She can be a bit of a nuisance when he is working."

As if to verify Diplodus' story, Brightglow swam over and nuzzled Lichten who chittered and rubbed her nose. Januelle and Richtor swam over to be with their sharrells. Lumbor certainly was a large one. Richtor had never ridden one quite as large. But he seemed calm. Strong, but calm.

The three friends guided the sharrells to the tack rooms where they proceeded to get the harnesses set up on the sharrells and on themselves. Lichten already had on his personal harness. The straps forming his harness were thicker and heavier than the ones for Januelle and Richtor. There were times when, while pursuing faster fish, it was useful to attach part of the netting directly to the hunter which could put added strain on the harness.

After harnessing, they led their sharrells through the stable and out to idle next to the buildings. Januelle and Richtor watched the sharrells while Lichten, being the strongest of the trio, went into the office to start bringing out bundles, tridents, and the other supplies. There was not enough room in the office to comfortably fasten all of the bundles properly to the sharrells' harnesses.

Once the supplies were laid in piles outside of the stables, Richtor and Januelle went over to the piles and handed items to Lichten to position properly on the harnesses. When a lot was being ported, balance of the items was important to maintain an optimum situation for speed and maneuverability. Lichten was, by far, the most practiced at this.

Januelle had specific places where she wanted some of the equipment she had brought. Other pieces could go anywhere and Lichten made use of them to keep the balance proper.

Once the bundles had all been fastened to the harnesses, Richtor swam back a bit and looked at the sharrells. He chittered softly. There was little indication of the torsos of the sharrells – there was so much dangling from, or snugged up against, their harnesses. Near the connector point, Lichten had placed only the bundles which could be snugged up. Dangling bundles could be a danger if the connection needed to be broken quickly and they could hamper proper connection.

Lichten, Richtor, and Januelle swam up to their sharrells and connected their harnesses to that of their sharrell.

"Ready to start?" asked Lichten.

"Let's go," responded Richtor. And they went.

Chapter 21 To the Pastures Again

*T*he group headed away from the shoal in the direction of the herd. They wanted to examine the pastures not currently in use by the herd. First, they would head to the herd to talk with Martus and Simton to see if they had any new information and to have a general idea as to where the other two pastures were located. As the shoal grew smaller behind them, they were able to see the herd more clearly - a large dark cylinder which slowly clarified into individual swimming fish.

As they got close enough for an individual channel to be effective, they heard Martus call out, "Hello. Again? What can we do for you today?"

They continued to ride their sharrells towards the two herders. There were, of course, more herders than just Martus and Simton - but they were the ones that they always encountered at this time of day.

"We have a few follow-up questions," said Richtor. "First, do you know if any of the other herders have noticed anything unusual during the night?"

"Yes, we talk a bit when we change shifts. But they don't know any more than we do. While it's true that the night shifts have a few creatures roaming that we don't see in the daytime, there doesn't seem to have been any real change over the past few currentflips. A decrease in the number of fish seen, of course."

"Oh," Richtor exclaimed. He was a bit sad that that appeared to be a dead end. "Anything new that you have seen?"

"No. What are you three doing? You seem to be prepared for a long excursion. I can barely spot your sharrells behind all the attachments. It looks like you are prepared for a trip to the other side of Ocean."

Lichten chittered, "better to have enough than to need something when you can't get it. Although, I agree that Richtor does tend to be a bit more careful than I would be. It's also true that, whenever I have gone on a trip with Richtor, we always seem to have what we need. And that's a good thing."

"We are going exploring. This is the week between finals and graduation and it may be the last chance for the three of us to head out together," said Richtor. "Our first stops are going to be the other pastures. Some of the things we've talked about involve things happening to the other pastures while the herd isn't there. We need to know how to get to them."

"That's not going to be easy," said Simton. "When we bring on a new herder, they are always paired up with an experienced herder to guide them between pastures. After a while, they learn just where they are. But to tell someone where they are? That's not easy."

"We might be able to tell them how to get to the hatching pasture," Martus said to Simton. "There are some recognizable aspects of the environment."

"True. But not to the other one," said Simton. "Do you still have those Deputy badges?"

Richtor and Januelle both reached into pouches connected close to them and pulled out the badges. Lichten shook his head and remarked, "I left mine behind."

"That's okay," said Simton. "Two are one more than I needed to see. If it's alright with Martus, I can take you to the unmarked pasture and then, from there, tell you how to reach the hatching pasture. It's about a two-hour swim on a sharrell, so I can get back here before our shift ends. Is that alright with you, Martus?"

"Should be fine," said Martus. "We're paired up mostly as a precaution. If nothing goes wrong, one is enough. Just make sure you check on me before you head off shift, Simton."

"Will do," said Simton. "Does that sound like it would work for you?"

"We'd really appreciate it," said Richtor.

Simton hefted her trident, and nudged her sharrell off to the side. As she moved off, the trio of friends followed in her wake.

After about a half-hour had passed, Richtor nudged Lumbor up to be next to Simton. "Do you think you'll be able to notice any variation about the pasture? Something different that might be relevant?"

"I doubt it," replied Simton. "As we discussed before, we don't go back to the pastures until we are ready to rotate the herd to one. So, I don't have that much to compare. I hope it's useful to you three."

"Januelle wants to take some tests," said Richtor. "to rule out some possibilities – or to verify if the test comes out differently than we expect."

"Yes?" Simton queried. "What kinds of tests?"

"Januelle! Can you come up here and talk to Simton about the tests?" Turning to Simton, he said. "Januelle knows all that information. I might describe them wrong."

Januelle came up on Widefin and took a place at the other side of Simton. "What's up?"

"I was mentioning to Simton about the tests you plan to do at the pastures – but you, of course, could do it a lot better than I could."

"They are a series of tests on the quality of the water around the pasture area. Checking for nutrient levels as well as traces of pollution that might not be easily noticeable."

"And you can do these tests while you are there?" asked Simton.

"I can do tests for the amount of phosphorus and nitrogen present. I couldn't bring an entire laboratory with me."

"It looked like you brought quite a lot," said Richtor with a grin.

"I brought some," replied Januelle. "But not enough to test for who knows what. I can only do a few tests at the pasture. For the other tests, I will gather samples and test them when I can get the samples back to the facilities at the Academy."

But, at the pasture, you can only do a couple of nutrient tests?"

"I will also use a portable microscope to examine the waters for anything unusual or anything known to cause problems."

"So, really, all you need are samples from the pastures?" asked Simton. "We could have done that for you and saved you the trip."

"Samples would have been a lot of it," said Januelle. "But I can look around and take other samples or examine things. Plus, this is only our first stop. Right, Richtor?"

"Right, Januelle. What you say also makes sense, Simton," said Richtor. "A lot could be done by all of you gathering up stuff. But the problem is that when you are looking for something unknown you don't know what is relevant and what isn't. I am not sure I'm really useful but it's important that Januelle be here – and for her to do it safely it is necessary to have someone, or some few, guard her and accompany her."

"You're too modest, Richtor," said Januelle. "Without you, we wouldn't be doing any of this. Not that I'm convinced that we should be doing this – it's really the responsibility of the Council and the Academy. But doing some extra field work won't hurt me and your excursions are often fun. It may even turn out to be useful to the shoal."

"Well, I'd sure love to be back on full rations," said Simton. "Since I'm younger, and smaller, than Martus the ration reductions haven't hit me as hard as they have him but I like starting the day with a full belly. If we can help, we will."

"You guys have helped a lot," said Richtor. "You have given us something to start on. And starting is often the hardest first step. You know the herds and you and Martus are the best sources of information about the herds."

"Well, perhaps," said Simton. "But you could get similar information from the other shifts."

"OK. We're all doing what we can," said Richtor. "About how much further is the first pasture?"

"Less than an hour," said Simton. "Do either of you follow the games of the Bluefin Marvels?"

"I do!" said Januelle. "They've had a great season so far."

As Simton and Januelle got involved in their sports discussion, Richtor allowed Lumbor to slip back until he was swimming alongside of Lichten once again.

"Welcome back," said Lichten. "I thought I might be by myself for the rest of the trip."

"Sorry about that. I wanted to ask Simton some questions and then something popped up that Januelle could answer much better and then Simton and Januelle started debating sports activities."

"So that's why I have the honor of your company," said Lichten with a grin. "I'm not all that excited about sports but you seem to actively avoid any discussion about them."

"I didn't have the best experiences during physical education classes," said Richtor. "For some reason, I seemed to always be the favorite target when the activity involved throwing. Even when there wasn't supposed to be a target, I somehow ended up getting hit."

"I suppose someone is going to fall into that role," said Lichten. "For myself, they always wanted me to lead the games. I'm not a leader. I'm a great participant and the team I was on often won. But I wasn't good at leading, didn't enjoy it, and don't want to ever do it again."

"I guess that looking at a person sometimes gives us ideas as to how that person is," said Richtor. "And that isn't always the person they are."

Up ahead, Simton raised her hand to indicate a stop. Richtor and Lichten looked around and finally saw a small algae cloud.

"This is the pasture we just left," said Simton. "It hasn't had much time to build itself up again."

"Wow, you can say that again," said Richtor. "Once again, thanks for coming with us and guiding us. We could have very easily swum past this without knowing it."

"Glad to help," said Simton. "Looking at it, I wonder whether we need to change our rotation speed."

Januelle spoke up. "That might make it worse. If you don't give the algae cloud enough time to recover, then it will get smaller and smaller."

"But won't it be larger when they leave it? Will having a larger starting point help it to grow?" asked Simton.

"I'm not sure. I believe it will depend on what is limiting its growth. Within a given period of time, there should be the same amount of algae available no matter how quickly you rotate through the pastures. I suppose that we could try that."

Januelle started working with her bundles. Richtor asked her if he could help with anything but she waved him off. "Thanks, but I know where everything is and how I've organized it. Just go over and rest while I work."

Simton went to Lichten and Richtor. "I want to head back to the herd. It isn't likely that anything will go wrong but it still makes me feel nervous to have Martus by himself."

"Sure," said Lichten. "How do we get to the hatching pasture?"

Simton looked around a bit to get her bearings. Finally, she said, "You go in this direction. In about two hours, you will see a mound of rough rocks. If you look closely, you will see some small caves along the seabed. There should be a large number of hatchlings not quite through the winnowing process. Be careful with them as they are the next iteration of the herd."

"There's nothing before we reach those rough rocks?" asked Lichten. "Nothing that might easily confuse us?"

"No. Nothing very large. There are a few rocks along the way and a small area of coral but they won't look like a mound of rocks."

"Okay. Thanks. We'll do our best and, if we can't find them it will be our fault and not yours."

"Bye," said Simton as she turned her sharrell and headed back in the direction from which they had come.

"Want to play a game of Glick?" asked Lichten. "I brought a board and pieces along."

"Of course, you did," replied Richtor. "No, I'm no good at Glick."

"Then, I think I'll take a nap. After Januelle finishes here, we'll be heading directly to the hatchling pasture."

"Okay. Sweet dreams."

Lichten detached himself from his sharrell and handed a strap to Richtor who connected it to his sharrell. Then Lichten allowed himself to slowly descend to the seabed where he hovered in a circle – continuing to rotate as he reached the seabed and settled into a temporary nest for a nap.

Richtor continued his vigil as Januelle took her samples and conducted her tests. His thoughts wondered here, there, and everywhere. He thought about his possible future, what might be causing the herd reduction, what their next steps should be. He had never had trouble finding things to think about – stopping his mind from thinking about them – yes.

It didn't seem like very much later when Januelle called out to say that she had finished her work. Richtor woke up Lichten and he swam up to be with them. Richtor handed the strap to Brightglow over to Lichten who quickly re-connected to his favorite sharrell.

"So, what did you find out," asked Richtor.

"Most of the results I won't be able to check on until I work with the samples at the Academy. But the nutrients that I could test seem to be in a good range. I checked for a couple of easily overlooked pollutants and they weren't present either."

"So, on to the hatching pasture?"

"I guess so. I have doubts that the results there will be any different," said Januelle. "But it will give me a chance to check on the hatchlings."

"What would you check on the hatchlings?" asked Lichten who now seemed to be fully awake.

"See if there are any developmental abnormalities," said Januelle. "I didn't see any in the adults but, if there are any, they might cause the winnowing to take out more of the population."

"Oh. Are you bundled up? Are we ready to leave?" asked Richtor.

"Yes. All ready. Can you guide us to the hatching pasture?"

"I think so," replied Richtor.

They nudged their sharrells and started moving in the direction previously indicated by Simton. Lichten, revitalized by his nap, took the lead. Even though the initial direction was given to

Richtor, once started on a vector, Lichten was much better able to keep at it with diversion.

The journey was made largely in silence. Lichten was scouting and Januelle and Richtor were each lost in their own thoughts. They passed over some large rocks but they couldn't be considered a pile in any way.

After a little more than two hours, they came upon the mound of rocks. They spotted a few hatchlings moving around and, while poking into some smaller caves that were present near the base of the mound, spooked a large number of hatchlings out – darting this way and that.

Januelle watched the hatchlings as they emerged. She succeeded in corralling one with her hands to look at it closer and soon released it.

"Well?" asked Richtor.

"They seem normal. I can't take inventory. Too many are hidden and I don't have a base number anyway. I'll get started on the samples and the testing. It should go faster this time."

Januelle drifted away from them to go closer to the center of the algae cloud. This cloud was much larger than the previous one. In fact, it was probably the largest of the three clouds that they had seen. That made sense, as the previous one had just been left and the current one was being actively eaten as food for the herd.

Lichten asked Richtor to play a game of Glick again but, once again, Richtor refused. "Sorry,

Lichten. I know you like this game but it just bugs me. I don't get it. I'd much rather play some type of game that involves physical exertions and reactions."

Richtor dug out a floating disk from one of his bundles. "Catch?"

Lichten smiled and responded. "Sure."

They moved away from the hatching grounds to not interfere with, or possibly harm, the hatchlings. Richtor made sure that Lichten could get some exercise from the period. The sharrells kept moving back toward the algae cloud. Realizing that they were probably hungry, they decoupled from their sharrells and allowed them to go feed on the cloud.

Richtor was getting a bit hungry, himself, but decided it would be better to just wait until after Januelle had finished her work.

Januelle did finish soon. She relayed that there were no surprises. It all looked about the same as it did at the previous pasture. She looked thoughtful.

"So, what's up now?"

"Tomorrow, we start seeing if we can find any problems with sunlight. We have done what we can about nutrients and pollutants. But first, let's do something about our own nutrients."

"Good idea," said both Lichten and Richtor. Richtor headed for Lumbor, who had most of the food supplies attached. Both of the sharrells seemed to be full. They were a bit sluggish and quite willing to be moved out of the cloud and stay still for retrieving food.

Richtor brought out three full days' rations as well as some snack packages. He brought out six of the snack packages as they would not last as long as the others. Taking the food over to one of the wider, smoother, rocks, he put the rations into a bowl, opened some vials of spices, and used a small scoop to move some of the spices into the bowl with the rations.

Mixing well, he divided the enhanced rations into three smaller bowls and handed two of them to Januelle and Lichten. They all hovered there, taking pinches of the meal between their fingers and slowly chewing and swallowing.

"Hey, this is pretty good," said Lichten. "It doesn't really taste like rations."

"Thanks. I guess," said Richtor. "I've brought along a sufficient variety of spices that I should be able to whip up a different tasting version each day."

"It has been a long day," said Januelle. "Thanks for putting the meal together, Richtor. It's good to not have to worry about that part of the day."

"So, what's the plan for tomorrow, Richtor?"

"I guess we do as Januelle has said. You said the next thing to test is sunlight, right Januelle?"

"Yes. Growth of algae isn't that complicated. Clean water, nutrients, and sunlight. It is possible, however, that the reduction in size of the algae clouds is not relevant - that something else is causing the herds to diminish."

"Do you think that is what is happening?" asked Richtor.

"No. A reduction in algae fits too well with the fact that other populations are also seeing a reduction. But a person should never rule out possibilities until the best current solution is found."

"Oh." Finishing his meal, Richtor rubbed his hands together. Any debris would be welcome food for whatever swam by. He then took a brush and wiped out his bowl and the mixing bowl. Lichten and Januelle passed their empty bowls to him and he wiped them out. He would leave the bowls out overnight. They would be clean by the morning.

"Anyone want a snack pack for dessert?"

"I'll have one," said Lichten.

"Not me," said Januelle. "I'm going to find a good area free of rocks and nestle down for the night. Unless there is something else you need this evening?"

"No. Have a good sleep, Januelle. Lichten, do you have any suggestions for tomorrow?"

"If we're going to be checking the sunlight, I guess that means heading to the surface. If we do that here, there shouldn't be any problems. The rotations of the herd - and the herders protecting them – discourage any larger predators from staking out a territory."

"That's right," said Januelle from an area on the seabed nearby. "Now, go to sleep."

"A good idea," Richtor remarked. "Have a good sleep everyone. I'll stay up and keep watch. After all, it's the times that you are not watching that cause problems."

"Wake me up after half the night," said Lichten.

"How about me?" asked Januelle. "When's my shift?"

"You're the one who worked today. Do you want a shift?" asked Richtor.

"Sure. We're all in this together."

"Okay. Lichten, I'll wake you up a third of the way through the night."

"Night."

Chapter 22 Checking Out the Surface

Richtor woke up and looked around. "Good morning," said Richtor to Januelle who, having had the final watch shift, was hovering around moving between the algae cloud, the hatching caves, and their sleep area.

"You probably don't need to actually patrol the area, Januelle," said Richtor. "Just stay alert."

"You watch your way. I'll watch mine," said Januelle with a smile.

"Should we let Lichten continue sleeping?" asked Richtor.

"Why not? Are we in a hurry?"

"I guess not. Since we don't know what we're going to do we don't really know how much time it will need."

"We each only got two-thirds of the hours we would normally sleep. I suggest we let him sleep for a bit more," said Januelle.

"Okay. What are we going to be doing today?"

"To check the sunlight, we need to get to the surface. Once there, I don't know what we can do. Take quick peeks above the water to see if there is anything obvious. I can take some readings about the amount of light and some spectrometry readings but, without a baseline, they would only be useful if we don't find out anything and decide to come back in a quarterflip to see if there are any differences. And that might not even be useful. I have heard some members of the Academy discuss a variation in light within, and between, currentflips. So, if we did come back in a quarterflip, we couldn't be certain of a difference. Only if we came back in two currentflips at about the same portion of the flip could we reasonably expect it to be the same."

"Wow. I see what you mean. Is it worth doing the tests and measurements if they can't be used for a while?"

"Probably not," said Januelle. "If we can't find any other leads then that's about our last possibility."

They hovered for a while until they heard Lichten wake up.

"Hey, sleepyhead," said Richtor. "Good of you to join us."

"It's not that late," said Lichten. "I had a short night. So did you two. Did anything show up?"

"I saw a couple of sharpfangs. I think one may have gotten a hatchling or two. They wouldn't have been any danger to us though, if I hadn't been awake, they might have gone after a few more hatchlings," said Januelle.

"Do you think that Sharpfangs might be the reason for the herd reduction?"

"I doubt it. How would that affect the other fish populations? And I haven't seen an increase in the number of sharpfangs. I suspect that their total population has been reduced just like the others. But I don't know. If we had baselines. Can't be prepared for everything."

"Hey, you're right. Maybe all of this will just be a short vacation and excursion before graduation. Even though Cheyelle gave us the Deputy badges in the possibility that we might come up with something, no one is really expecting it."

"So, what are we doing now?" asked Lichten.

"Let's have one of the snack cakes to start our day," said Richtor. "And then we'll mount up and head for the surface. Right, Januelle?"

"Right."

"Do we head up to any particular spot?" asked Lichten.

Richtor looked at Januelle who said, "No. I don't know, at this time, that it will make any difference as to where we surface."

"Surface," said Richtor with a shiver. "Do you think I should put on sunblock before we head up?"

"Shouldn't be necessary as long as we pay attention to how long we are exposed," said Januelle. "But, if you feel more comfortable, then I can coat your upper side."

"I'll continue without block today," responded Richtor. "If we ever expect extended time at the surface then I'll gladly take you up on that offer."

As Richtor was talking, he was rummaging through the bundles attached to Lumbor. He found three of the snack cakes and distributed two to Januelle and Richtor. He took a bite out of one. Still tasted pretty fresh. Probably wouldn't by the end of the week. Still, who knew how long they would be out? It was completely possible today would be the end of their trip. If so, he might suggest that they hang out for a couple of days at the nearby Griegor Canyon.

But, for now, let them just continue doing their investigation. Richtor finished his snack cake and brushed off his fingers and lips. He looked at Januelle, who was just finishing, and Lichten, who looked like he would prefer to eat a couple more.

"Would you like another, Lichten?"

"Well, if you're offering then I wouldn't mind," said Lichten.

Richtor dug out another snack cake and handed it to Lichten. He watched his friend scarf it down. Richtor smiled. No leftovers around Lichten. But he was larger and stronger than he or Januelle. Richtor wasn't even sure that the two of them, together, could tackle Lichten. Not that they would try. When they were younger, they sometimes got into wrestling fights. Lichten wasn't quite as large or in such good shape then – but he still usually came out on top.

Lichten brushed off his hands. "OK, do we go?"

"Sure," said Richtor.

The three friends got themselves connected to their sharrells and, with Januelle taking the lead, slowly started upward to the surface.

It wasn't that far to the surface – only about 17 or 18 bodylengths. But, in their classes, they were told that they should ascend and descend slowly if possible. At this depth, it wasn't that important – the most that might happen is that would get a headache. But, if they did end up going to Griegor Canyon, which was more than 500 bodylengths deep in places, the advice would be more important.

They weren't in a hurry. As they ascended, Richtor noticed colors reappearing that were muted, or absent, at the levels at which they normally lived. He could see other details more clearly, although the light was hurting his eyes a bit. That was another good reason to surface slowly.

Some of the fish nearby were rarely found at the lower depths. Even though he had had problems with the campus field trip to the surface, there were still a lot of interesting things. Richtor decided that he would work to get rid of his inhibitions about the surface and try to go on more excursions there by himself. He had been told that the feathertail was a very tasty fish. The feathertail only lived near the surface and did not do well in a herd.

Reaching an area close to the surface, the three disconnected from their mounts to examine the surface on their own. While their sharrells might be willing to breach the surface, the connection would not work in the same manner as it did when they were both in the water and the effect would be very clumsy.

As Januelle was in the lead, it was not surprising that she breached the surface first. She went up, up, and out very briefly before her body hit the surface and she came back down.

"That was kind of fun," said Januelle.

"Showoff," said Richtor with a grin. "Did that help you to see the sky better than just moving your head above water?"

"Probably not. In fact, I was spending so much time just enjoying the sensation that I didn't pay that much attention to the sky."

"Ready to look again?" asked Richtor. "Shall I join you?"

"And me!" added Lichten. "You may not need my eyes but we came as a group and might as well do it as a group."

"Sure, the more the merrier," said Januelle. "We can compare observations."

"One, two, three," said Richtor. On the count of three, the friends pushed their heads out of the water. They had tried to face three different directions – though they had not decided upon that before they rose.

Moving their tailfins back and forth with a slow, but powerful, stroke they kept their heads above water for almost a full cycle.

As they relaxed, their heads came back down under the surface.

"Wow," said Richtor. "That brings back memories. Not particularly good memories but memories, anyway. About how much time can I be exposed without risking sunburn?"

"About four or five cycles, in total," said Januelle. "Our skin is totally vulnerable unlike that of the feathertails that I saw you admiring."

"If we lived closer to the surface, would we become less vulnerable to the sun?" asked Lichten.

"Maybe eventually," said Januelle. "But maybe not. It might take many generations before we adapted to this depth."

"Did anyone see anything interesting?" asked Januelle.

"I think I may have," said Richtor.

"Me too," said Lichten.

"You first, Lichten," said Januelle.

"It wasn't as bright as I remember and the sky wasn't the same color that I remember," said Lichten. "Of course, I haven't been up here often – but more often than Richtor."

"When is the last time you came up here, Lichten?"

"It was for some wrangling competitions that the stable sponsored. It was about four currentflips ago. One of the activities had us breaching while riding on a sharrell. The trick was to stay connected while that happened. I disconnected twice but managed to stay connected the third time."

"And the sky looked different from the way it does today?" asked Januelle.

"I think so. I never breached by myself and I was spending most of my attention working with the sharrell but I am pretty sure the sky was a light blue rather than white, gray, and black. I also seem to remember it being brighter but I might not be remembering correctly. I am pretty sure about the color."

"And you, Richtor?" asked Januelle.

"It's been a lot longer since I came up here – but I did breach by myself. All of us in the class did. But I thought it was so interesting that I kept breaching, and staying out of the water as long as

I could. That's how I got such a painful case of sunburn."

"I agree with Lichten," continued Richtor. "The color of the sky was different. Much brighter and a definite blue."

"That's my opinion, too. Did either of you see a line of darker sky while looking up?"

"Darker sky?" asked Richtor.

"Yes. Almost a line but without clear edges," continued Januelle.

"No. I didn't," said Richtor. "But I can take another look." Saying this, Richtor pushed his head above the surface and tried to keep it there while he looked over as much of the expanse of sky as he could."

"Yes. I can see it – I didn't notice it before. How about you, Lichten?"

"I thought I saw something but I don't have enough experience with looking above surface to have known it was something special."

"Well, I can't claim that I have that much experience either," said Januelle. "I have heard of something called clouds, talked about within the Academy, which can vary in colors and block the sky so it no longer appears blue. But the appearance of a straight line was never mentioned."

"When I think of a straight line, I think of directions," said Richtor. "One end of the line points one direction and the other points the opposite direction."

Lichten chittered. "I guess that's true. So what?"

"So, if the area that looks like a straight line isn't a normal part of the sky, wouldn't it make sense that it would originate at one end or the other?"

"That's right!" exclaimed Januelle. "But which direction?"

"How can I know? How could any of us know? We should go the shortest distance first and, if that doesn't work out, we can decide if we want to try the other way," said Richtor.

"You're the leader of this excursion, Richtor. I'll do whatever as long as I'm back for graduation. Januelle?"

"That's as good of a rationale as anything," said Januelle. "We certainly can't go both directions at once."

"How do we keep track of where we are going and where we have been?" asked Richtor.

"That's one advantage of following a straight line. We should be able to use that as a guide. We'll need to mark direction when we sleep. Maybe we can mark our forward direction with a rock while two of us nestle down," said Lichten.

"Let's swim back a little," said Richtor. "Do we want to do this? Why do we care if a line is being made or where it comes from?"

"Sunlight!" said Januelle. "We don't have any baseline to compare against but this line obscures the sky. It has to make some difference about the amount of sunlight. And it's possible that the rest of the obstruction of the blue sky is associated with that line. I think it's our only lead and we should try to follow it."

"You're the scientific head of our trip," said Richtor. But that only answers the first question. Why do we care what is making it?"

"We might get an idea as to whether we can expect it to be temporary or permanent," said Januelle.

"Oh. Well, I'm game. How about you, Lichten?"

"Same as I said before. As long as I'm back for graduation."

"Does anyone know what exists in each direction?"

"Remember that the Jordech Jungle's seabed is higher than here. That means that there is some type of slope heading towards the surface in that direction. The line doesn't quite point to the jungle but one end is mostly that direction. There's probably some type of above surface mass that direction. That would certainly pose a stopping point for us."

"What about the other direction? Does anyone know what is that direction?"

"Orangegill shoal is that direction," said Lichten. "I've gone there a few times to sell sharrells for the stable. I think that Pearly Shell shoal is also that direction but I don't know how far. I guess I really don't know what is towards the stopping point of that direction. But the seabed at Orangegill is deeper than here for Bluefin."

"Sounds like we should head in the same general direction as the Jordech Jungle. All agreed?"

Januelle and Lichten nodded.

"Okay. Might as well start out. Lichten, could you get your head above water and give us a direction?"

"Sure." Lichten forced himself back out of the water for a half-cycle or so. "Got it. Let's go connect to the sharrells and leave.

They swam back down to where the sharrells were, once again, nibbling on the algae cloud. Reconnecting, they nudged the mounts and, with Lichten in the lead, continued their search.

Chapter 23 Tridents in Hand

*T*he three friends started off in the direction that Lichten had determined was where the line pointed – more-or-less towards the Jordech Jungle. They weren't sure just what would be there after the jungle. While Plidioch recited a lot of details about the various shoals that she had encountered as she roamed around Ocean, since it was originally a fully oral tale there was no associated map. Some maps had been created based on descriptions made by Plidioch and others but there was little reason for the people of the shoal to move around very much within Ocean.

As their sharrells proceeded on their way, Januelle browsed through her bundles close to her connection point. From one, she pulled out a small stone cube with a glass top inlaid onto the hollowed-out cube. She looked at it and started muttering to herself.

"What's that?" asked Richtor. Januelle was always bringing along new equipment that Richtor had never before seen. So, he wasn't surprised when he didn't recognize a device but he was curious. Januelle didn't just examine things as a matter of course. She was either trying to figure out how it worked or it was something she thought would be of use to them in their excursion.

"It's a new device that one of the people at the Academy has been playing around with. They call it a compass," said Januelle. "They asked me to bring it along to test it."

"Test it?" asked Richtor.

"Yes." She carefully handed the cube to Richtor. "See the needle floating under the glass?"

"Yes. What about it?"

"No matter how you turn the box, the needle will continue to point to the same location. Can you see a rock that appears to be pointed to by the needle?"

Richtor looked around. He looked one direction where the needle pointed and did not see anything easily noted. But looking the other direction, the needle seemed to point to a large rock, in the distance, with some criecraws scuttling around it. "Yes. I have one spotted."

"Turn the box around," said Januelle.

Richtor did as instructed. The needle continued to point to the large rock - though, as they continued moving, it was no longer pointing exactly to the rock. "Wow."

"The needle always points the same direction according to the person from the Academy. It uses magnetism. The needle has been magnetized."

"I understand magnets. The factories use them a lot to be able to manipulate ores without having to touch them. But a magnet has to be attracted to something. To what is the needle attracted?"

"We're not sure yet," said Januelle. "But it seems to work. Notice that the needle has been darkened on one end. That allows us to keep track of which end is which."

"It's neat. What good is it?"

"Look at the needle. Where does the lighter end point?"

"A little bit to the right of our direction of travel."

"Can you be more precise?" asked Januelle.

"I suppose. If I turn the box around so one edge is perpendicular to the needle. There. The needle points about 20 degrees to the right of our direction of travel."

"And if we keep traveling 20 degrees the left of the lighter end of the needle, we will keep going the same direction."

"That's neat. So, we won't have to surface?"

"Not as often. We should still check occasionally because it is dangerous to assume that the line in the sky is completely straight and will always point exactly the same direction."

"Got it," said Richtor. He was about to hand it back to Januelle when Lichten allowed Brightglow to fall back and line up with them.

"Can I see?" asked Lichten.

"Sure," said Januelle. Richtor handed the box to Lichten who turned it around and around, watching the needle.

"I love it. I wouldn't need it near anywhere I really knew – I can use the things on the seabed as landmarks. But on a trip like this it can really be useful to not get lost around unfamiliar areas. Neat." He handed the box back to Januelle.

"It needs a way to attach firmly to the harness," she said. "I'll make note of that."

Having to hold it all the time made Januelle anxious that she might drop it. She put the compass back into the bundle. "I'll pull it out once in a while to check," she said. "But we all can keep to a given direction."

"Sure," said Richtor. The three continued on their path.

In addition to trying to keep to the path, they were keeping track of what landmarks were present as they went. Relying on the permanence, or reliability, of the straight line in the sky seemed rather precarious. In addition, the seabed gave them some idea as to what was happening – a continued rise in the seabed indicating a shallower part of Ocean, and other possible things around them as they moved.

At that point, the depth seemed to be very similar to that of the Jordech Jungle. As they approached a dense algae cloud, they stopped and disconnected to allow their sharrells time to forage. The three decided that it was time to eat their lunch.

The larger meal, for them, was at the end of the day just before going to sleep – or take the watch shift, whichever happened to have it for that night. At wakeup time, and throughout the day, they relied primarily on the snack packs. Richtor retrieved four of them from his bundles, recognizing that Lichten would be wanting two of the wrapped fish, kelp, and moonflower snacks.

"Do you think that our herd could make use of this algae cloud?" asked Richtor.

Januelle, who was chewing a bite of her snack, blinked and looked thoughtful. After she had finished chewing and swallowing, she said. "It's a little far but that's a possible solution. This place could be made to work if it isn't staked out by any other shoal. But maybe a search could be made closer to the shoal to see if there any other usable algae clouds."

"Of course, that would only address our current problem," continued Januelle. "If we don't know what is causing the problem then we have no way of knowing whether it might get worse.

And our making use of another algae cloud, or perhaps two, only addresses our shoal's problem. If other shoals are also having problems, as it appears, then we have to make sure that any newly added pastures are not already being used by another shoal. If expansion is used to address the issue, then we need to make sure that neighboring shoals are aware of what algae clouds we are using."

"Whew!" said Richtor. "I thought it would be simple."

"Maybe not simple," said Lichten. "but at least it is a possible short-term solution. Good going, Richtor! Do we head back now?"

"I don't want to," said Richtor. "I won't feel satisfied until I understand. What do you say, Januelle?"

"I agree. Maybe we won't find out what is going on. But finding out could be very important and useful."

"Okay," said Lichten. "Everyone done with lunch?"

Richtor and Januelle nodded. Richtor, who was messier than either of the other two, wiped himself off as well as removing crumbs that had gotten stuck in his harness.

The trio headed over to their sharrells, who had obviously gotten their fill, and reconnected.

"I'm going to take a fast check of the surface," said Lichten. "We haven't checked lately to make sure we're still following the path of the markings in the sky."

"Good idea," said Richtor. "I'll come with you."

The two headed up to the surface and pushed their heads above the water. Lichten stayed above for almost a cycle but Richtor got tired and allowed himself to submerge again quite soon.

"Are we still following properly, Lichten?"

"Mostly. We are off a little. We'll check with Januelle's compass when we get back to her. The line seems a little clearer now."

The two headed back down to where Januelle and their sharrells were waiting. First, Lichten, who had the best sense of direction of the three did a comparison of the direction that they had been swimming with the orientation of the line in the sky as it presently was. They were not swimming exactly in the right direction. It was good that they had used this time to verify.

"Either the line has shifted or I started moving off our primary direction," said Lichten. "We need to adjust our direction a bit."

"That's okay," said Januelle. "Though, with your sense of direction, I would bet that the line has shifted."

"How about checking against your compass?" asked Richtor.

"Good idea! If the direction, according to the compass, has shifted then it is definitely the line in the sky that has moved."

Januelle reached into her bundle near the harness connection and pulled out the compass. "What direction should we now be travelling?" she asked Lichten.

Lichten pointed. Januelle responded. "Yes, the line has shifted direction a little. But the variation is only about five degrees. And it shouldn't make any difference as we are hoping to reach a destination where it points. The actual path isn't important."

"But we should check our course a bit more often. Right?" asked Richtor.

"Sounds good," said Lichten and Januelle at the same time.

Richtor and Lichten reconnected to their sharrells and the three nudged their sharrells along the shifted direction. Having just eaten quite a bit, the sharrells were calm but not very energetic. It didn't matter much. They knew they would need to turn back within half a week's travel to make it back in time for the graduation ceremonies. But since they didn't know what – or if – they would find anything there was no reason for hurry.

There were more fish than usual darting around the algae cloud. Richtor wondered what they would do if the shoal ended up needing to make use of the cloud as an additional pasture. This high up in the water, he was able to see a lot of fish that he did not normally encounter.

It seemed rather peaceful moving through the area with fish darting back and forth as he and Lumbor moved along, following Lichten, on the path to who knew what. This close to the surface, the colors were more visible and vibrant. Richtor decided that he would visit the higher areas more often – there was a lot of beauty present and he could certainly be more careful about sunburn.

Lumbor jerked quickly to the left. Something darted past Richtor's shoulder heading down very quickly. Richtor brought Lumbor to a halt as he examined the area. The fish were rapidly leaving the area. He saw another flash darting by from the corner of his eye.

He called to Lichten to ask his opinion. As he did, a sharpfang came into view heading for Lumbor. Then he spotted another sharpfang and then yet another. The peaceful stroll had disappeared.

Chapter 24 Under Attack!

Sharpfangs usually did not hunt as part of a pack. But whether they were operating together or each individually, there were a lot of sharpfangs active at the moment. Richtor sent out a shout, both mental and oral, to Lichten and Januelle to warn them and possibly get some help.

One sharpfang got too close to Lumbor and grazed his flank. Lumbor jerked to the side and Richtor, using the magnetic connection, was tossed aside as the sharrell was attacked.

Richtor swam back over to the sharrell and pulled the trident out of the holder on Lumbor's harness. Lichten might be a lot better than he was but he could still defend himself and his sharrell. The trident had the traditional three points on it but it had sharp blades along the sides of the tines including on the outside edges. It did not make an effective sword as it was not the correct shape to swing through the water in a swiping fashion.

However, effective or not, it could be used both in stabbing and as a slashing blade.

Richtor swam over to be between Lumbor and the direction from which the sharpfang seemed to be coming. As he calmed down, he became aware that there were not as many as he originally guessed. The speed, and lack of expectation of danger, made them multiply in combination with his fear. There seemed to be three attacking Lumbor. In the distance, he could see Januelle and Lichten each doing their own fighting. Lichten had already killed one sharpfang and there was blood starting to permeate through the water. The blood would attract other predators but hopefully they could be away from there before that happened.

Richtor used the trident in a quick movement coming up and into an approaching sharpfang. The outer point and the outer edge both slid along the side of the fish. The blood came out quickly but the momentum of the fish carried it into Lumbor's side who bolted to the side. Luckily, the sharpfang was no longer thinking about attack.

The sharpfangs seemed to be ignoring Richtor which seemed strange. Sure, Lumbor was a larger target but he was also more capable of general defense than Richtor. There were two sharpfangs left who still seemed very interested. They moved around Lumbor in a circle making it difficult for Richtor to guard both of the sharrell's flanks.

Rumblings in the Reef

A sharpfang dove for Lumbor's left side. His fangs, longer teeth that jutted out from his mouth even when closed, cut another gash into Lumbor who started to panic. As the sharpfang moved away, Richtor jabbed at it and succeeded in getting it caught on two of the prongs of the trident. With the sharpfang stuck on the trident, it was difficult to continue to wield it as a weapon but removal of the not-yet-dead sharpfang did seem to be a good idea. Richtor swung the trident at the third sharpfang who easily dodged it.

Suddenly, a silhouette appeared between Richtor and the surface which was no longer very far away. Lichten jabbed all the way through the sharpfang and then used the edge to slice the sharpfang on Richtor's trident into two parts.

"Are you okay?" asked Lichten.

"I seem to be. The sharpfangs concentrated on attacking Lumbor. I'm not sure why."

"He's carrying all the food, silly," said Lichten. Some of it has got to be smelling pretty good to them now."

"Oh, right. Well, thanks for coming along. It made it much easier to finish."

"Not a problem. Let me remove the sharpfangs from our tridents and then move away from these clouds of blood."

Lichten had stayed connected to Brightglow, having used the non-magnetic connector. Richtor had to go after Lumbor who seemed to be calmer now but still moving the wrong way. Richtor quickly caught up to the slow moving Lumbor and gave him a few strokes on his flanks, being careful to avoid the wounds. While the wounds seemed fairly shallow, they were still bleeding quite a bit. Richtor swam to the other side of Lumbor and opened up the medical kit near the connector on Lumbor's left side. He pulled out a roll of adhesive tape and tore off a strip long enough to cover the gash on Lumbor's left side. He took out a tube of antibiotic ointment. He then tore off another strip for the right side, carefully put the roll of tape back in the medical kit. Swimming over to Lumbor, he could put ointment on and then cover the wounds with the strips of adhesive tape.

With the wounds temporarily attended to, Richtor reconnected and he and Lumbor swam over past the cloud where Lichten and Januelle were waiting.

"Sorry for the delay," said Richtor. Lumbor received a couple of gashes. I don't think they're bad but, if the idea was to get away from the blood, I thought we should make sure he wasn't bleeding before we moved along."

"Sure. That makes sense," said Lichten. "You aren't hurt. Right?"

"No. How about you, Januelle?"

"No. I only had one come my direction and it didn't seem to really be attacking me - more on the way towards you. You seem to have been a very attractive target, Richtor."

"Not me. Lichten thinks they were attracted to our food supplies. Is that normal, Lichten?"

"No. Not really. I would guess that they are hungrier than usual. It's probably all part of the problem."

"Why did we meet them here?" asked Richtor.

"Fish are going to come to the cloud to feed. That makes it a great hunting ground. If they just stayed in the area, other fish would avoid it so they probably swim a circuit between various hunting areas."

"So, this should be expected?" asked Januelle.

"To a lesser extent. As I said, they may be extra hungry. It is surprising that so many arrived at the same time. They may be adapting to conditions."

"Adapting?"

"Yes, if they work together – even independently and not part of an actual pack – then they can attack larger fish"

"Okay. Are we ready to head off again?" asked Richtor.

"I believe so," said Lichten. "Januelle, you know more about health and medical needs. Should we attend to Lumbor's wounds now or is it alright to proceed?"

"It should be fine. There's no reason to think they should be infected. They bled for a while before you covered them. Right, Richtor?"

"Correct."

"That would allow anything from the fangs to be washed away if they were surface gashes. You put on ointment before bandaging? They were surface gashes, correct?"

"Yes and yes."

"Then I think we're safe to proceed, Lichten"

In all of the chaos which occurred during the fracas with the sharpfangs, no one was exactly clear on their desired direction. A general direction but not good enough to start.

"Do you want me to surface again to check direction?"

"No. we did a crosscheck on the compass," said Januelle. "I'll just pull it out and check." She checked her bag, pulled out the compass, and looked at it. "That way. They really need a way to attach it to harnesses."

With those words, the three headed off. As they moved away from the cloud, there were fewer fish in the area around them. Richtor resumed looking at distinguishable formations to help guide them back when they returned.

Except for the fact that the ocean just seemed to be less active – fewer fish in the water and activity on the seabed – all seemed pretty much the same as it was during previous trips around the area. Richtor had only been this far this direction once. The class did a longer distance field trip – an overnighter. They went all the way to a slope so shallow that their tops were out of the water even while they were still swimming just above the seabed. Granger had actually gotten stuck and a couple of others had to pull him back out to slightly deeper water. He had followed the teacher and the rest of the class but he didn't go to the edge for long. His sunburn had been only two currentflips prior to that trip and he remembered it all too well.

The water was getting shallower but it was also getting darker. He didn't mind swimming around in the dark but it was more difficult to notice formations and they all needed rest at some time. Richtor called out. "Hey! Do you think it might be a good idea to rest for the night? I am not sure when we reach whatever we are going to reach but we should try to be rested when we reach it."

"It's okay with me," said Lichten. "Januelle?"

"Sure."

"Let's go over off the path a bit," said Lichten. "It's dark enough that it's hard to be sure but I think I see a small algae cloud over there."

They swam in the direction Lichten mentioned but, as they did, a shadow moved overhead in the direction of the original alga. They stopped. The shadow continued its movement. Soon it was no longer visible.

"Whew!" said Lichten. "I'm sure glad that you got your sharrell's wounds covered, Richtor. That narrowmouth is heading for the blood. I'm not sure there's enough for much more than a snack for it. Let's go a little farther than I originally thought."

"Okay. Do we need to backtrack to here when we leave tomorrow?"

"I'm not sure. What do you think, Januelle?"

"We'll take our bearings at the surface and decide tomorrow. The most important thing is that we not get so confused that we can't find our way back to the shoal."

"That would never happen," said Richtor. "We can all tell direction well enough to go back."

"Probably. But we're still close enough that it wouldn't take us long to get to familiar areas even if we were off a little bit. None of us know how much farther we are going."

"Not more than about three more days," said Lichten. "We're going back for graduation. Remember?"

"I remember. I want to get back for it but they'll give us our certificate whether we are part of the procession or not. Why is it so important that we be there?" asked Richtor.

"I expect Diplodus to be there. And I expect Krangor to be there as well. I want Diplodus and Krangor to both be there to offer me an apprenticeship."

"Why?"

"Because then both offers would be in the open and I can make a decision there and then. Plus, if they each really want me to come on board, they may adjust their offers a bit to try to get me to come."

"What kinds of adjustments?"

"Oh, number of work units per day probably. But, the more important part is to have the number of years of apprenticeship as few as possible. Once I have completed that, I can negotiate for myself – even set up a new business."

"That's really clever, Lichten," said Januelle. "I've never seen this side to you before."

"I just want to move towards independence as quickly as I can. I am okay with working in a stable and I am okay riding out with Krangor and finding wild sharrells to train. But what I really want to do is to have an area stable that serves more than just our shoal. I would have different breeds of sharrells for different work. And if I grow the business large enough, I can have several apprentices of my own – and maybe a junior partner eventually – and have time to keep working on developing new breeds."

"Januelle's right. I haven't seen this side of you before, either. Okay. We'll definitely turn around in three days whether we find the answer or not."

They arrived at the small cloud that Lichten had spotted earlier. It was now dark enough that none of them could see anything very clearly – not even Lichten who had the best night vision of the three of them. Sometimes the water was still somewhat light even at night. Richtor wondered why that was the case. Maybe he would remember to ask Januelle.

They all disconnected. Lichten had offered to prepare dinner that night so Richtor went to Lumbor and stroked him a bit. The mucous covering his scales was heavier towards the area of his wounds. That was a good sign but the mucous couldn't help the healing process if the wounds were still covered by the tape.

Richtor laid one hand on Lumbor, just beneath his gills, and with the other hand he pulled off the tape in one continuous motion. Lumbor jerked but calmed back down quickly. Richtor used his hand to spread the mucous over the gash, sealing the gash and allowing the mucous to help the healing.

Richtor swam over the sharrell to the other side and repeated the process there. Swimming over a sharrell was always better, if possible, as it did not scare them as much to have movement near that they could see with their peripheral vision.

Richtor rubbed off the excess mucous from his fingers and moved over to where Lichten had prepared their dinner. The basic rations were much the same each day but they each had their own methods of seasoning and modifying them. Alternating the preparation gave them each a chance to enjoy, and share, their own tastes.

Rumblings in the Reef

Richtor had brought over the last of the snack cakes and they each had one for dessert. There wasn't enough left for Lichten to have two this time but the snack cakes were probably what had produced the odor that attracted the sharpfangs. Rations were made with processed fish and kelp and other things. Snack cakes used fresh ingredients and, as such, would not keep as long and the smell of decay was strong.

Januelle offered to take first watch that night. She led the sharrells to the cloud as Richtor and Lichten swirled around to make their own nestling spots for the night.

Chapter 25 Journey's End

Richtor had the third watch for that night so he was awake when the water and the surface became lighter. He had tried to keep an eye on the sharrells but the dark had been so deep during the night that he could only make sure there were no indications of trouble. He was relieved to see them all floating in sleep, having eaten to satiation. They would be sluggish but, as far as Richtor knew, there was still no big rush even if they did have a deadline. The water continued to become shallower and the seabed was now no more than six or seven bodylengths in depth.

Richtor glanced around. This close to the surface, there were different fish swimming around, more floating vegetation, and more life scuttling, burrowing, and creeping along the seabed. Being near the fissures gave the Bluefin shoal an advantage in that the general temperature of the water was higher and that led to faster, and greater, growth of both animals and vegetation. But, otherwise, the variety and amount of life was proportional to the depth.

Richtor enjoyed these quiet hours in the morning. He almost hated to wake Lichten and Januelle up. At the rate the seabed was rising, it seemed unlikely that they could proceed much farther. Of course, it was always possible that the rise of the seabed would be temporary and that it would go down again. Richtor had only been this general direction once, with the campus field trip, but he couldn't be sure that he was heading the same direction the class had gone.

He swam over to where the sharrells were sleeping. He looked at the wounds on Lumbor. They appeared to be almost gone. The mucous sealed it away from the ocean and had mild analgesic and healing properties. At least, that's what they said in class. It seemed to be true.

Richtor checked all three sharrells to see if there were any signs of the harness rubbing anyplace. His efforts were probably unnecessary. Lichten would be checking automatically every time he approached one of the sharrells. He was just putting off waking them up.

Richtor reached into the bundle for snack cakes for a treat for morning and then remembered that they had eaten the last of the cakes the previous evening. He should have planned for some more durable breakfast treats.

He took a small net out of one of the bundles. He unfolded it and took it by one end and swung it around. These nets were weighted at the edges. If he swung it at a fish, it would wrap around the fish and trap it.

He pulled a small flattened woven basket from another of the bundles. He opened the top, pushed at the bottom and opened it up. It was now a small lidded basket to hold any fish that he caught for breakfast.

It had stopped getting lighter. He was fairly certain that it was not as light here as it was closer to the shoal where they first surfaced to see if they could find any clues. He wondered why that was – and whether it had any relevance to the goal of their trip.

A small school of gordies was swimming nearby. They weren't very large but they were tasty and, if he could catch a dozen or so, they would make a great breakfast for the three of them.

Richtor moved slowly along through the water. There weren't a lot of people who hunted around here on a regular basis. The fish did not become alarmed as he approached them. Once within throwing distance, he took one edge of the net and swung it around the school.

As designed, the net touched a number of the fish and then, using the fish as a fulcrum, it continued to move around until the far end was now close to the near end. They were trapped. Richtor moved away from the school which was agitated but appeared to be uncertain as to what was happening and was remaining in the same area.

Away from the school, Richtor examined his catch. There were seven gordies. That was a good total. He usually got more in the first swing than he did in later swings. Even if they weren't specifically anxious about his presence, they would still be nervous. He carefully transferred the gordies from the net to the basket and latched the lid. The fish inside would keep it afloat in the water as the basket, itself, was not heavy enough to sink.

He headed back to a different area. He didn't want to deplete any specific school. He glimpsed a few feathertails moving around. They did not group into schools but, since they liked similar food and surroundings, if a person found one then others were probably nearby. He swam over to where two feathertails were close together and swung his net. He missed one but did get the other. Unfortunately, he had to move his catch to the basket before he could open the net again for the next swing.

Richtor quickly went back, deposited the feathertail into the basket and returned. This time he was successful in getting two feathertails. Soon, he had a full basket with eight gordies, three feathertails, and one chewdor. He didn't often spot chewdors. They were larger than the gordies but not large enough to consider a gordie prey for their next meal.

Having carefully folded up the net, Richtor swam back to Lichten, Januelle, and the sharrells. As he put the net away, Lichten swam up to him.

"Good morning! It looks like we're going to have some fresh food for breakfast. What's in the basket?"

"Eight gordies, three feathertails, and a chewdor," said Richtor.

"A chewdor! Can I have it?" asked Lichten.

Richtor chittered. "Sure. You're probably the only one who could eat all of it anyway. After yesterday, I don't want to risk having any whole dead fish with us."

Richtor looked over toward Januelle, who was starting to move as if she were ready to awaken. Lichten swam down towards her. As he got near, her eyes opened.

"Hello! What's up?"

"Richtor and I are up. How about you?"

"Give me a few cycles. These nights that we have to keep watch don't give as much rest. Is there a reason to hurry?"

"Richtor found a chewdor for breakfast!" said Lichten.

It was now Januelle's turn to chitter. She and Richtor were both well aware of Lichten's appetite.

"Okay, you near starving almost graduate. I'll get up." They all slept with their harnesses on but, since the bundles were all connected to the sharrells harnesses, all they had to do to sleep was to smooth out a nestle.

Januelle, with Lichten, swam over to where Richtor escorted his basket containing their breakfast.

"Here, Lichten. Grab the chewdor so the basket has more room available." As Richtor cracked open the lid, Lichten inserted his hand and pulled out a medium-sized fish which seemed to be almost as wide as it was long. Lichten held it carefully with one hand, short talons embedding slightly in the chowdor's sides.

"Your turn, Januelle. There should be three feathertails and eight gordies."

"Can I have two feathertails? They're my favorites."

"Sure, take what you want. We will release whatever we don't eat. I don't want to take time to preserve them and we don't want them attracting scavengers."

"Good idea," said Lichten as he took a large bite out of the chewdor. "I'll do my part to reduce the work you'll need to do to release the extra." After swallowing, his mouth turned into a large grin.

Meanwhile, Richtor was repeating the transfer process with Januelle. As she put her hand into the crack to retrieve her first feathertail, a gordie popped out making its try for freedom.

Richtor twisted his body to reach out with his other hand. He succeeded in grabbing it but Januelle called out. "Hey! Keep the basket still, please. There's not as much difference between a feathertail and a gordie as there is for a chewdor."

"Sorry," said Richtor. He bit off about half of the gordie in one bite. There was no reason to put it back into the basket when it would soon be his turn to pull out a fish.

Januelle pulled out her first fish. The feathertail had a long, bifurcated, tail with the top part extending out several digits farther than the bottom part. It was a bit larger than a gordie but the tail would be the most easily distinguished aspect when reaching for one in the dark.

Lichten had now finished eating the chewdor. He swam back to Richtor and the basket. "That was good. Can I have dessert?"

Richtor grinned. "Sure, there should be two feathertails and seven gordies present. But Januelle has first dibs on one of the feathertails. She wanted two for breakfast."

"Can I have the remaining feathertail? They don't provide a lot of food but they make a great dessert - especially after a chewdor which has a lot of meat but not that great of a flavor."

"Go for it," said Richtor. He also got hungry but he didn't care much exactly what he ate. Come to think of it, he had less resistance to hunger than his two friends. But he was more reluctant to express it than Lichten and about anything would work to satisfy his hunger.

Januelle was now ready to pull out her second feathertail. No more feathertails! Richtor pulled the basket closer to him so he could use one hand to grab while the other hand held the basket. His hand went in. Out it came again holding a wriggling gordie.

Richtor wished that he could grab more than one at a time but, holding the basket, that just wasn't possible.

"What's left?" asked Lichten.

"Six gordies," replied Richtor.

"Can I have one?"

"You really don't have to ask. Go ahead."

Lichten reached in to grab a gordie and soon pulled one out. Richtor repeated the process for himself three more times. Five gordies was a rather large meal for him. He thought he might end up as sluggish as the sharrells.

"Do you want a gordie, Januelle?" Januelle shook her head. "Lichten?"

Lichten gave a short burp sending a bubble up to the surface. "No, I've had more than I should have had. I'll have to work to keep up with Brightglow and not have her tow me."

"I feel about the same way," said Richtor. He opened the basket lid and the remaining two gordies swam out. They appeared to be a bit confused but soon darted off away from the three friends.

"Richtor, can you pop up to the surface to get our bearings?" asked Januelle.

"Sure. Lichten shouldn't have to do it all of the time."

Richtor swam up – not very far to go – and soon returned. "That way. Is that what you figured, Lichten?"

"More or less, except I'm pretty sure you got the directions backwards, Richtor." He pointed in the opposite direction of which Richtor had pointed.

"I'll check the compass," said Januelle. She pulled the compass out. "Yes, Lichten is right. Sorry, Richtor."

Richtor sighed. "Well, I really figured that if we differed then Lichten would be the one who was correct. OK, that way." He pointed in the opposite direction – and almost the exact same direction as Lichten – and Januelle and Richtor agreed.

"Let's get connected. The sharrells shouldn't have to eat again until late tonight but I don't know where we'll be at that time."

Richtor and Januelle aligned their magnetic connectors to their sharrells while Lichten re-fastened his non-magnetic connection to Brightglow. They all headed towards the agreed upon direction. The seabed did appear to continue to be becoming more and more shallow although it was not a steep slope. Still, There were no significant reverses such that it became deeper.

Within a couple of hours, the depth of the water had about halved. It was only two or three bodylengths in depth now. Without disconnecting from Lumbor, Richtor headed towards the surface. It was awkward since it was not a rigid, fixed, connection but he was able to get his head above the surface. Looking up, he could tell that the line in the sky had much more defined sides. They were off in their direction a bit and he would tell Januelle and Lichten. Still, it didn't seem to matter that much. The line must be far up in the sky.

Submerging, Richtor told his friends about the slight shift in direction. They nudged their sharrells. "The line in the sky is more solid but not as straight."

"What does it look like?" asked Januelle.

"Those puffy things in the sky are called clouds, correct?"

"Yes."

"It looks like a cloud. Kind of puffy but much darker than the surrounding clouds."

"Could you see anything in our direction of travel?"

"I didn't try very hard. Just getting above the surface still connected to Lumbor wasn't that easy. Next time, we can stop and disconnect and we can all look more carefully."

The slope did not change much. Within another couple of hours, there was barely enough depth to stay submerged while connected to the sharrells. They all disconnected. Lichten watched the sharrells while Richtor and Januelle surfaced.

They both surfaced at about the same time. Januelle surfaced with her face facing in the same direction as they had been swimming. Once again, Richtor came out facing the opposite direction. He heard a gasp from Januelle and quickly turned around.

"It's not a good idea to be surprised while above the water," said Januelle. "I think I swallowed some air. Look!"

Richtor looked and, in spite of having heard and watched Januelle, let out a gasp of his own.

Chapter 26 What does it Mean?

Januelle and Richtor had returned to Lichten and the sharrells and Januelle was now obviously taking charge of the trip. "You should surface and take a peek too, Lichten. Then we can talk about it."

Lichten disconnected from Brightglow and moved up to above the surface – which was now only about a bodylength above them. They had learned from Richtor's experience and did not try to surface still connected to their sharrells. The water was getting so shallow that neither Januelle nor Richtor had reconnected after doing their own examination of the surface

Lichten joined his two friends. "What is that mound of land above the surface?"

Richtor responded. "You heard about that in geology class. It's called an island. They aren't that large. Or, at least, Plidioch didn't mention any that took a long time to go around. Of course, after the first couple that she circled she didn't bother. It's possible that there might be a larger one."

"Right. I don't remember it from geology class but I do remember from Plidioch's narration. We didn't come this far on the field trip, did we?"

"Some of the kids started to panic when the water got too shallow. The teachers stopped at that point," said Richtor.

"I have been out this far before," said Januelle. "It was part of a field trip sponsored by the Academy. But the island doesn't look the same."

"What's different?"

"The big piece that goes up high into the air. It looks more like our fissures than just a piece of dry seabed."

"So, it looks hot? How can you tell? Is it that close? It didn't seem that close," commented Richtor.

"What did you see?" asked Januelle.

"I saw a big piece of dry seabed jutting into the sky. It looked like some of it was really bright, and moving, and there were clouds around the piece of land. At the top, there were lots of black clouds coming up and connecting to that line we have followed in the sky. How about you, Lichten?"

"Same as you, except the part that was moving seemed to be coming from the top and moving towards the bottom. It reminded me of our fissures as they build themselves up and we eventually have to knock the tops off."

"Right!" said Januelle. "And the reason that rock moves is that it is very hot. When it is very hot it doesn't have to stay in one place and gravity will take it downward. In the factories near the fissures, this means that as the opening of the fissure moves up, what comes out moves back down towards the seabed. Here, it just moves down towards the bottom of that piece of seabed that sticks up. But you could say that it is moving towards the real seabed - under the surface - but it doesn't make it that far."

"What about those black clouds that are coming up?"

"I don't know about them. But the reason that they are moving towards the shoal is because of something called wind. Wind moves the air from one place to another - just as currents move water from one place to another."

"Wow!" said Lichten. "Do you think we can get extra credit for this?"

"Silly! We've already completed finals. We're just waiting for graduation."

"Oh. Right! Hard to change habits, I guess."

"Easy enough to do," said Richtor. "Knowing about wind doesn't have much importance for our daily lives."

"No, it doesn't," agreed Januelle. "Or, at least, we don't think that it does. This smoke may be making a difference for us. It is something different from the last time I visited here."

"Why is it moving towards our shoal?" asked Richtor.

"I don't know. Maybe the winds just normally go from this island towards our shoal. I don't know."

"Okay. So, we know some things are different from what you saw before, Januelle. How could this affect the herds?"

"We have been investigating what might interfere with the amount of sunlight available for growth. Wouldn't lots of stuff between the sun and the surface of Ocean reduce the amount of sunlight? I am certain that it is darker here than it was when I was here last."

"That makes sense. But there isn't that much of the black smoke in the air. We can see the edges of it. Surely, a line of smoke couldn't make that much difference in the amount of sunlight?"

"I don't know. There's a lot that I don't know. But remember that the black line of clouds was just part of all of the clouds. If the black smoke is helping the rest of the sky to be cloudy then that might do it. I'll have to talk it over with the people at the Academy. I'm good at science but I'm just an almost-graduate. I don't have enough experience. I need some more opinions."

"Sure," said Richtor. "Sorry. I didn't mean to lay the entire problem on your back."

"Okay," added Lichten. "What do we do now? Do we keep searching for possible problems? Do we just head back to the shoal? We don't expect you to know all the answers but you are the leader for analysis."

Januelle swam around silently for a while. Lichten moved over to the sharrells to make sure that the harnesses weren't rubbing badly and that they were in good health. He was certain that they wouldn't be hungry until the end of the day.

Richtor looked around at the life around him. Everything here had a lot more sunlight available. The variety, and profusion, of sea life was amazing to see. This shallow, he had to make sure that he didn't accidentally run into anything coming up from the seabed. He twisted this way and that, maneuvering around small pillars of rock or coral. On the seabed, he could see a large variety of criecraws although the type he usually ate appeared to be absent.

It wasn't just the amount of life that was amazing, it was all of the color. It was beautiful. Life at the shoal was beautiful also, of course, but so differently beautiful. This was dazzling. They were almost, but not quite, too beautiful to eat. Richtor reached out to snatch a fat small, smooth skinned, fish. He popped it into his mouth. Yuck! He didn't know for certain as to whether or not it was edible but he did know he didn't want it inside of his mouth. Luckily for him, and for the fish, he had not closed his teeth on it before spitting it out. It lazily swam away.

Not willing to just grab the next fish swimming by, Richtor examined them as they passed. He was still hungry. It had been about four or five hours since breakfast. He snatched a type of criecraw as it scuttled back towards a sheltering rock. Biting into it, he smiled. These criecraws had more meat and a much softer shell and better flavor.

"Hey, Lichten," Richtor called. "The criecraws are really good here."

After eating a few more criecraws, Richtor's hunger was not as pressing and he was able to look around again. No sharpfangs. He wondered why that was the case as it appeared there was plenty of prey for their hunts. He swam back to where Januelle was hovering.

"Can I help with anything? If you're hungry, the criecraws are delicious. Don't grab the small, fat, red and orange fish though. They taste terrible."

"That's good to know," said Januelle. "I'm trying to think of what questions will be asked when I return to the Academy."

"Why?" asked Richtor.

"I want to be able to answer their questions. Making a good guess at their questions gives me an idea as to what we should look for while we're here."

Januelle grew silent again for a few moments and then spoke. "Most of the questions would require us to stay here for a few weeks – maybe even a quarterflip or two. That would give us an idea as to whether the smoke is increasing, decreasing, or staying about the same. Staying awhile would allow us to take note of how things are changing."

"But we can't do that. We have graduation to attend and we are going to have to move forward with our lives after that – even if it might be a choice of going nomad for a while," said Richtor.

"Is that still a possibility?" asked Lichten, who had approached them as they talked near the sharrells.

"It's still a fallback solution. I know that I don't want to do that for the rest of my life. But I certainly don't want to commit to something in which I will be miserable for the rest of my life. Better to be a nomad for a while than someone who gets the reputation of not being reliable."

"I can see that," said Lichten. "But you'll lose momentum if you go nomad for a year. People will start to forget you."

"That's not all bad. Maybe they'll forget the stuff they didn't like and remember the stuff they did."

"Maybe. But you can't count on that," said Januelle.

She continued. "Back to our current problem. Most of the things that would be most useful would take time which we all agree that we don't have. The next best thing that we can do is to try to take a baseline of things that can be measured. Then, whenever whoever comes back, they won't be starting at the beginning. They can compare against our baseline and see if there is any change."

"That makes sense," said Richtor. "What would be important? Do we have what we need to do that?"

Januelle chittered. "Remember that I have half of a laboratory packed up into bundles and brought with me. Since I don't know what will be important for the analysis, we should take as many samples and measurements that we can think of."

"We'll help however we can."

"The most vital measurements will probably be from above the surface," said Januelle. "Since we are working from the view that this is a problem of reduced sunlight, we have measurements about sunlight and potential obscuring situations. We also have measurements on how that might be affecting life below the surface."

"Lichten, since you seem to do the best at keeping above the surface, you can do most of the measurements there. Richtor, you can help by taking measurements down here. Both of you bring your measurements back to me. Some I'll need to analyze but I'll need to record all of it."

"How long should all of this take?" asked Richtor.

"Do you have an appointment?" asked Januelle.

"Just graduation. Will we be able to make it back in time for graduation?"

Januelle chittered. "Sure. It might take us until dark. We might even finish before dark. But we can start heading home tomorrow. We'll get back with a couple of days to spare unless we encounter something on the way."

"Something?" asked Lichten.

"Well, we can't really count on being home until we're there," said Januelle.

"That's a bit pessimistic, isn't it?" asked Richtor.

"I hope so."

"Okay, Richtor. Here is a thermometer. Take readings in several locations. If they are the same, you don't need to worry about where it is, we can record one number. If they aren't, come back to me and we will figure out how to proceed. Lichten, here is a thermometer for you. Same instructions for the upper areas."

"What are you going to do, Januelle?" asked Lichten.

"I'm going to collect samples from the water. Then, I will do inventories of sea life contained within the samples. I am the only one to be able to do that. After you get your temperature samples, we will do some exposure samples in the air. We can do equivalent tests in the sea to determine how much light is penetrating at what depths." She was digging into her packages as she spoke. Handing thermometers to Lichten and Richtor, she said. "Okay. Move out."

"Aye aye," said Lichten and Richtor together. It was kind of fun to have one person coordinating everything. It probably wouldn't have been nearly as fun if it happened all of the time. Lichten swam up and Richtor swam around.

There didn't seem to be any significant variations in the temperature according to where he was taking the measurements, except once when he took a measurement within a pocket in the seabed. He realized that he needed to keep the depth constant to have a good comparison.

The measurements continued for most of the afternoon. Around 8th hour, Januelle told them that they could close up. She worked on packing her samples away along with the equipment.

"We have a couple of hours until dark," she said. "I suggest we start heading back. See if we can find a cloud for the sharrells to use as pasture."

"Sounds good," said Lichten.

"Fine with me."

The three friends reconnected to their sharrells and headed back in the direction from which they came.

Chapter 27 A Journey Home

*T*he path home was not exact. It didn't need to be. They were just planning to flip around and head back the direction from which they had come. They were all confident that that would get them back into recognizable areas and they could correct their course from there. In fact, not going exactly the same way might allow them to discover things that would be of benefit to the shoal.

Richtor examined the seabed as they moved along. The seabed was lowering, or the ocean was getting deeper, very gradually. He could see the colors muting and disappearing. And the number of fish, and other life, could be seen to decrease. From what he could recall from his classes, this was not unusual. The only thing unusual was the total amount - the decrease was expected but the gross numbers were not.

The sharrells were fully active again. It was easy to tell that they had worked off their morning foraging and were looking forward to the next one. It was not dark yet, but it was getting that way. Richtor hoped they could find an algae cloud before sight became difficult. They could give free reign to the sharrells and they would probably find a cloud on their own – but there was no guarantee that it would be in the same direction to which they wanted to go. If they became insistent, it would probably be okay to allow them their freedom to move as the cloud would probably be quite close and any deviation from their desired route not that substantial.

"Hey, Januelle!"

"Yes, Richtor?"

"Is there anything you want us to actively do on the trip back?"

"Not really. It's unlikely that we will have missed something coming out that we will notice on the way back. But keep your eyes open, of course."

"It's about dark," said Lichten. "I think Brightglow can smell a cloud nearby. Is it okay to let them leave the path?"

"Sure. As long as it isn't too far away. If we get truly lost then there isn't much we can do. I brought a copy of 'The Voyages of Sebaria' but I don't think there's enough detail to help us to find ourselves again if we get lost."

Lichten allowed Brightglow to follow her nose and she moved almost perpendicular to their current path. Widefin and Lumbor followed along. Just before it got too dark to see well, they saw the amorphous column of an algae cloud. Richtor removed a couple of provision bags from Lumbor and then detached himself to allow Lumbor to head into the cloud. Brightglow and Widefin soon moved over to forage along with Lumbor. The three sharrells had gotten used to each other's company over the past few days.

"My turn to make the rations edible," said Januelle. She took the provisions from Richtor and placed them on a flat rock nearby. Various criecraws and other seabed creatures scrambled to move away. She grabbed a criecraw as it moved away from the rock. Appetizer!

Richtor and Lichten tried to give Januelle space in which to work in peace. Since they were now heading back to the shoal and graduation, the conversation took up that thread once again.

"Just why are you so anxious about getting back in time for graduation, Lichten?"

"I know that I can't start off on my own business directly after campus graduation. I don't have enough work credits available and, even though I have a pretty good reputation, no one is going to lend me enough to get started with my own business. And, truthfully, there are things that I really need to learn that weren't covered in classes or in the work that I did outside of class hours."

"Yes," agreed Richtor. "And..."

"Graduation ceremony is the primary job fair for the campus. It takes place after you have received your grades, and graduating position, so groups and people know how you rank. All the major business segments have people attending. Having them there gives the best chance to have them compete against one another and get the best starting wages and most open position."

"I can see that but what areas are you wanting to work in and will they be willing to negotiate?"

"I think so," said Lichten. "I have a good reputation dealing with animals. I can do most tasks from general care, to wrangling, and to hunting. For that matter, I am pretty good at preparing food from the catch. So, we have the stables and corrals. Diplodus's stables are the largest, the best stocked, and the most often used. But there are a couple of other stables and it is even possible that someone from Orangegill or Pearly Shell will come to the ceremony."

"OK. I can see how that might create some competition."

"That's not all. The primary wranglers will also be there. They are the ones who obtain the sharrells for the corrals as well as gentling them before transfer."

"Some don't gentle," said Richtor.

"Yes. But I won't consider them. I am only interested in high quality businesses."

"So, what is your dream, Lichten?"

"I want to have the area's best source of sharrells. Not just our shoal but something good enough that people will come from all around the area to me to get a sharrell that they want. I want to breed sharrells, in addition to gentling wild sharrells. I want smarter, gentler, ones for children. I want strong, docile, ones for hard hauling, fast and maneuverable ones for hunting, and such."

"I'm sure you can do it. A lot of work, though. But if I can ever help, you can count on me."

"Thanks," said Lichten.

"Dinner's ready," called out Januelle.

Lichten and Richtor swam over to the rock where Januelle had prepared three large bowls of food for them. Lichten was in the lead and he had slowed down to a hover before Richtor had even arrived.

"Dig in," said Januelle. While Januelle, and the others, made use of spoons and knives in the preparation of the food, no such thing was present during eating. No mess was really possible with the sea happy to take care of any spills or waste. All three friends took a handful of their dinner and started to eat.

"Hmmm. I like this combination," said Richtor. "Not really spicy but it has a pleasant connotation. What's in it?"

"Ground blue kelp balls. I was introduced to them by a friend at a potluck."

"Certainly good," Lichten murmured around a mouthful of food. His bowl, which had been filled almost twice as full as that of Januelle and Richtor's, was just about empty.

"Any plans for tomorrow?"

"No, not really. Get back to the path. Continue," said Januelle. Now that they had found something and were finished with the excursion part of their trip, Januelle had stayed the de-facto lead of the group.

"OK," said Richtor and Lichten.

"I'm going to go make a nestle over there," said Lichten.

"I'll take first shift tonight," said Richtor.

"Fine with me. Will you clean up from dinner, Richtor?"

"Sure. Not a problem."

"OK. Goodnight."

~   ~   ~

It was another eventless night. Lichten, who had the last watch shift, swam up to check on the sharrells' harnesses. Still no problems. There really shouldn't be a problem unless a load was maldistributed or the harness had been attached incorrectly. But it was much better to be proactive.

Lichten had forgotten which container had the fish net and basket. He decided that it would work just as well to make a miniature pen for a bunch of criecraws. He moved around and found some flat rocks that could be piled upon each other. He made a circle with them that was about two hand spans high. The criecraws could crawl out but not quickly or easily. He hunted around the flat rock that Januelle had used in dinner preparation. As he thought, although it was largely gone now, there were a number of criecraws and other scavengers that had been attracted to the food debris. Not having had a good reason to leave once they had arrived, there were a couple of dozen that he could easily spot.

The criecraw claws weren't large enough, or sharp enough, to cause any significant problems. Still, they could be annoying so he picked out two at a time to be able to hold them from behind. Doing such, he had to move back and forth between the flat rock and his temporary pen a number of times. Finally, he had a number that he thought was reasonable for breakfast.

"Daytime, folks," called out Lichten.

Usually, Richtor was an early riser but he had had a rather restless night's sleep. He stretched his body out, tail moving back and forth such that he shot out from his nestle of the night. Just stretching his torso out didn't cause such an explosion but it was so hard not to move his tail while he was yawning. Maybe Januelle would know why that happened.

Januelle started moving around at about the same time that Richtor succeeded in returning to the sleep area. "Good morning," said Richtor to his two friends. "Anything special about today?"

"Nothing planned. We should get back to familiar territory today. That will make things more comfortable," said Januelle.

"I have some criecraws penned up for breakfast," said Lichten. "They're over there." He pointed over in the direction of the cloud where their sharrells were sleeping – having gorged themselves the previous evening.

Lichten stayed back while Richtor and Januelle scooped up the criecraws that they wanted for breakfast. After they finished, he moved in and ate the rest. He felt a bit full – maybe a couple of criecraws too many. But he didn't expect any real activity today. Just another day moving through Ocean.

"Should I check the surface?" asked Lichten.

"If you want," replied Januelle. "I don't expect any substantial change. We do know where the line of black is coming from – sometimes that extra knowledge can make a person see things differently. Maybe you'll notice something. At any rate, it won't hurt."

Lichten moved himself up to the surface – which was considerably farther from the seabed than it was yesterday afternoon. Richtor moved to get things prepared for the days trip. Not much to do. He had already cleaned up from dinner and there wasn't any mess from the breakfast the three had shared.

Lichten returned. "You're right. Nothing special. We aren't travelling quite the same direction as the cloud. Should we change directions to follow it?"

The three swam over to where the sharrells were floating and sleeping. Januelle took the compass out of the pouch nearest the connector and looked at it. "Let's just get back onto the path we were on and keep going. According to the compass, we are going back along the path that did exist. Perhaps the wind has changed. I think that is more likely than us not noticing we weren't heading back the same way."

"Okay." The three connected to their sharrells and started moving back to the path that they had been taking the previous day. As they had diverted for only about a half-hour's distance, they reached their last point on the path quickly.

"I recognize those corals," said Lichten.

"So do I," said Richtor. "Plus, over there is where we hovered while we were deciding whether to move away from the path for forage."

"Okay. Let's continue on the old path."

The three nudged their sharrells back to the path from which they had diverged the previous day. They continued along for a couple of hours and then a number of shadows started appearing over their heads, moving just below the surface.

It wasn't one large shadow, such as would be made by a widemouth but rather a pack of fairly large animals. Most predators were territorial rather than pack-oriented so they probably weren't active predators.

"What's that above us?" asked Richtor.

Lichten, who had already been looking above them, smiled at Richtor and said, "Quarrells!"

Chapter 28 Swimming on the Wild Side

Richtor spoke up. "Quarrells? Aren't they dangerous?"

"Sure. And so am I," said Lichten. "But they aren't malicious. They don't attack unless they are provoked or feel threatened."

"Quarrells are closely related to sharrells, aren't they?" asked Januelle.

"They believe so. I have never succeeded in following the lessons in biology class on that subject. I would think that you would be the one who would know that."

"I'm interested. But a person has to pick and choose what to study and wildlife isn't one of my main interests. I probably am not the best person to be science liaison on this trip. Then again, maybe I am most appropriate because I am still a generalist. Still, I can't tell you much about what is known about interrelationships between species."

Lichten continued. "In general shape and configuration, quarrells and sharrells are very similar. But quarrells are larger, smarter, and their lobe fins have evolved into arms - but without hands as we have. What they have at the end of their lobe fins look more like pincers than anything else."

"Like a criecraw?" asked Richtor.

"Not quite. Sharrells and quarrells are both vertebrates. Criecraws are crustaceans and their shells envelop, and connect to, their muscles. You may have seen those large gloves that people use in the factories when they are fabricating metal objects. I think they call them mittens."

"Yes."

"Well, the ends of their arms - might as well call them that - look more like mittens than the sharp, hard claws of the criecraws. But they are still strong. There isn't the delicacy to manipulate that we have with full hands and fingers but they can grasp tighter than we can."

"So, do they use tools and weapons?" asked Richtor.

"When they can," said Lichten. "They can fashion some crude tools but nothing delicate or intricate. They are really good at making use of things they can scavenge. For example, some fish have long sharp horns for defense. The quarrells find those – or claim them from the bodies of their prey – and make use of them."

"Why did a herd of them swim overhead?"

"Not a herd. A pack," said Lichten. "Sharrells are in herds for safety. Quarrells are in packs for hunting and it does give some additional protection for any young quarrells."

"Do they hunt us?"

"Not usually. They prefer prey that doesn't organize its defense. We wouldn't consider them to be very smart. Not being able to make tools has probably hindered that development. But they are definitely smarter than sharrells and can coordinate, and work, together for common purposes."

"To answer the original question. It is a bit concerning that they are moving this close to the shoal – although, as you may have noted, they weren't traveling the same direction that we are. That is, they aren't moving towards the shoal. But this looked more like a migration. They usually only do that when the food supply in their original area starts to run out."

"So, this movement may be associated with the overall food supply problem?" asked Richtor.

"Possible. What do you think, Januelle?"

"As I said, I haven't studied wildlife that much so I don't really know. But it makes sense."

"That's not good," added Richtor. "But it is good they aren't heading towards the shoal's herds."

"Yep."

As they talked, they continued their way following, more-or-less, the reverse of the path they took to the island. Some of the seabed was beginning to look familiar though it was probably due to having seen it when they were travelling the other direction rather than being that close to the shoal.

Now that the excitement of the quarrell pack was past, the journey was proving to be rather boring. Richtor tried to revive his interest by examining the surrounding areas much more intently than he usually would have.

The seabed was at about one-half the depth that it was at the shoal although much of the colors were already subdued or missing. At about two bodylengths, there was effectively no red left to be seen. They were now past four bodylengths and he could see orange only in his imagination.

It wasn't quite true that red and orange had disappeared, of course. It was just that he saw them as black rather than as a color. At the depths of the shoal, blue was about the only color still discernible. Even though a person couldn't see the color red at these depths, being red was an advantage to many fish as it allowed them to blend into the surrounding blacks and greys.

He watched a poacher eel swim by with its overlarge head attached to its sinuating body. The extra-large head allowed it to swallow larger prey but it looked peculiar with the head being almost three times as wide as the body. The bone structure of the head was very light so as to not throw off the distribution of weight for the eel.

The gordies were not as common at this depth but there were more feathertails. He couldn't see any chewdors at all. It was really along the seabed that the variety of life changed a lot. The ubiquitous criecraws were present, of course, but there were a number of other crustaceans in addition. One peculiar one had its head, and eyestalks, in the middle on top with six arms and pincers radiating out from the body. Richtor remembered having read about it but couldn't recall any details or even the name. He wondered if they were as tasty as criecraws. Sometimes he felt that his stomach was about as active as Lichten's – he just didn't eat as much.

"Hey, Januelle," called Richtor. "I haven't been seeing any chewdors lately. Is there a particular reason for that?"

"They are more common at greater depths. You might think that, being a larger fish, they would prefer shallower water with a larger number of fish available to be prey. But, because of their size, they are not a very speedy fish and it works better for them to hide among the rocks on the seabed and jump to catch fish. So, the deeper seabeds work better for them."

"Okay. Is there anything I should be looking for, or noticing, at this depth?"

"Check out the vegetation," replied Januelle. "It gets anchored both ways – as something descending into the water from a floating main body and as something embedded in the seabed but sending up fronds towards the surface. In combination, at this depth, they keep some type of vegetation present between seabed and surface."

Richtor looked around and noticed the phenomenon of which Januelle was talking. Fortunately, there were few areas where both top-growers and bottom-growers overlapped. That would cause virtual curtains to be navigated around. The bottom-growers had little balls, filled with gas, about every half bodylength that forced the strands to go up rather than drift in the current.

"Januelle, are these balls the same as the ones you used as spice for our dinners?"

Januelle looked at some of the kelp in the area. "Related, but not the same. I guess it would be worth trying. Remove a couple – but not consecutive ones such that it would hurt the plant."

Richtor nudged Lumbor closer to the nearest ground-based kelp. He took a short knife out of his personal pouch and cut off one of the balls pulling the strand upward towards the surface. He moved the sharrell up, skipping the next two balls, and took off another ball.

"This won't hurt the plant?"

"No, it shouldn't," said Januelle. As long as it can still reach up so that it filters the water correctly and reaches up towards sunlight then it will replace the balls in a week or two."

Richtor punctured the two balls, allowing the gas to escape. They would pack away much more easily if they were deflated.

As he looked around, he noticed at least three different types of plants anchored on the seabed. The ones which started at the surface were all the same type of plant, as far as he could see. Not being anchored, they would move around along with the waves and current – their dangling fronds working as sails in the current. Sometimes they caught on the upward bound branches of seabed anchored plants and formed a temporary wall until shifted, once again, by the currents.

They continued to move along but, at this place, the environment reminded Richtor of the Jordach Jungle. Within the areas of vegetation, he could spot fish moving into and out of the fronds.

Suddenly, Richtor saw a sharpfang darting out of the fronds. It was chasing a gordie and winning the race. Soon the gordie was caught in the mouth of the sharpfang and, with a couple of large bites and swallows, the gordie was now becoming part of the sharpfang.

Lumbor moved a bit away from the fronds and Richtor allowed him the movement. Unless very hungry, sharpfangs were only a nuisance to people and larger animals. They were fast but not particularly maneuverable and it was easy to grab one over the top after they had gone by. Of course, a bite was a bite and a sharpfang bite hurt. There was a chance of infection although, since sharpfangs were predators rather than scavengers, the bite was less likely to contain too many pathogens.

Moving around within this vegetation, Richtor was finding it unusually difficult to be certain he was continuing to follow the original path. He certainly didn't remember this patch on the way out.

He could see Januelle and Lichten up ahead - still in sight but not very close. During his examinations of the fish and vegetation, he had allowed them to go ahead. He called out to them.

"Hey, Januelle. Hey, Lichten." Januelle and Lichten stopped their sharrells and turned around.

"What's up? Why are you so far back?"

"I've been looking around at the fish and stuff."

"Interesting, isn't it?" said Januelle. "This trip has reminded me of how fun it can be to wander out of the bounds of the shoal. The shoal isn't a desert but most of the living plants and animals around the shoal have adapted to that environment. Being at a greater depth, there just isn't enough sunlight for earnest plant growth. Of course, we do get some variants near the fissures that you won't find around here."

"What I was calling about is that all of this life around me and the dodging and twisting I have to do is making me less certain that we are heading the right direction. Januelle, could you check your compass and see if we are still on course?"

"Sure."

"I'm pretty sure we're still on course," said Lichten.

"It's okay, Lichten. It doesn't hurt to be certain. If we are backtracking accurately, we shouldn't encounter anything that we didn't encounter on the way in. Do you remember these seaweeds? I don't."

"I don't either," said Lichten. "But it could have been a hundred bodyflips to either side and we wouldn't have seen it."

Januelle examined the compass. "We've moved off course a bit but it's not really a significant amount. We should move about five degrees to the right."

"Fine. Thanks," said Richtor.

By this time, Richtor had caught up with his friends. He could have spent a lot more time looking at the area. Maybe he would come back again someday. It was only about a day and a half away from the shoal.

The three friends continued on their way, after having shifted their direction just a bit. In a few more hours, they started seeing signs of the locale of the shoal. Richtor felt relieved. This expedition was his responsibility and anything could happen at any time. While possible within the shoal, that wouldn't be likely to be his responsibility.

Now that they were in the correct general area, they decided to find somewhere to settle in for the night and head in to the shoal the next morning.

Chapter 29 Discussions

Januelle had the last watch shift for that night, so she took care of rounding up breakfast. They had found a very small algae cloud before settling in the previous night. Large enough for the sharrells to forage. It was, of course, fully possible for the three friends to eat algae but they didn't have the ability to sift it directly from the water that the sharrells and other grazing fish had.

Usually, when the food processors – unpopular to call them factories – were preparing algae cakes as supplemental food rations for the shoal, they would round up a large number of algae in a fine-sieved net and then use tools to tighten it around the algae until it clumped together into an irregular block. The people at the shop would then break off, or cut off, sections from the block and put them into molds where they would further compress, and shape, the rations.

Even though she had brought quite a bit of equipment in the possibility of the need for testing, or analyzing, material, that assortment had not included a tool that could be used for sieving. Januelle wanted their breakfast together to be a good one. It might not actually be their last breakfast together but, depending on what paths they each took in the future, it could be. Richtor had caught wild fish. Lichten had rounded up criecraws. Maybe she could do a combination of criecraws with some type of vegetation. She examined the local florae to see what could be used.

She remembered using the pods as seasoning but that wasn't sufficient for a substantial meal. She wished she had spent more time on the more practical survey of edible life in Ocean. She had seen Richtor spit out the one fish when they were near the island and that had reminded her that not everything was edible for them – though most of the moving animals would probably only make them sick. But who wanted to spend the day sick?

Her best chances were to stick with plants or animals that she recognized. She looked around. There were a few rocks piled here and there on the seabed. Often, sea life would make use of such for protection when not actively moving. She decided to head down and look around.

As she approached one of the rocks, she saw quite a few criecraws moving around. For some strange reason, perhaps because they were so numerous, criecraws seemed to just ignore anything around them. Of course, they did scuttle along the surface of the seabed. It was difficult for anything without arms and hands to lift them off of the seabed to eat. She hadn't thought about that before.

Criecraws were fine but she wanted something special. She moved around the rock. She spotted a small piece of a seaweed's stipe which had broken off – probably during some type of surface storm. She used the stipe to search around the edges of the rock.

A tentacle popped out from under the rock. It grabbed at the stipe. Januelle pulled it backward and the soft head of an animal poked its head out as it moved after the stipe. It was a blue-striped decapus. She didn't care that much for decapus but she knew that many people did. And it would be special. Decapus usually had to be individually hunted and they did not cultivate well.

If she had still been attached to her sharrell, she wouldn't have had a chance to approach the decapus this closely. But she wasn't. She used the stipe to slowly encourage the decapus, who had not yet noticed her hovering above the rock, to move out farther.

Finally, the decapus was out far enough and Januelle pounced. The decapus immediately tried to move back under the rock but Januelle was too fast for it. It wrapped three of its tentacles around her arm. She pulled back on her arm. The decapus started moving its tentacles quickly. Januelle pulled her arm up to her face and quickly bit down on a spot near the spot below its eyes and above where the tentacles started spreading. Even though the decapus became still, the tentacles maintained their grip.

Januelle slowly peeled the tentacles off her arm. She lay the decapus on the top of the rock and then started creating a pen, as Lichten had done previously, and quickly started putting criecraws into it.

Once done, she swam over to where Lichten and Richtor were nestled and called to them to wake up. Lichten woke up abruptly, reaching for a trident that he had laid down close to him before sleeping. Richtor opened his eyes and then bent his spine to bring his tailfin up. He had never been flexible enough to bring his tailfin all of the way to his head but he had seen some hatchlings do it before they grew very large.

"Breakfast is ready. There are criecraws to grab and a decapus to divide. Lichten, would you be willing to do the honors of splitting it. You can take the largest portion, of course."

Lichten headed over to the rock and, using the sharp side edge of the trident, split the decapus into three unequal pieces with Januelle's and

Richtor's being pretty similar in size and configuration.

"All ready. Shall we dig in?" asked Lichten.

"Sure, you first," said Januelle.

Without hesitation, Lichten grabbed a criecraw from the pen with his left hand and carried his portion of the decapus in his right. He swam to the side to allow his friends to start their breakfast.

Breakfast was soon over and they were all reconnected to their rather sluggish sharrells. They weren't close enough to the stables for their mounts to start hurrying along to get back to their familiar goal. But the trio saw more and more things that told them they were near the shoal.

"We should probably report to Cheyelle," said Richtor.

"And I will need to report back to the Academy, as well as return the test equipment and get the samples documented and recorded," said Januelle.

"I don't think I need to do anything in particular, do I?" asked Lichten.

"We should probably all report to Cheyelle, as she may have questions that any one of us might be the best to answer," answered Richtor.

"Anyone want to race?" asked Lichten.

"No, not really," responded Januelle. "But if you two want to do such, then go ahead."

Richtor looked at Lichten who looked back. "I guess not," said Richtor. "We've done this trip together. Let's stay together."

Richtor, who was on his sharrell between those of Januelle and Lichten, reached out his hands to both sides and the three friends swam on, for a while, connected together.

They had dropped their hands once again, after a while, and noticed a shadow moving over them again.

"Another pack of quarrells?" asked Richtor.

Lichten replied to both of them, staying only on a private mental channel. "No, that's a widemouth. I haven't seen a widemouth in this area for many flips. We don't want to attract its attention. I suggest we slowly move, with our sharrells, down to the seabed."

"Is it going the same direction that we are? Is it headed toward the shoal?" asked Richtor.

"Not quite. At least, I don't think so. But it might hit our herd."

"Oh no," said Januelle. "Is there anything we can do?"

"We sure as everything can't fight it." Lichten looked around. He spotted a small school of fish. He wasn't sure what type they were but it didn't really matter.

"Willing to take a risk?" asked Lichten.

"For the shoal? Sure," replied Richtor. Januelle nodded.

"If we can persuade this school to move perpendicular to the route of the widemouth, it is possible that it will change course to chase them. But we'll have to be pretty close to the bottom of the widemouth, in order to chase them up and past the widemouth so it will notice them."

"But that would divert it?"

"Not for certain. But there's a decent chance it might work. There is a non-zero chance that it might spot us first and we would be a much more solid meal than a school of smaller fish."

"How do we do it?"

"I have the most practice, so I should come up behind the school and try to direct them. I will be moving, on Brightglow, from side to side and pushing them upward. We'll want them to go past the widemouth about a bodylength in front of it and moving towards the side. Then, we'll want to stay below the school so that the widemouth sees the school first and turns after them."

"Got it," said Richtor. "When do we do it?"

"Now. Or a little before now, if it were possible."

"What do we do?"

"As I said, I'll come up from behind and try to herd them. You two act as barriers on the sides so isn't easy for them to head that direction. I'll try to keep you informed about changes of direction, since you will need to be ahead of me."

"OK," said Richtor. He moved Lumbor over to one side of the small school of fish. Januelle took the other side.

"Let's start," said Lichten. He moved Brightglow between Januelle and Richten and to one side - away from the direction in which he wanted the school to move.

Lichten and Brightglow moved forward. The school moved away. Januelle and Richtor stayed on the sides. "A bit right and up," said Lichten.

In this manner, they continued to move the school upward and over towards where the widemouth had been seen heading. Luckily, for its size, the widemouth moved very slowly through the water. His course continued to point very close to the shoal's herd.

Richtor, on Lumbor, got behind Lichten and Januelle a bit and the school started to move off in his direction rather than forward toward the widemouth.

"Richtor, get back into position. Come from the side to persuade the school to get back into our pen."

Richtor attempted to follow directions, urging Lumbor to move faster. They angled in, forcing the school to retreat in order to not run into them. Soon, the formation was moving forward as needed.

The large shadow of the widemouth was now noticeable overhead. They were close enough to see some of the details of the belly of the widemouth. It was quite pale on the belly with a few scars from where smaller predators had nipped a bit from the wide expanse. Due, in part, to its large size, the widemouth was not very maneuverable. If it was annoyed enough, however, it could be a dangerous predator. Normally, it operated more as a grazing animal – though the food matter it took in was in the form of fish and other higher animal life.

Lichten started moving the school into a vector which would intersect the widemouth's path. This was the most dangerous part of the exercise. In order for the widemouth to see, and smell, the school to allow it to divert its course, the school had to be in front of it and preferably a bit to the desired direction of diversion. There were going to be a few moments when the three friends had to drop down quickly with their sharrells hoping that the momentum of the school would continue moving them into the desired path.

They rose steadily higher. Januelle and Richtor kept to the sides of the school, although their sharrells were getting more and more fidgety and hard to control. Lichten, with his mastery over his favorite mount, didn't have that problem but he was dealing with determining that precise vector to accomplish their goals.

They were close. The school was almost to the same height as the widemouth. Faster and faster so the momentum of the school would be difficult for them to break out of.

"Now," said Lichten on a tight channel to Richtor and Januelle. They each directed their sharrells downward at a steep angle, being careful to not touch any of the fish in the school. As they reached a depth of a couple of bodylengths below the widemouth, they stopped and turned around.

The school was starting to break up and become less concentrated. But they were in front of the widemouth. It saw them. The school continued to swim in the same direction but much faster now as they could no longer ignore the widemouth. The widemouth slowly changed its direction. It scooped up a few of the stragglers from the school. It continued the shift in direction chasing after the rest of the school. Success!

Chapter 30 Back to the Shoal

*T*he three friends joined little fingers across the three of them, in acknowledgement of a job well done. They watched the widemouth continue in its journey – this time in a direction which would, unless perturbed again by some unknown event, keep it on a safe path away from the shoal.

"Well," exclaimed Richtor. "Are we ready to continue back to the shoal? Since the widemouth was heading that general direction, we are mostly on course."

"Sure, let's go."

Each was lost in their own thoughts as they continued along towards the shoal. After a couple of hours, their sharrells started moving perceptibly faster. It was obvious that they had reached "the home stretch". They allowed the sharrells free reign as there wasn't a good reason to restrain them or to provide specific instruction.

As they moved, they all looked around at home. Would their excursion be of use to the shoal or was it just a last campus trip with friends before moving into the working stage of adulthood?

The trio started to reign in their sharrells as they tried to go faster and faster as they approached the stable and corrals. It felt like they were unintended participants in a sharrell race where each was certain that they would win a wonderful prize if they crossed the finish line first.

As they approached, Lichten sent out an alert to Diplodus such that he would be ready for them as they arrived.

"Back a bit early, aren't you?" asked Diplodus as he met them outside of the stable office.

"Well, we didn't take the full time. But I don't think we're really early," replied Richtor.

"Successful trip?"

"Maybe." Richtor was aware that the information they had collected might be of value – and it might not. It needed to be evaluated first. Spreading information too early could be very bad.

"We had a great last-of-the-class-years trip, Diplodus," said Januelle. "Thanks for helping. The sharrells were great. I loved being taken along with Widefin."

"That's good," said Diplodus. "Lumbor work well for you, Richtor?"

"Yes. I should tell you that he got a gash from a sharpfang a few days ago. We treated it and I think it is all healed but I thought you should know."

"Can you show me?"

Richtor disconnected from Lumbor. Januelle and Lichten parted from their sharrells too.

"Right here," said Richtor as he pointed to a spot which was not quite blended in with the rest of the scaled surface.

Diplodus leaned forward and used a finger to probe the area, trying not to scrape off much mucous. Lumbor continued to hover, though it was obvious that he wanted to get back to the corral and his feeding area.

"I don't see any long-term problem," said Diplodus. "Thanks for telling me and thanks for taking good care of him."

Januelle started the process of removing all of her pouches and containers from Widefin's harness. She carried each over to the outside wall of the stable office and then returned to detach the next one.

Richtor and Lichten disconnected their parcels. Richtor found that there was quite a bit more food than he expected. It could be taken to either the campus or the creche where it would help them with their overall budget. Lichten had very little connected – just where his trident was harnessed for easy removal and a few other supplies oriented towards taking care of the sharrells.

Once they finished with their packages, they went to Widefin and asked Januelle if they could help.

"Not right now," she replied. "I have almost all of the equipment and supplies detached. But I would appreciate help getting them to the Academy."

"Sure."

Having detached everything from the sharrells' harnesses – and a few items from their personal harnesses – they were ready to take their sharrells into the stables to remove harnesses and store them away.

"We'll be taking the large pile with us as soon as we settle, Diplodus," said Richtor. "Is it OK to leave this food here for a while until I can come get it?" He spoke to Lichten. "I guess that you'll just take your stuff along with you?" Lichten nodded.

"It would probably be better for you to place the food inside the office – just in case someone or something swims by and is hungry."

"Okay. Thanks."

The three led their sharrells into the stables and proceeded to remove the animals' harnesses as well as their own. Most were placed back in storage on the walls of the rooms while Lichten left his personal harness on. He would use it to help carry his personal items as he was helping move the packages and equipment for Januelle.

The three met up outside of Diplodus' office. Januelle distributed parcels. Lichten was willing to attach a couple of pouches to his harness in addition to his personal items. With their six hands, the three started off toward the Academy building with Januelle in the lead. The Academy building was close to the center of the shoal near the central statue garden.

Without the sharrells, they struggled with their burdens, resting a couple of times on the way to the Academy building.

"How in Ocean did you get all of these supplies over to the stable, Januelle?" asked Richtor.

"It took two trips and Geordo helped me."

"Geordo?"

"Yes. He's a member of the Academy. He helped me check out the equipment as well as to decide what types of things I might need to do to investigate things. In addition, he has been assigned to head the investigation into the herd decrease."

"Oh. So, we're kind of working with him and whoever he is working with?"

"Yes – except that he only has himself on this."

"I'd think this would be considered serious enough to warrant a few people to help."

"Perhaps. But they would need to have something specific to do. I'm afraid that the Academy is excellent at measurements and discussion but not that great at investigation or experimentation. I can't decide if that is a good reason to try to move into the Academy or a good reason to avoid moving in."

"Yes?" asked Lichten.

"If I moved into the Academy, I might be able to use their resources to start doing more active, and proactive, work in the sciences. However, I would be a very junior member and I might not be allowed to do anything except assisting others for a number of years."

"That doesn't sound that bad as long as you had an opportunity after the apprenticeship finished." Said Richtor.

"Sure. It's fair – apprenticeships are to help the senior folk and much of the learning is achieved by listening and watching. But there's always the danger that I might start drifting and just find it too easy to follow along and become an expert discussion person."

"What are your other options?"

"I could be a science teacher on campus. There would always be problems with budgets and equipment and supplies but they would allow me to conduct experiments as long as I do them safely. If I focused my work on something – metal fabrication, for example – I could work within a factory. There's not a lot of need, or jobs, for a generalist in the factories."

"Any leanings?" asked Richtor. He was always interested in people's career choices due to his own dilemma. And he respected Januelle's approach to life and her studies.

"I think I'm leaning towards becoming a teacher. That won't stop me from working with the Academy so I can combine some of the good from both."

"And the bad?" asked Richtor with a grin.

"I'll have to deal with one set of politics either way."

"I guess that's true," said Richtor much more seriously.

The trio makes it to the front entrance of the local Academy offices. Januelle sat down her packages and entered through the doorway. She soon came back out with a somewhat older, but not that much older than they were, male. He had very interesting markings - almost circles along his body near his tailfin.

"OK, Januelle. We should first just put the equipment back where it belongs. Then we'll store any unused supplies."

"Is there anything for us to do?" asked Lichten.

Lichten looked over to Januelle.

"Oh, yes. Geordo, these are my friends from campus, Richtor and Lichten. Guys, this is Geordo, a member of the Academy. Geordo has been very helpful."

"Hello, Geordo. Pleased to meet you," said Richtor.

"Same here," said Lichten.

"We were all on the same trip together. Lichten and I helped to tote Januelle's stuff from the stable. Is there anything we can help with?"

Geordo gave a mild grimace. "Stuff. Hmm. No, I don't believe you can help with any of the stuff right now. Januelle and I know where everything goes and we would spend more time telling you what to do with it than to do it ourselves. Thank you for your assistance."

Januelle looked at Richtor and Lichten, amusement in her eyes. "After we get things put away, I will need to go over our investigations with Geordo. Do you think that you two know enough about what we did, and have found out, to present a summary to Cheyelle?"

Lichten and Richtor nodded and swam away. Lichten was the only one left with any burdens and he was so used to carrying around his personal equipment that he hardly noticed.

They continued swimming towards the center building, where they might find Cheyelle – if she had any time.

"Do you think Geordo didn't like me calling the equipment and supplies 'stuff'?"

"Where would you have gotten that idea?" said Lichten with a smile and a small chitter.

Richtor also chittered. "I supposed you wouldn't appreciate me calling your trident a fork."

"No, I wouldn't. But I doubt anyone would. More likely, they would just say 'things'. That would be OK with me. I guess some people are a bit more sensitive."

"Oh well. Live and learn," said Richtor.

They now approached the center building. They entered into the front office. As usual, Wayroll was hovering around behind the desk pedestal.

"Hello Richtor. Hello Lichten. Back already?"

"I guess so," replied Richtor. "Is Cheyelle in and available?"

"She's in. She doesn't have any meetings scheduled for another hour but I don't know if she is available. Do you know how much time you think you'll need?"

"Depends on whether she has any questions and, if so, whether we can answer them. We can present our findings in just a few cycles."

"I'll see whether she wants to see you now. Wait here." Wayroll swam off into the corridor.

"Do we know what we want to say?" asked Lichten.

"I think so. Do you want me to start off?"

"Sure. This was your trip and you started it all off."

"Okay."

At this point, Wayroll swam back in. "She has a half-hour to give to you. I'll take you back."

As they followed Wayroll back to the Council head's office, Richtor thought back to the last time they had seen her. That time it was only Januelle and himself. This time it is Lichten and himself. He guessed that, with only him in common, it did make sense that he would take the lead in any discussion.

They arrived at the office door. Wayroll pressed the pulse plate and then slid open the door without waiting for a response. Once Lichten and Richtor had made it through the door, Wayroll closed it behind them.

Cheyelle continued looking through some written pages that were spread out on her pedestal. She looked up, took a breath, and smiled.

"Hello Richtor."

"Hello."

"You are Lichten, are you not?" asked Cheyelle.

"Yes."

"I am pleased to meet you. I hear about some of your activities with the stable and the wrangling crews. You seem to have a good way with the animals."

"We seem to get along."

"Good. I assume that, with you being here in my office, there is something to report?"

Richtor tried to stop his dorsal fin from twitching – which caused him to wriggle from side to side. "We think so. We're not sure of all of the ramifications."

"Where is Januelle?" asked Cheyelle.

"She's finishing up with Geordo at the Academy."

"She feels you can give the report?"

"Yes."

"Then I'm sure you can. Proceed."

Richtor took a breath and started. "We started with the premise that a reduction in the food supply most likely was caused, at some point in the food cycle, by a decrease of sunlight."

"Why did you believe that?"

"We examined various possibilities for reduction in the herd size and it seemed to be the best reason left."

"Go on."

"If the sunlight had decreased, we figured there had to be a reason. As we explored the surface, we encountered a very dark line of clouds in the sky. That dark line was surrounded by other clouds. We could not see any blue in the sky."

"Interesting," said Cheyelle.

"The clouds, if they stayed present, might account for the reduction in sunlight. But that pushed the question back another layer. What was causing the clouds?"

"You're doing a good job of presenting, Richtor. Continue."

"With a line in the sky, we thought we would try to follow the line. A line goes both directions, of course, but we thought that we had a good idea what existed in one direction so we followed it the other direction."

"After a few days, we came upon a land mass that continued above the surface of the water. Januelle called it an island."

"Yes, I know about islands," said Cheyelle. "Continue."

"There was a high area on this island. It had areas on it that reminded us of the fissures. From the top, a stream of smoke came out and connected with the line in the sky. Januelle said that the winds at that height must be pushing the smoke into the line that we saw."

"Any sign of it stopping?"

"No. Januelle said that it was impossible to speculate without having a baseline of how it had behaved in the past. We then proceeded to create baseline measurements that could be used by the Academy in the near future to determine how conditions were changing. That is the main thing that Januelle is discussing with Geordo."

"Since Geordo is leading the Academy investigation, I am sure that I will hear more about this. What more do you know at the moment?"

Lichten spoke. "This lack of food is affecting most of the life around us around the seabed. We saw a Widemouth on the way back. It was heading in the direction of our herd. We managed to shift its course."

Cheyelle's face had paled at mention of the Widemouth. "Thank goodness."

"Anything else?" asked Cheyelle.

"We saw an algae cloud that was as large as the ones we rotate our herds to. Perhaps we could find, and make use, of some additional pastures to increase our herd's food supply?" added Richtor.

"That's a good idea. I'll ask the herders if they think that would help. Anything else?"

"I don't think so. I hope it was helpful."

"You have come back with more than I expected. It may be quite useful. I didn't really think you would find anything, I admit," said Cheyelle. "But I didn't see anything to lose and all three of you are very capable, each in your own way."

"As I said, I didn't have any expectations but I think you have done a great job. We may not know the reasons, or what has happened, or how long it may happen - but, thanks to you three, we have a better knowledge of things that are present. And even, perhaps, some ways to work around them. I'd like to get more information about that widemouth."

She continued. "We'll wait for a report from the Academy to do anything specific - but there's no reason not to see if we can start expanding the herd with additional food. Thank you."

"You are welcome," said Richtor. "We enjoyed doing it," said Lichten.

"Anything else?"

Richtor shook his head. "No, I don't think so."

"Do you still need the badges?" asked Cheyelle.

"I guess not," said Richtor. He placed his badge on the pedestal.

"I left mine back in my room. Can I bring it later today or tomorrow?" asked Lichten.

"That should be fine, Lichten. Just give it to Wayroll at the front pedestal. Thank you once again. Happy Graduation! Goodbye." She pressed a pulse plate near her pedestal.

Wayroll came soon, opened the door, and escorted Lichten and Richtor back out.

As the friends left, Lichten spoke to Richtor. "Only two days to graduation."

Richtor looked startled and then replied, "I guess so. See you then. Thanks, Lichten. I hope we'll continue to be friends and see each other."

"Hey, not so sad. I'm sure we will see each other unless you go nomad or become a hermit."

"I don't think so but I still don't know." Lichten moved off toward his room at the dormitory. Richtor went to the statue garden to think.

Chapter 31 A Good Night's Rest

Richtor woke up after a long night's rest. It was a good one. He still didn't know, for certain, what he wanted to do past graduation but he felt like he and his friends had done as much as they could to investigate the herd problem. He hoped that what they had done would help. At the least, he could remove it from his list of concerns.

He looked around his room. Since the new hatching would not move in until the beginning of the next campus academic year, he didn't have to worry about moving for about a quarterflip. He would still be able to continue to eat in the dormitory food area until then. But he would lose his student stipend in a couple of weeks. It was fair. He didn't have to worry about immediate living needs but, since he no longer had his job as student, he would no longer have any income.

Still, the day would come soon. He had been in this room for ten currentflips – about half of his time on campus. Before that time, he shared a room with another from his hatching. He hadn't stayed in touch with him. His name was what? Richtor couldn't recall at the moment. He thought it might have begun with "Mor". It would come to him.

The meeting with Cheyelle seemed to have gone well. It would have been nice to keep the badge but he could understand why that wasn't possible. Some souvenir would have been nice. Something to look at and say "I remember that trip".

Richtor supposed that it was reasonable to reminisce over his past currentflips in classes. Tomorrow would effectively end that portion of his life – and almost all of the conscious, sapient, part of his life. Crechelings learned something but they were largely living entities to be kept under control. Not as bad as during the winnowing but bad enough. He hadn't even gotten his official name until he had entered the campus academy. He was just "Squirmbox" until then.

Richtor was unaware of another Richtor in the shoal. Of course, his full name was Richtor Bluefin, being a member of the Bluefin shoal. He had heard that there was another Januelle in the shoal, besides the one that he knew. Her full name should be Januelle B Bluefin but that was only necessary in larger circles where there was a possibility of confusion. He wondered how many "squirmboxes" there had been over the currentflips.

He looked around his room. It didn't have many personal things. Not a lot of academic awards as in Januelle's room. He had gotten one for second place in a Science Fair during fourth year. It wasn't that it worked out so well – but no one else had even thought of the possibility of the experiment.

And as for physical accomplishments – they just didn't give out awards for "managed to not get tangled in the net during hunting practice". He wasn't particularly weak – he was able to help others when they needed it. But no one would pick him first for a team playing water waffle. No one would call him out of a crowd to move a heavy object to a different location.

All that was fine with Richtor. A little better than average grades because he did know how to study and he worked hard at it. So, what were his strengths? If he met people at Graduation tomorrow, how would he present himself? What aspects of his life would act as recommendations for a job, position, or situation?

He was loyal. He treated people as well as he could – even those who, he felt, did not treat him that well. He was reliable as long as there wasn't a specific time deadline. He never told lies although he certainly did not always volunteer information. It wasn't his responsibility to make sure that the questioners phrased their questions well.

Inventiveness. Creativity. Extrapolations. These were his greatest strengths. But how could they be best used? In what position would these traits be best valued?

Richtor decided that he had wandered around in his own thoughts for long enough. Maybe a tour of the statue garden would help his mind to work through the issues. The statue garden was his favorite place for relaxation.

Richtor left the dormitory in a wide sweep which took him all around the building. He was feeling nostalgic and wanted to store things into his memory as he could. In the same way as the campus building, the dormitory had grown out in a spiral and then up in layers. Normally, there were no decorations anywhere on the building. Now, there was a banner above both entrances to the building. The banners had the words "Congratulations on Graduation Day!" in big letters.

People of the shoal didn't celebrate that many days. The biggest one was the move from the creche to the campus academy and dormitory. This was the formal acceptance of a hatchling as a member of the shoal. A person got their first dormitory room and roommate – usually one other, sometimes three others. They received their official name about which they had some input. And they started classes on campus.

Making the move to the campus was not without its drawbacks. You could no longer kill, or eat, any of your fellow hatchlings. Although more allowance was made for behavior in the lower grades, you were expected to behave according to shoal manners.

Graduation was the transition of your job from student to whatever you could be accepted into. Your work units were no longer tied to attendance and grades but, rather, the various dynamics of the economy of the shoal.

In spite of several economics courses that he had successfully completed, Richtor still could not understand the way work units were calculated and distributed. He did know that, for members of the shoal, no one received more than twice the amount of the least paid one. Anything more would be absurd. What could they constructively spend it on? More food? A bigger shelter? A private sharrell or their own stable of sharrells? It was silly to think of such but, at least, it was a clear limit within the shoal. It might be very useful if a person wanted to start a new business – but what could they do before they had the experience and to accumulate work units or create partnerships?

No, the amount of work units was not a factor in his decision. There were some options where he could decide on his own. There were other options where he operated independent of the shoal – but that had its own set of limits and complications. Most options were a form of apprenticeship and, in such cases, it had to be by mutual agreement. He could not just decide he wanted to farm the kelp beds without acceptance by the supervisor.

Working at the creche was the strongest draw for him at present. Flexibility and inventiveness were mandatory to work with extremely independent and erratic crechelings. And adults rarely died while teaching anymore – the safety protocols seemed to work adequately. He had heard of a few missing fingers but they were rare.

Working with the crechelings could be argued to be the most important task within the shoal. Survival of the shoal depended upon a continued flow of hatchlings moving through their stages until they were a productive part of the shoal. The crecheling stage was the most difficult with the highest mortality rate.

As he swam slowly amidst the statues in the statue garden, he mused what it might be like to be a sculptor. The shoal only supported one full-time sculptor and they were chosen by the community as a whole based on every-ten-currentflips competitions. Once chosen, a community sculptor rarely lost her, or his, place until they were quite old.

But those were unproductive musings. He greatly enjoyed the sculptures but his creativity had never been expressed in that form nor within any of the other arts. He looked forward to continuing to see what Angella might produce. Perhaps it was just pride in his hatching but he thought Angella might become one of the community artists someday.

Freeform use of creativity. That was the key to his future. Within certain limits, that could be used in working at the creche. The politics, and structure, of the campus would not allow such flexibility.

Art would fit the criteria but he was not an artist. Sebaria was an artist, of the type that he could implement, as an explorer but that might be more of a vocation for a nomad. He couldn't see how one could do that within a shoal.

His maneuverings had brought him to the central sculpture. The twisted columns seemed to rise up and up. He wondered whether his future would ascend too.

Tomorrow was another day. Tomorrow was Graduation Day.

Chapter 32 Graduation

*I*t was a big day for the hatching as well as all of the campus. People often attended from the general population. Perhaps it was nostalgia for many – remembering their graduation ceremony and launch into adulthood. There were some who wanted to be first in the queue to congratulate them. The Hatching Elite group would have multiple people waiting for them. Starred certificate graduates often had one or two approach them. But, even among the general hatching, some would be approached because of familiarity with their work from volunteer work, or awards, or general acknowledgement by the shoal.

Those who did not get approached would still find a position. The shoal made sure that all who remained were contributing. There were continued opportunities, through the Academy, to enhance learning in new areas and the possibility of volunteer work to get them into places where they did not initially shine. All could shine if they wanted and all were part of the shoal.

Richtor's fellow graduates swam around the central sculpture garden. The central sculpture offered a focus for the ceremonies while the area was kept clear of any other obstacles. It made a great assembly place for all kinds of occasions. Richtor had attended a concert during the previous halfflip. He wasn't as interested in music as some. He, himself, could not play any instrument to the extent that others would want to listen. And his channeling was fine for speech but there was nothing special about it to enhance a concert. He had heard about the female from the Pearly Shell shoal who could play shells in a special manner so he had attended. He understood how she had gotten her reputation.

A heavy pulse went through the water, calling everyone's attention to the center. Administrator Radistron was present along with many of the teachers of the classes that were taken by the graduating class. Being the only one to be speaking, she could have reached them all with water pulses but she opened up a broadcast mental channel to everyone so they could hear clearly.

"We are here to celebrate the achievements of our hatching class. They have made the long journey from the hatchery to the creche and upward through the currentflips to now. Each one of you is exceptional in your own way and we are happy to have you join us in the everyday work of the shoal."

She paused at this point and a set of vibrations moved through the water as those in attendance all moved their tailfins back and forth in unison – or close to unison. There were always a few who couldn't quite get in sync with the others. Richtor was in that group figuratively but not literally. He did have rhythm.

"We shall now proceed to announce your names. When you are called, please come forward to get your certificate from the teachers present here at the center. First, however, please let me acknowledge those who have striven especially hard within the campus – recognizing that all have their own focus and that may not always mesh with the classes on campus."

Administrator Radistron proceeded to list those who were part of the Hatching Elite group. Occasionally, there would be a vocal cheer for a name listed. There were a number of cheers when Angella's name was called and Richtor made sure to exclaim when he heard Januelle's name called.

Administrator Radistron then listed the graduates who had achieved stars on their certificates. While this was a longer list than those who were part of the Hatching Elite group, it was still fairly short. The hatching was only about sixty people in total. He was relieved when his name was called from the starred list. He heard a couple of cheers and looked around to see Lichten mouthing a call. He wasn't sure who the other was.

Richtor headed forward to pick up his certificate. With a smile, Teacher Gregov handed it to him. He swam away and was happy to see Overseer Waveur and Administrator Flondeau nearby and heading toward him.

"Congratulations, Richtor!" said Waveur. "I knew that you would reach this point and I am not surprised that you received your star."

Flondeau held out his little finger and Richtor hooked his finger onto Flondeau's. Flondeau said, "I extend my congratulations to you as well."

Since there was much official business still going on, the conversation was kept in a tight private band to not disturb others.

"Have you thought more about joining the staff of the creche? We would certainly welcome you," said Waveur.

"Thought about it? Certainly. I haven't done much other than to think about it – and other possibilities – for months."

"Have you come to any conclusions?" asked Flondeau.

"Well ..."

At this point, Cheyelle swam up to take part in the small grouping.

"Hello, Coordinator," said Waveur with some surprise flashing across his face.

"No need for formality," said Cheyelle. "This isn't a formal occasion – more of a celebratory one. The next stage after a long journey from the hatchery."

"Congratulations, Richtor," continued Cheyelle. "I wanted to reach you before you made any commitments."

At these words, Waveur's look of surprise shifted into a rather serious, deadpan, version.

"Waveur, Flondeau. I would appreciate it if you didn't talk about these next items for a day or two. We will be making a formal announcement at that time and that would be better than having the information drift out into the shoal. Such drifting information often is distorted by the time it reaches the final person."

"Certainly," said Waveur. Flondeau nodded.

Richtor looked uncomfortable. "While I certainly hope that we have provided information to help, I don't know of anything that extraordinary to take note of."

Cheyelle smiled. "And that is part of the reason why I am over here to talk with you."

"Excuse me, but I don't know what you – or Richtor – are talking about," said Waveur.

Richtor started to talk, but Cheyelle motioned to him to allow her to take the lead.

"If I am the one to tell you, then I can make sure that I understand the story well enough to tell the shoal in a couple of days. Richtor, feel free to correct me."

"We all know of the problem with the herd having dwindled. For most of us who have pedestal jobs, the reduction in rations just means that we are a little thinner - something that many of us find no problems with."

Flondeau smiled and nodded. He had been known to take up more of the doorframe than would be good for bidirectional traffic. He was already thinner than he had been.

"But," continued Cheyelle. "that is not true for those who are more active. We have allowed some increase in rations for those who are active and working for the community. Overall, the shoal cannot afford any additional reduction in the herd."

"Yes, it is certainly a topic of discussion. Our staff talks about it too. Most of them have tasks on the active side and some are getting much thinner than optimum for their health," said Waveur.

"Yes. Richtor and Januelle came to the Council offices a few weeks ago. Maybe just a couple of weeks ago?" Richtor nodded at this last correction. "They had been discussing the food situation and, with their friend Lichten, had taken a trip to the Jordech Jungle."

Waveur nodded his head.

"They had found – or it would be more accurate to say that Januelle had taken measurements – that indicated that our problem with the herd was a more general problem. It was something affecting the life of Ocean – or this area of Ocean."

"They had talked with the herders but, quite rightly, they did not get much information from them. Richtor wanted authorization from the Council so that they could continue to investigate with greater leverage talking with people. The grouping seemed to be a good one to me. Januelle could handle the scientific portions, Richtor was leader and instigator, and Lichten could both protect and be of use with any animals encountered on the way. I gave them the authority for which Richtor had asked."

"That all sounds reasonable," said Waveur. Although Waveur was not currently a member of the Council, he had been at one time before deciding that the Creche needed him full-time. He was used to having his thoughts, and advice, solicited and felt no reluctance to comment on Cheyelle's narrative.

"Yes. They proceeded to talk with the herders and discussed possibilities among themselves. Then Richtor organized an expedition. Yes, Richtor?" Richtor was raising his hand to give input.

"I wouldn't call it an expedition. It was just the three of us going on a trip during the week after finals and before graduation. An excursion, possibly, but not an expedition."

"Fine," said Cheyelle. "An excursion. They didn't discuss it with me before leaving." Richtor started to raise his hand again as she added, "and they were not required to do so. My authorization was for them to investigate. It was not to order them to do, or not do, any particular thing – though, I admit that, with Januelle and Lichten present to restrain Richtor's more exuberant tendencies, I felt comfortable that anything they did would not be too irrational." She smiled.

"They reported back to me two days ago. That's right, isn't it, Richtor?" Richtor nodded.

"They had discovered, or examined, three different things. Any one of the three would have been of use to the shoal but, together, I can fully say that they have given the shoal great help in both working on the crisis in the short-term as well as giving us a good direction for investigation for the future."

"Speaking for Januelle and Lichten, who I wish were here, we are glad that we could be helpful," said Richtor.

"What were these three things?" asked Waveur.

"One was the possible problem, and things to investigate concerning the problem. There's not much use in going into detail about that although I will go into a bit more specifics when I give my talk to the shoal. It concerns a decrease in sunlight which affects plant growth, which in turn directly affects the general fish population."

"I see," said Flondeau.

"The second I feel almost embarrassed to mention," said Cheyelle. "We certainly should have thought of it but then we were not particularly aware that our problem was a food chain issue."

"As you know, Waveur, and you also may know, Flondeau," continued Cheyelle. "Our herd is rotated between three pastures. They make a complete rotation once per quarterflip. We harvest from the herd once per halfflip. If the problem is food scarcity, as we now believe it is, then increasing the pasture food supply should allow the herd to increase in size once again."

"That makes sense," said Waveur. "And ...?"

"Richtor and his team noticed, and reported, that there are other large algae clouds in the general area. I have discussed it with the herders and it is possible, though not without inconvenience, to increase our number of pastures to four or five. If we are to maintain harvesting frequency, it will mean that they will have to be moved between pastures more often but, in theory, it should work."

"So, we would have our full rations back again?" asked Flondeau with a hopeful face.

"It will take a couple of quarterflips but, yes, that is possible. There are some things that I, and the Council, need to do – to make sure we are not barging into the areas of other shoals. Everyone is hurting and we don't want to cause undue conflict."

"And the third item?" asked Waveur.

"Something that Richtor reported on only very briefly. I don't think you thought it was that important," she spoke directly to Richtor.

"What was that?"

"Your diversion of the widemouth. I suspect Lichten was more in the lead for that action but it was very important. If the widemouth had encountered our herd, it would have been a disaster. Thank you, Richtor."

"A diversion?" asked Waveur.

"Yes, on their way back to the shoal, they encountered a widemouth heading in the direction of the shoal's herd."

"Oh my," said Waveur.

"Yes. Oh my,"

"You said that you wanted to reach me before I made any commitments?" asked Richtor.

"Oh, yes. I have been talking with the other Council members and we think it would be useful for the shoal to have a troubleshooter."

"What would a troubleshooter do?"

"Investigate. Hopefully, this specific problem will be resolved in a currentflip or two. But the shoal continues to grow and, if we succeed in keeping the food supply in sync with the growth of the shoal, we may double in size before the current hatching makes it to graduation. Growth always has problems - usually unforeseen."

"So, you're offering this new position to me?" asked Richtor. "Why me?"

"Your teachers all say you're a pain in the dorsal fin, Richtor," said Cheyelle. "But most of them, with a couple of notable exceptions, say that you contribute greatly to the classes - bringing original questions to the classes and forcing even the teachers to learn a bit more. This is not a skill that fits into a regular job position. But it is a skill that we can value and make use of. What do you say?"

"We would miss having you at the creche, Richtor. But it sounds like a grand, and glorious, opportunity."

"Will the position last?" asked Richtor. "I could change directions in the future but I probably won't change that much myself. Are you offering the position to be counted upon for a couple of currentflips or for the ongoing future?"

"Who knows what the future may bring? Our intention is that this position continues indefinitely. If you do as well as I expect and the shoal does continue to grow, you should be able to consider it to be secure."

"You have yourself a graduate," said Richtor. "This sounds just like what I was wanting - it just didn't exist for me to dream about."

"Congratulations," said Waveur. "Perhaps you can still visit the creche, and help out, on some weekends or when you are free?"

"Possibly. I don't know."

"You can report in to the Council in a week. Happy graduation, Richtor, and thank you once again. I want to head off and thank Lichten and Januelle." With that, she swam away from the group.

"I wonder what would have happened if Cheyelle had come over just a few cycles later," murmured Waveur.

"Who knows? Just part of the overall mystery."

Epilogue

*O*f course, life continued after Graduation day. Richtor went to work for the Council. Although he was given the new title of "Troubleshooter", the definition of that was very broad. He could not just swim around looking for, and waiting for, an emergency. He filled in for shoal positions when they needed extra hands or when someone was unable to work and they could not find a replacement. A "problem" was a need. There were few days when Richtor reported in for the day that he did not have an assignment.

Richtor didn't mind. The primary thing that he didn't want was to be stagnant – to keep doing the same thing day after day. Cheyelle said that he would be accompanying the Academy's next excursion to the island that he and his friends had reached. The Academy had already started a process of surfacing on a weekly basis, at the same time of day, and measuring the amount of light. There was some variance but it seemed to stay within a range. Up some days, down some days.

Since there was no previous initial reading – no baseline measurement, no one at the Academy could be certain that the amount of daylight was less than previous currentflips. But that was just true for academic proof. All of the Academy members had seen the sky without clouds before and they were certain that the cloudy/smoky sky prevented much of the sunlight from reaching the ocean.

So far, there had been no ideas as to how they might stop the volcano from emitting smoke or any guesses as to how long it would continue to do such. It was hoped that the measurements from the coming excursion would be able to be compared to the numbers that Januelle took and any change could be detected. They did expect to need two such excursions and measurements before any more-or-less reliable comparisons could be made.

Januelle did decide to become a science teacher at the campus. She was presently assigned to teach ninth and tenth currentflip students. It was not clear as to whether she would be able to take time off to go along with the excursion. She had put in the request and, in addition, the Academy had sent a request but the campus did not always find it easy to find substitutes for science classes.

Rumblings in the Reef

Lichten had been offered an apprenticeship with a group that found, and gentled, wild sharrells. He had accepted the position. He had an overall plan of building up work credits, then working full time with Diplodus for a half-dozen currentflips, then open up a second stable which would focus on longer distance trips and where he could breed sharrells which were better aligned with specific needs. He had talked it over with Diplodus who agreed with him that the shoal could support a second public stable and they should be able to work together.

The herders, with the political work of Cheyelle and the Council, succeeded in adding two more pasture areas for rotation of the herds. The size of the herd has been increasing but the restricted rations have not been removed yet.

Richtor still has the dream of following in the wake of Sebaria and exploring a good portion of Ocean.

Charles K. Summers

List of Publications

Technical
> ISDN Implementor's Guide, Mc-Graw Hill, 1995.
> ISDN: How to Get a High-Speed Connection to the Internet (w/Bryant Dunetz), John Wiley & Sons, 1996.
> ADSL: Standards, Implementation, and Architecture, CRC Press, 1999.

Non-Fiction
> The First 100: Ideas and Interpretations, Charles K Summers, 2020.
> The Second 100: Ideas and Interpretations, Charles K Summers, 2022.
> The Third 100: Ideas and Interpretations, Charles K Summers, 2025.

Middle-grade and Young Adult Fiction
> The Taylor Twins and the Ghost Club, Charles K Summers, 2013.
> The Taylor Twins and the Pirate Cave, Charles K Summers, 2023.
> Rumblings in the Reef, Charles K Summers, 2025

https://charlesksummers.com

https://charlesksummers.substack.com

www.ingramcontent.com/pod-product-compliance
Lightning Source LLC
Chambersburg PA
CBHW072025020726
47501CB00006B/1960